The Body

A Spirit Trilogy Novel

d. Nichole King

The Body

Limitless Publishing, LLC
Kailua, HI 96734
www.limitlesspublishing.com

Formatting: Limitless Publishing

ISBN-13: 978-1-68058-195-9
ISBN-10: 1-68058-195-3

Dedication

To my firstborn, David Michael.
May you always keep your caring heart
and your love of fantasy.
You make me so proud.
I love you, dude.

Chapter 1

The town square was deserted. Football Friday night had a tendency to do that to Villisca, tonight especially, being the first round of playoffs.

I adjusted my scarf and peered over at Lucas behind the wheel. He grinned, his glowing green eyes shining back at me.

Windows to the soul, indeed.

Turning his attention to the park in the middle of town, he slammed on the brakes. I threw my hands out in front of me, using the dashboard to block my lurch.

"Lucas!" I cried out.

He didn't answer.

My gaze teetered to him, my voice low, confused. "Lucas?"

Eyes still locked on something outside the Jeep, he shook his head. "Uh, nothing. Never mind."

"No," I said, grabbing his hand. No way he'd stop the car for "uh, nothing." I knew him better than that. "What did you see?"

Lucas looked at me, grazing the tip of his tongue over his lip. Surely he couldn't be considering hanging onto this lie.

"What is it?" I repeated.

"I thought I saw—"

"A demon?"

"No. Something else."

I studied him for a second, worried. "What color was the aura?"

Please say it's not that.

He hesitated, his eyes shifting out the window again.

My stomach dropped. Sometimes, I hated being right.

"Black," he answered. "Look, Carrie, since August, since what happened, I've been a little on edge. I thought I saw the glow, but I didn't. It's gone."

"Black? Is that a—"

"A Soulless One. Cambion. Half-demon, yes."

"Here? Why?"

"It wasn't one, though." Slight irritation crept into his tone. "Cambions have bodies. They don't disappear into thin air. I'm just being paranoid."

I laughed, releasing my sudden tight grip on him and choosing to ignore his moment of impatience. "Being paranoid is *my* thing. You need to stick to *your* thing."

Lucas smiled, his lone dimple sinking into his cheek. "And what is my thing?"

"Um…being hot and sexy?" I asked, because I didn't think he'd agree with me.

He snickered, the sound making my heart twirl

inside my chest. "Right. The dead guy as the epitome of sexiness? I doubt it."

"Dead boyfriends are all the rage in Europe," I teased. "Everyone has one."

"That'll be the day," he said, taking one last glimpse out the window before inching the Jeep forward.

***

Lucas and I sat on the bleachers, me wrapped up inside my new bubble coat, shivering from the cold. My boyfriend wasn't much help, and by the look on his face, my discomfort was killing him—well, figuratively.

"I can go grab a blanket from home and be back in five seconds flat," he said, giving me a onceover.

"Being warm defeats the purpose of an outside football game in November, doesn't it?" I grinned. "At least around here."

He wasn't smiling. "Say the word and I'm gone. It'll be like I never left."

"Sit back and enjoy the game, will you? I'm fine."

Lucas glared at me. I glared back harder until I started giggling. Finally, the corner of his lips tugged upward and he relaxed. Threading my gloved fingers through his bare ones, I pulled him to my side. I loved having him close. If only he could feel me like I felt him.

He shook his head. "I'll only make you colder."

I yanked again. "I don't care. I want you here," I said, emphasizing my point by patting my hip.

In the last few months, I'd gotten used to the chills he sent through me. Those tiny tingles that spread goose bumps over my skin were the same ones that made my heart fly high. Under the glow of the stadium, his eyes glistened like two emeralds. I watched as he pushed his hand through his dark hair, the short locks falling over each other. Man, he was gorgeous.

The roar of the crowd brought me out of my reverie. Lucas and I jumped to our feet—okay, I jumped, Lucas eventually stood up—with everyone else, cheering. Villisca's defense ran off the field after a blocked field goal. Being a life-long football fan, close games always fired me up. I shot Mike a thumbs-up as he led his offense out from the sidelines. He couldn't see me, but later when he asked, I wouldn't have to lie.

I glanced at the scoreboard. Two minutes left in the third quarter: Villisca up by six. Captain Mike Carson needed to make some magic happen to win by three TD's—his personal goal for this game.

I shivered again. Lucas's eyes cut to me, two sets of dark lashes kissing each other. He frowned and opened his mouth to say something.

I pressed my index finger to his lips. "Nope. Not a word."

Sitting back down on the bleachers, I noted a group of girls snickering by the fence line below us. They nodded at Lucas, and couple of them flashed him a seductive grin and waggled their fingers at him.

Seriously? I'm sitting right here!

I sighed and scooted a little closer to him.

Maybe I should sit on his lap...

"Hey, what's wrong?" Lucas asked.

I leaned my head on his shoulder. "More staring."

He kissed my head. "Why does it bother you so much? You know I don't care if they think—what did you say earlier? I'm hot and sexy?" He chuckled at the look I shot him. "All that matters is what you think...which is?"

He knew. Oh, he so knew.

"I think they should be wildly jealous of me. I have the perfect boyfriend."

"Eh, perfect might be pushing it. Extraordinary."

I rolled my eyes. Why did he always have to bring *that* up?

"Really though, why does it bother you?" Lucas asked, sweeping two fingers down my cheek. I hoped the girls were watching. "Are *you* jealous?"

I made a face at him. "Maybe a little."

"I'm yours. And because I don't have a heart to offer, you can have my soul."

"Easy to say when you don't know where it is," I teased.

"True."

I snuggled up to him. "What happened with Megan this week? Any news on the search?"

Megan was the witch that worked with me at my grandma's antique store all summer. Though, I didn't know she was a witch until a few months ago. Now, she was at college in Iowa City and training with her witch-aunts in her spare time.

Lucas took a quick survey of the field. "Megan's tried a tracking spell, a memory potion, several charms—nothin'. If only I could remember something—anything—it would help."

I grimaced. "Uh, you're letting a witch-in-training give you potions?"

"Care," he said, hugging me to him, "she can't hurt me. Besides, she's getting pretty good."

The officials blew their whistles, indicating the end of the third quarter. I clapped along with the crowd. Mike said he loved hearing when the fans were enthusiastic.

At the start of the fourth, East Union ran the ball—or tried to. Villisca's defense blocked like they'd studied from their opponents offensive playbook. Clearly, Mike's hard work analyzing film with the team was paying off. I'd hardly seen him outside of class.

I sat back down, leaning against Lucas, who had remained seated, frowning. I couldn't figure out why, but I braved the next question anyway. "Has Susan been replaced yet?" I asked, my voice cracking a little.

Despite what Megan and Lucas said, I had a hand in the town necromancer's death. We all did. Granted, the escaped demons of Lot 310 did the pushing, but if it weren't for us, Villisca would still have a necromancer to direct the ever-present influx of spirits. Now, Vanessa Miller—Megan's mom— and Lucas had to deal with them all.

Lucas sighed, and I couldn't help wonder what filtered through his mind. "No. Not yet. It's strange, though. According to Megan, a replacement necromancer coming to town doesn't usually take this long."

I swallowed the guilt-induced lump in my throat. "Why is it then?"

"Could be any reason. The chosen one isn't in town yet. Or not of age. Or is still being trained."

"Yeah, you lost me."

Lucas scanned over the crowd before answering. "Necros need training, like witches. They have the abilities they need, but somehow those abilities have to surface."

"How?"

"No idea."

"A Necro gets some sort of supernatural calling though, right?"

Lucas shrugged. "Supposed to."

"What happens when someone gets the call?"

When he didn't answer, I lifted my eyes to him. He seemed lost in thought, his lips forming a hard line.

I nudged him. "Hey."

"Yes?" he said, as if he hadn't heard my question.

"What happens when someone gets the call to be a necromancer?" I repeated.

"I don't know. I guess it might be different for everyone."

All of a sudden, the East Union fans exploded into cheers. Great. Just great. The opposing team scored with a forty-one yard option pitch out. I slumped against Lucas's wool coat. A long, white cloud billowed out of my mouth.

"Blanket option is still available," Lucas reminded me.

"Still ignoring you," I said, eyeing him and

taking the last sip of hot chocolate he'd bought at halftime. I set the empty Styrofoam cup on the floor then accidently kicked it under the bleachers. Oops.

I watched Mike run out with the kick return team. Again, I shot him a thumbs-up that he wouldn't see. Why he asked me to do it was beyond me, but I always did.

With the score tied up, I cheered along with the cheerleaders.

"LET'S GO, BLUE JAYS, LET'S GO!"

On the fourth round of cheers, with a lot of prodding from me, Lucas reluctantly stood up. He offered me a small grin, as if he hadn't just been spacing off again. What he had or hadn't seen earlier in the park was probably still on his mind.

We were here to cheer on Mike, and I wasn't about to let Mr. Distracted stop me.

I squinted until I found Mike on the thirty-one yard line. Oh, what I wouldn't give to have Lucas's eyesight! The intensity of close games always made me a little nervous for him.

For good measure, I did *another* thumbs-up.

After a short huddle, the offense broke and set up for the next play, which gained only two yards. I bit my nails through my gloves and bounced on the balls of my feet.

Lucas grabbed my wrist. "Stop it. Mike will pull it out, Care. He always does."

Oh, so now *he's paying attention?*

"Yeah, I hope so. He said some college scouts would be here. He needs this."

Team captains, Mike and Logan, lined up the players again—the same I-formation Coach was so fond of. Mike moved to the left end, opposite his usual position. Our quarterback, Logan, took the snap and handed the ball off to Brandon. Mike circled back and took the hand-off in a reverse. Then he ran behind Brandon and moved quickly to the middle where the defense had left a gaping hole.

I bit down on the top of my gloves enough to feel it on my fingers. Sometimes I wished I didn't know so much about the game and the dangers it could pose. My dad's football career had ended at the University of Texas after a serious knee injury took him out. To this day, it gives him trouble.

The defensive tackle broke free of Villisca's guard and took off toward Mike. From his position, there was no way Mike could see him coming. Nor would he see the other defensive lineman push through the stronghold of his teammates.

I sucked in a mouthful of cold air and held it. It always put me on edge when Mike got tackled. So far, he'd always jumped back up, ready to start the next play.

But this time was different.

The two East Union players collided with Mike from both sides. Next to me, I felt Lucas's body go rigid. He'd seen it clearly, and his posture scared me. I stared at him, eyes wide with fear.

"Lucas, what happened?"

He didn't reply, his eyes focused on the field.

Oh, God! He's not even pretending *to breathe!*

"Lucas, talk to me. What's going on?"

Without waiting for an answer, I followed his gaze back onto the field. The East Union players were already on their feet, high-fiving each other for reading the play and for the subsequent tackle. Mike still didn't move.

Coach Morrison rushed out and knelt beside his team captain. Then he signaled the ambulance. Red and blue lights lit up the stadium. A quiet hush fell over the crowd. No one moved.

"Lucas," I whispered, clutching his coat.

Quickly, I searched the crowd until I found Mike's parents and little sister, Mandy. She sat on her mom's lap while her dad made his way down the bleachers. He crossed the track and ran to his son's side.

"No," Lucas mumbled, his pupils expanding over green irises.

My mouth went dry. I'd heard that tone in Lucas's voice before, and I didn't like it.

After a while, heads lifted upward toward the sky as the sound of blades slashed through the air. I covered my mouth, following the helicopter as it landed on the football field.

I jerked on Lucas's arm, forcing him to face at me. "Just tell me. Please."

Lucas's hand grazed over my cheek.

Is Mike breathing?

"Barely," Lucas murmured.

"What?"

"You asked if he was still breathing, and I said—"

I shook my head. "No, I didn't ask that."

Lucas pulled his hand away from my skin and examined it, concerned. "You didn't say anything?"

"No."

His lips twitched as he studied me for a moment.

Cautiously, he placed his palm back on my face.

What's he doing?

I turned back to the field and gasped. What I saw, I shouldn't have seen. I was only human with no supernatural abilities.

Silver mist, clear as the Caribbean, began to rise out of Mike's body.

Chapter 2

NO!

I shook my head frantically. "Please, God, no."

Lucas's hand fell from my cheek, and the mist disappeared from over Mike's body. I grabbed for Lucas's hand.

Bring him back!

I squeezed harder. Somehow, his touch had allowed me to see what he saw.

Gripping as tightly as I could, I stared back out on the field. The paramedics were strapping my friend on a stretcher. Tears formed in my eyes.

"Why isn't it working?" I threw off my glove and folded my bare palm into Lucas's. "Let me see!"

Lucas's gaze wandered to our hands, lost in thought. His brows furrowed, and I wondered if he was worried or if there was something else behind the expression.

Desperate, I watched the paramedics load Mike onto the helicopter. Nothing else—just what my regular human eyes saw.

"Carrie, I don't—"

"Did you see it? Was that what I thought it was?" I didn't care that I was almost yelling at him.

"Come on," Lucas said, picking up my glove and shoving it at my chest. He grabbed my hand and held on too tightly.

Halfway around the field to the exit, Lucas spun around to face me. "What did you see?" he demanded.

I swallowed, shooting a glance out to field before answering. The helicopter blades whirled at full force.

"Silver mist," I answered, my eyes rising to meet his. "His spirit coming out of his body. That means he's dead, doesn't it? Now he's a…"

"No. No, Mike's alive." Lucas pushed his fingers through his hair. "What the hell is going on?" he muttered to himself.

"Alive? Then what *did* I see?"

Hardness that he tried to cover up filtered through his voice. "Exactly what you thought it was. Mike took a bad hit. The guy on the left rammed his helmet into Mike's ribs, and something cracked. When the other guy slammed into him, the force tossed his head back, maybe breaking his neck—I'm not sure. But the shock to his body stopped his heart momentarily."

Fear folded its arms around me and held on for dear life. "His heart…stopped?"

"Momentarily."

"And his spirit?" I croaked out, half holding my breath.

"Back in his body."

My attention jerked to the field as Mercy One lifted into the air. It was the second time this sort of fear had gripped me. Three months ago, I'd stood by as a demon almost dragged Lucas to Hell. The nightmares hadn't stopped.

Numb from the inside out and without a word to Lucas, I turned away and started to jog toward the Jeep. Nothing mattered except getting to the hospital.

Lucas appeared at my side in an instant. "Where are you going?"

"Isn't it obvious?" I snapped.

"Carrie, what's the point? They won't let you see him tonight. You'll just be sitting around in the waiting room watching the minutes drag by," Lucas said. I wanted to scream at him for his lack of caring. He must have seen the disgust on my face because added, "We'll go first thing in the morning. I promise."

"What's the difference between sitting at the hospital waiting or sitting here and waiting?" I shook my head. "I don't care if I see him tonight or not. I have to go."

Lucas huffed and turned away from me.

"He'd do it for me," I said through gritted teeth.

What's gotten into him?

Glowing eyes locked onto mine. With his eyebrows raised, he shifted his weight, perturbed.

Whatever.

"I'm going. Are you coming or not?" I asked, not sure if *I* wanted him to come at this point.

Finally, he conceded. "I'll drive."

"Thank you."

As I slid inside Lucas's Jeep Compass, I cast a final glance at the field. Villisca fans were on their feet, clapping less enthusiastically. Honoring their injured captain, the Blue Jays had just scored.

*****

Mike's parents sat in the corner of the emergency lobby. A table with children's books and toys stood in front of them, but Mandy ignored it, cuddled up on her mother's lap.

The little girl peered up from under her mass of blonde curls as Lucas and I walked in. She forced a small smile when she saw me. Mrs. Carson gave her a slight nudge, and she slid off her mother's lap and ran to me, throwing her arms around my waist.

"My brother's hurt real bad," she said, pressing her cheek against my stomach.

"I know, sweetie. I saw it."

"Carrie," she whimpered, "I don't want him to die."

The fear in her voice made the blood drain from me. I stared up at Lucas, hoping my next words weren't a lie. "He's going to be fine. Good as new. I promise."

Frowning, Lucas averted his gaze, and my heart jumped into my throat. I squeezed my eyelids shut and held Mike's little sister tighter. She sniffled and wiped away her tears.

Mike's mom, with her blonde hair pulled back in a messy bun, shuffled over to us. She looked tired and older than she had only hours ago.

"Thank you for coming, Carrie," she said. "And

Lucas. It would mean a lot to him to know you're both here."

Mandy released me and swung around to her mom, resting her head against Mrs. Carson's hip.

"Have they said anything yet?" I asked, and then held my breath.

"The CT scan showed the worst of it, we think. A concussion, shattered collar bone, three cracked ribs, and fractures in his neck."

The hit had been hard, and even though I knew how dangerous the sport could be, the long list of injuries made me dizzy. How could he ever be okay again?

She continued, "The EKG is normal. They're doing an MRI right now. If you want to stay, it'll probably be a long night."

Lucas and I took two seats on the opposite wall from the Carsons, next to a window. I watched the other people crowding the lobby. Some bit their nails impatiently, a few seemed as if they were napping, and the rest had some hospital periodical in their hands that they pretended to read.

An hour passed, but it felt like days before a tall man in a white lab coat entered the lobby. Mike's parents rose to their feet, his dad's arm wrapped securely around his wife's shoulders. As much as I wanted to be in the circle, Lucas held me firmly in place. I didn't protest; I wasn't a family member.

Lucas's breath tickled my ear when he leaned in to tell me what they were saying. "Mike's resting in recovery. They're keeping him comfortable with morphine." Lucas paused, listening. "The MRI showed nothing unexpected: a concussion and a few contusions. His neck injury is better than originally expected. But he'll need surgery to repair his clavicle."

I didn't need to hear the worst of it from Lucas. I saw it in Mrs. Carson's face.

"Mike will never play football again."

***

One play.

Ten seconds off the clock.

And Mike's football dreams had been smashed into a thousand pieces. Would his parents tell him now? Or wait until he was home to crush his heart? Not all pain could be controlled with morphine.

Mandy peered at me over her shoulder before following her parents down the corridor to Mike's room. I gave her a reassuring smile, and she turned back around.

"Let's go," Lucas said after they'd left. He gathered my coat off the chair where I'd laid it earlier. "We probably won't be able to see him tonight." He handed me my stuff, and I set them on the chair next to me.

"No. I wanna stay. Maybe…"

Lucas didn't understand; I needed to see Mike tonight. Hear him say something. Anything. Just so I'd know he was all right. After what I saw through Lucas's eyes on the field, I had to know for sure.

Lucas stood up, ready to leave. "Care, it's getting late, and your—"

"If you want to go then go. No one is stopping you," I snapped. "I thought Mike was your friend too," I murmured, eyeing him.

They weren't best friends by any stretch of the imagination. I was the common denominator between them, but they acted civil, even jovial sometimes, around each other. Except this attitude Lucas had today: his tone of voice, trying to keep me from coming, wanting me to leave now—it wasn't like him. And it was starting to piss me off.

Emerald irises stared back at me, hard and distant. He leaned forward, brushing the hair off my shoulder. I flinched away.

Lucas's expression was unreadable. "Fine. We can stay if that's what you want."

I slumped back into the chair and crossed my arms. Lucas sat hunched over, elbows on his knees, eyes downcast. Neither of us touched each other.

I looked up when the sliding glass hospital doors opened. My trigonometry teacher, a.k.a. Coach Morrison, followed by six of Mike's teammates dressed in jeans, hurried into the lobby. He spotted me immediately.

"Carrie," he said, rushing over. "How's Mike?"

Since the Carsons hadn't told me what the doctor had said, I rattled off the info I'd received when I first arrived. "His parents are seeing him now. I'm not sure how much longer they'll be."

Coach nodded, and he and the rest of the team fanned out to find seats. I studied the clock too long, counting the hours. After all the time we'd been there, the waiting area had emptied steadily. Still, the room suffocated me.

What's taking so long?

I cracked my knuckles, something I never did,

and watched the double doors that lead into the main hospital.

Lucas's hand slid onto my thigh, stopping it from bouncing. I took a deep breath, held it, and let it out slowly.

Minutes ticked by in silence. Finally, I saw Mandy round the corner. She ran to me, beaming.

"He's alive, Carrie!" she spouted. "You were right. He's going to be okay." Then she giggled. "He called me a squirt."

I laughed. "You are a squirt."

She cocked her head to the side, corkscrew curls sliding into her face.

"A cute one," I added.

She yawned. "I think we're going to get a hotel room. I'm tired."

Voices drew my attention to where Mike's parents stood with Coach Morrison.

"I'm so sorry," Coach said.

"Not your fault, Don," Mr. Carson assured him, placing his hand on the coach's shoulder. "These things happen."

When Mike's mother noticed me, she walked over. "He's drowsy, but he asked to see you. Room 106."

I nodded. "Thank you." Crossing the floor to Lucas, a small weight lifted from my shoulders. If he was asking for me, maybe he would be okay. "Come on."

Lucas shook his head. "No. You go. I'll wait here."

I rocked back on my heels. "You don't want to see him?"

"He wants to see you. Not me."

For a split second, I thought I saw him waver into transparency, losing concentration. He stretched his shoulders backward. "I'll warm up the Jeep."

I puffed out a sigh. "Whatever." When I walked through the double doors, I didn't look back.

Mike's room was halfway down the hall. I paused just outside his door, closing my eyes and taking a moment. Mike had always been so solid, tough. It was hard to imagine him broken and beat down. In my head, I pictured him in a full body cast, unable to do anything. No way it could be that bad…right?

I jumped when a hand fell on my shoulder.

"Sorry," the nurse said. "Are you Carrie?"

"Yeah."

"He's been asking for you, but he needs to rest. Ten minutes, okay?"

"Sure. Thanks."

She wandered down the hall, and I reached for the door handle. Before I saw anything, the sound of machines buzzing and beeping caught my attention.

That can't be good.

The room smelled like latex gloves. It made my stomach hurt.

Stopping just inside the door, my gaze drifted from the foot of Mike's bed up to the light blue blanket spread over him. His arms, dirt still dotted over his skin, lay to his sides, tubes poking out of his veins.

A neck brace hugged his head, immobilizing

him. Bruises stained his cheeks and one eye.

"I can hear you breathing, Carrie," Mike said quietly, his voice more gruff than usual.

I straightened up and took the last few steps to his bed. Next to his head, I could see small cuts all over his face from where his helmet and chin guard dug into his flesh.

"Hey," I said, smiling. "How are you? You look good."

"Humph." Mike forced a laugh. "Cut the bullshit, Carrie. I look like crap."

I cleared my throat. God, I hated seeing him like this. "Yeah. You do."

"Did we win the game?"

What? Seriously?

"Uh. I…I don't know," I stammered.

"What the hell? Does *anybody* know?" The beeping on one of the machines sped up. "We better not have lost, damn it! *That* would make *this* suck even more."

The red line spiked in quick succession. "Uh, Mike…" I pointed to the screen.

"If it's not flat-lining, it's fine."

Stealing a quick peek at the door, I worried that a nurse would come running in at any second and throw me out for overexciting her patient. "Mr. Morrison is in the lobby right now," I said, lamely pointing toward the hallway.

"What? And you didn't ask him?" Mike's hazel eyes widened, and I wondered if the morphine drip wasn't working as it should.

"Do you want me to?" I squeaked out.

Mike sighed, exhaustion coating his voice again.

"Nah. Ask on your way out, though. If you leave, they may not let you back in."

"I'll do that."

"Man, I really got myself banged up this time, didn't I?" He smirked, catching my eye. "You forgot to do the thumbs-up thing, didn't you?"

I tried to smile. "I'd never forget that." I leaned back against the wall. "Mike, you—"

"I'll be okay."

"They said—"

"I won't be able to play football again, yeah, I know. There are worse things in this world than shattered dreams, Carrie. Dreams change all the time. I can have a different dream, but I only have this one life."

"What about—"

"Hey, stop. Different doesn't mean bad. It just means different. Maybe I'll coach," Mike said. "It's not like I was going to make a career out of playing football anyway."

I didn't know what to say to that. That last thing I wanted to do was to feel sorry for him. He'd probably hate me if I did.

"Where's Lucas, by the way?" he wondered.

I stuffed my hands into the back pockets of my jeans. "He's...I don't know. Something crawled up his ass and died."

"Whoa, Carrie's swearing?"

I chuckled. "Hanging around you too much."

"Or not enough." He waggled his eyebrows.

"Shut up." I'd have slugged him if I knew for sure it wouldn't kill him. "He's been acting off today."

"Well, you know where to find me. I'll be here all week." He grinned, flirting more like himself.

I poked a finger at him. "Keep that up, mister, and you'll be here longer."

"Ten minutes are up," the nurse said, walking in with a blood pressure machine.

"Tomorrow?" Mike asked me.

"Yeah. See you then. Good night."

I made my way toward the door.

"Oh, and Carrie?" Mike said, stopping me.

I spun around. "Yeah?"

"Don't forget to find out the score of the game, will ya?"

I breathed out a laugh. "Sure."

"Good night, Carrie."

Chapter 3

A gust of cold air stung my cheeks as I left the hospital. From the corner of my eye, I noticed Lucas watch me as I slid into the Jeep. He didn't say anything or ask about Mike, and I didn't acknowledge his presence. It was a long drive back to Villisca.

When he pulled into my grandparents' driveway, I had the door open before he came to a complete stop. I heard him say something, but I didn't turn around. A sliver of guilt tugged at me as I slammed the door and ran into the house without looking back. Once inside, though, I pushed the feeling away.

He's the one with the mood disorder, not me.

Tucked in a blanket of warmth under the duvet, I forced Lucas's less than pleasant attitude out of my mind and thought about Mike. I envisioned going to one of his games at some hotshot college. His name filled the announcer's box.

"Mike Carson with another spectacular catch."

"Carson with the eighty-five yard touchdown."

"Number 57 breaks five tackles for the first down."

Instead, he would have to settle for coaching some mediocre junior high's failing football program. He'd probably love it.

Then, the picture changed. Mike lay on the ground in the middle of the field, silver mist rising from his chest. Higher and higher it rose until the smoke formed into the spirit version of my friend. He flashed me a sideways smirk and thumbs-up, winked, and disappeared.

I rolled onto my stomach, snagging an extra pillow to hug. No matter how hard I tried, I couldn't get the vision out of my head. Sure, his spirit had re-entered into this body where it belonged, but still…what if it hadn't?

I shivered. Usually, I loved the sensation because it meant Lucas was nearby. Not tonight, though. Tonight, I was probably alone.

God, I hated it.

I scanned the dark room. Nothing except blackness and silence. I touched the pillow beside me, hoping. Warm cotton greeted me, and I frowned. Disappointed, I lowered my hand onto the duvet. No trace of coolness settled around me.

"Lucas?" I whispered. "Are you here?"

I wasn't surprised when I didn't get an answer—not after how I'd left things in the Jeep. I'd been so absorbed in myself, I hadn't even cared to hear whatever he'd said when I left. It wasn't like me.

And it wasn't like him to let me go.

Maybe…just maybe…

I tossed the blankets off and stepped my bare feet

onto the wood floor. Walking to the chair in the corner of my room, where Lucas often sat, I strained to see or feel something. Mist. Breath. Anything.

There was nothing.

I ran my hand over the microfiber. The seat wasn't any cooler than the rest of the room.

Yes, I was alone.

In one motion, I ripped the comforter off the bed, twirling it around me. I collapsed on the chair, imagining Lucas's arms folded around me. Cradling me. Telling me that everything was going to be okay. Somehow when the words came from him, I believed them. Today, though, he hadn't said much worth believing.

I held my breath, trying to fight the swell rising in my throat. Until now, he'd been so understanding, so eager to comfort me when I needed him. After a night like tonight, the old Lucas wouldn't have left me alone. He would have appeared in my room regardless of my sassy attitude.

What changed?

Then it hit me.

Lucas. Mike.

Car accident. Football accident.

Lucas, during life, was like Mike now. Only, Mike survived—his spirit didn't stay outside his body. Mike could change his dreams. Lucas couldn't even remember his. Yes, Mike was the lucky one.

How could I have been so selfish? Thinking only of me—and Mike. I'd completely overlooked Lucas and what all this meant for him.

Concentrating on my boyfriend, a new wave of pain washed over me. Unfamiliar pain. Pain that didn't belong to me.

With my hands wrapped around my stomach, I doubled over, crying out. Oh Lord, it hurt, like my insides were falling out of my body. Not only that, but my head and my heart throbbed as if something squeezed them. Gasping for breath, I heaved in air, trying to calm the slew of emotions ready to spill out.

Then it passed. Just...evaporated.

Strange.

Quickly, I untangled myself from the blanket, leaving it in a heap on top of the mattress. I fumbled in the dark for a clean pair of socks in the dresser, and threw on the clothes I'd worn all day. Figuring I was already in trouble with Grandma and Grandpa, I needed to be back before they got up. I checked the alarm clock.

Can I get there and be back in less than two hours?

I had to try; I had to see him tonight.

The door creaked a little when I opened it, so I left it open. I cringed when the stairs groaned as I descended. In the mudroom, I slipped on my shoes and grabbed a jacket on my way out the door. My silver Honda Civic purred to life, and I was extremely grateful for such a quiet car.

I sped down the highway faster than I'd taken it since August, when demons were chasing me. I'd only been to Lucas's house in Red Oak once, on my birthday in October, but already, the way had been ingrained into my memory.

Lucas lived on the back edge of town, a lone house surrounded by empty space and trees. It only took me fifteen minutes to get there, ten minutes shy of what it should have taken.

I hugged my arms around my chest, blocking the cold wind, and hurried up to the front door. Taking a deep breath, I silently prayed that he wasn't upset, even though he had every right to be; I'd acted like a spoiled brat.

The door opened as I raised my hand to knock. Lucas stood there, dark hair sticking straight up, his eyes heavy. Shirtless and barefoot, he wore only a pair of jeans that hung low off his hips. From the way he squinted at me, I probably woke him up and he'd materialized quickly.

Without a word, he stepped aside and let me in. He raked his fingers through his hair and sighed.

"Hey," I said as soon as he closed the door.

"Hey, yourself."

I swallowed. *Where do I start?*

Thankfully, Lucas broke the silence. "I wondered if you'd show up tonight."

I worked my gaze up his body, starting at the floor, slowly taking him in. Lingering on his lips a little longer than necessary, I finished my visual climb until I rested on his eyes. "I'm sorry."

"Look, Carrie, I think we need to talk."

Uh-oh.

"Yeah, sure."

He didn't take my hand, and I felt rejected. We sat on the sofa—at opposite ends. I grabbed one of the decorative pillows, placing it on my lap to play with the ends. Nervous habit.

I didn't dare peek over at him. Already, the tension in the room crept around my neck, ready to strangle me.

"Early this morning, I went to see Becca."

Immediately, my eyes flicked up to him. Becca, a ghost who lived on the beach in California, had been the one who helped Lucas figure things out after he'd died. She taught him how to concentrate and conjure a body so that he could be among the living, still a part of this world.

His jaw tightened. "Carrie, she's gone."

I shook my head. "Gone? Like on vacation?"

How did this happen so soon?

"No. Gone. Disappeared."

"You don't know that. She could have—"

"Carrie, listen to me!" His voice rose, making me sit back. "The doors were busted in. Windows shattered. The beach house destroyed. I found Lulu, her cat, living in a box in the bedroom. She hadn't been fed in God knows how long." Lucas paused. "Becca is gone."

A chill raced up my spine. "Maybe...maybe she found her soul. Crossed over."

"You know as well as I do that didn't happen." Lucas's low voice sliced me. Yes, I knew, but the other two options were too unbearable to consider. "Ghosts who maintain a body, who pretend they're not dead, don't feel the pull of their souls anymore. She stopped feeling it a long time ago; it's why she sent me here. She faded away."

I hugged the pillow to my chest, goose bumps forming over my skin. Closing my eyes, I sucked in a deep breath. The last option was that a demon had "recruited" her. Taken her to Hell and turned her into one of them. No, I wasn't going there.

When I opened my eyes, Lucas was staring at me. Fear shot through me at what he might say next.

"Carrie, I need to double my efforts. I'm feeling the pull of my soul less and less as it is. Remember what Susan said?"

"Yeah," I squeaked out. "That you wouldn't feel it in corporeal form."

"I have to find it. I have to know."

"This is what you've been thinking about all day, isn't it? It's not about Mike, or what you saw in the park." My voice shook as I spoke. Deep down, I wanted him to find his soul too. I just didn't want him to take it yet. Selfish, I know.

Again, Lucas pushed his fingers through his hair, and I wondered if he'd done that a lot when he was alive. "I've been distracted. What happened between you and me in the bleachers, with you being able to see what I was seeing, I freaked out. I don't understand how you could do that."

Well, if that freaked him out, no way was I going to mention that in my bedroom, I was fairly certain I could feel his inner pain.

"Incenamus?" I asked. It had to be the rare soul-connection we shared. A connection that fused the souls of two people—one living, one dead. "Susan said it holds powers that even she didn't understand."

But we can't ask Susan now, because we helped kill her.

"The thought crossed my mind. I'm going to see

Megan tomorrow and tell her what happened."

"You don't think it's bad that I saw that, do you?"

Lucas slumped into the sofa. Resting his head back against the cushion, he stared at the ceiling. "I don't know what to think."

"I haven't been having visions of you lately. Not like before," I said.

"Makes sense. We're seeing more of each other now than then."

I inched closer until our knees touched. "What about Mike?"

He tilted his head toward me. "What about him?"

"About what happened today? How Mike could've died and been like you."

The corner of Lucas's lips turned up, revealing his dimple. "Nah. Mike wouldn't be like me."

"That's not what I meant. I mean that Mike was given a second chance at life," I said, taking his hand, "and you weren't."

Lucas sat up a little and brushed his two fingers down my cheek. "Mike will be fine, you know that, right? Cocky as ever, I'm sure."

"He's not cocky."

Lucas smirked. "Only when it comes to you."

"What? And you're not?"

"I have a reason to be. He doesn't."

I rolled my eyes. "You two need to cut the testosterone war down a few notches."

My boyfriend pulled me into him, kissing my hair. "Never."

"So, you're not jealous?" I asked, snuggling closer, remembering my earlier admission.

Lucas went quiet for a few seconds. "Maybe a little." I couldn't help the smile spreading over my face. "But not for the reasons you think."

"What other reasons are there?"

I sunk deeper into him, the tension draining out of me. Lucas's chin rested on the top of my head. "When we arrived at the hospital, I noticed the fatigue and worry in his parents' eyes, and I thought of my own folks. Were they like that after my accident? Then I saw Mandy and how she ran up and hugged you, wondering if her brother might die. Do I have a sister? Does she still think about me?"

He paused for a second, and I looked at him, waiting from him to continue.

"I want to know that they're okay. That they're happy," he murmured.

"You will," I said. "You'll find whoever it was at the crash site, and they'll tell you what you need to know. You'll figure out who you are."

Lucas squeezed me tighter.

"By the way, I did get a second chance," he said, brushing a thumb over my chin. "I got you."

I laughed softly as his lips lowered to mine. "Some second chance."

***

The sun poured in through the window, waking me up. Alone on Lucas's sofa, I sniffed at the faint aroma of sizzling bacon coming from the adjacent room. Something crashed to the floor, shattering, and Lucas swore.

I sat up and rubbed the sleep from my eyes.

Lucas appeared in the doorway to the living room holding a silver tray. At the sight of him, I covered my mouth with a hand to stifle the giggles.

His hair was a mess, locks stuck together and flying in all directions. Grease stains splattered on his white t-shirt, spreading down to the hem.

I pulled my lips between my teeth and bit down, clearing my throat. The smile I tried to suppress slowly stretched across my face.

"Sorry," I muttered, acting innocent.

Lucas flashed me an impish grin. "I made you breakfast. Consider it a peace offering for acting like a jerk yesterday."

Cautiously, I peered over the back of the sofa to see what he'd made. A white plate sat on the tray containing scrambled eggs, three strips of bacon, and...was that supposed to be toast? Beside the plate stood a tall glass of orange juice, which, judging by the stains on his clothes, was probably the second glass. I crinkled my nose, and then realizing that this was Lucas's apology, I scratched the bridge as if I'd had an itch.

"I made pancakes too, but um, I was kinda going for a peace offering and not a burnt offering, so..." Lucas sat the tray on the coffee table in front of me.

"This is perfect," I said. "Thank you for going through all this trouble."

Lucas took a seat beside me. "Oh, no. No trouble at all."

I filled my cheeks with air, puffing them out. "Really? Your clothes seem to tell a different story."

As if he didn't know, he pulled his shirt away

from his body and studied it. "Hmm. Guess I got a little on me."

"Yeah, just a little bit." I stabbed my fork into the pile of eggs, taking a bite. "These are good!"

Lucas sighed, relieved. "Oh, thank God."

I glanced at him, holding his stare. "You *doubted* it?"

Smirking, he shrugged. "Nope. Just praying."

"Burnt offering?"

"Something like that."

"Right…" I drew out the word. "So, you actually have food in your kitchen?"

"Not much. I ran to the store while you were still asleep."

I picked up a piece of bacon. "These look good."

"Yeah," Lucas agreed. "*Those* three do."

With my mouth full, I eyed him suspiciously.

He shrugged. "I bought a whole pound."

I almost choked. After taking a long drink of the OJ, I twirled a dark lock of his hair between my fingers. "This is really sweet. Thank you."

"I owed it to you. Finish up," he said, standing up and pecking my cheek. "We'll head to the hospital to see Mike then you'll have to go home and face the music."

I groaned. He was right. I hadn't intended on falling asleep at his house, but I didn't regret it. Right now my cell phone was probably ringing on the dresser in my room.

Out of nowhere, Lucas appeared sitting beside me, fully dressed in clean jeans and a long-sleeve, green shirt that matched his eyes. Wow, he was sexy…and very distracting. Finally, I gave up eating cold eggs and excused myself to freshen up in the bathroom.

I splashed water on my face and combed through my hair with my fingers. It wasn't much, but whatevs. It would have to do for now.

When I walked out, I heard Lucas fumbling around in the kitchen. I tip-toed over to the doorway to snoop on him, even though I knew he could hear me breathe.

Scanning over the kitchen, I wondered how I hadn't smelled the smoke that filled the whole house, or how Lucas managed not to burn the kitchen to ashes.

Wet paper towels, egg shells, and black disks—pancakes?—littered the linoleum at the base of the garbage can. More breakfast scraps cluttered the counter along with...yeah, those squares *were* toast.

Lucas was on his hands and knees wiping up spilled orange juice.

"You don't cook much, do you?" I asked.

"I thought we established that a long time ago." He swiveled his head around, bobbing his head in approval. "Really, not too bad for my first time."

For the second time that morning, I threw my hand over my mouth to stop the laughter. It didn't work, though. In a flash, Lucas was in front of me, pressing his lips firmly against mine. My hand gripped the back of his head, and I melted in his embrace, my knees buckling under me. To keep me from falling, Lucas spun me around and pushed me up against the refrigerator, his hips digging into mine.

His mouth moved to my neck and he nibbled on

my earlobe. Ripples raced up my spine, shooting off fireworks into my chest. I whimpered as Lucas's tongue caressed mine. My fingers found their way into his hair, grabbing handfuls of it.

Pinpricks of pleasure glided under my skin, making my blood morph into liquid desire. Months ago, Lucas told me that even though he couldn't feel my touch, my kisses, like I did, he felt them stronger on the inside. He'd compared it to people losing one of their senses: when one is gone, the others strengthen. For him, my touch resonated in his mind, his heart—his soul.

I hoped the intense rocking waves in my stomach was what he meant. Maybe, just maybe, it would make up for the lack of him feeling my physical caresses.

Cool fingers ran down my arms, leaving warmth in their wake. I slipped my hands under his shirt, gliding up his sides. Muscles rippled under my palms, and I couldn't stop the unwanted thoughts from consuming me.

No, he didn't feel it. He couldn't feel the heat transferring from my fingertips to his skin, couldn't feel me pressed against him, couldn't feel me kiss him. Thinking about it, the excitement drained out of me.

Lucas's mouth slowed at the same time, almost as if he'd read my mind.

Looping a lock of my hair around a finger, Lucas's eyes searched mine. He pulled the hair out in a curl, letting it fall over my shoulder. "What's wrong?"

I wished he *could* read my mind, because then I

wouldn't have to say it out loud. Speaking it made it real, and I didn't want it to be real.

Taking a long breath, I dropped my gaze so I didn't have to face him. I loved him so much, but…

With my back against the refrigerator, I slid to the floor. Lucas lowered himself too, squatting in front of me.

"It doesn't mean I don't love you. That I don't want you more than anything in this world. If I could figure out a way, I swear to you, I would. I'd do anything," he said, tenderly caressing my cheek.

I peered up at him. A glint of sadness flashed across his eyes, and I wondered how he knew exactly what I'd been thinking. "I don't understand how you touch me and don't feel it."

Lucas took my hand and pressed it to where his heart should be. "I do feel it, baby. I feel it right here."

I lowered my head again, still unable to comprehend how he worked. For me, each time he touched me fueled my desire, and I wanted him more. How could he reciprocate that?

Lifting my chin to meet his gaze, Lucas ran a thumb over my lips. It tickled in a sensual way, leaving me desperate for him.

"I just want you to feel this," I murmured, and hooked my arm round his neck, easing his mouth to mine. "To feel me."

I kissed him, willing something to happen. For Incenamus to kick in, for the universe to finally give us a break.

"I do," Lucas said, both palms gripping my face. "Every time you sink into me when I do this." He kissed my nose. "And this." My forehead. "And this." My lips. "Every time you shudder. When you moan, I feel you. I feel you all over, and I long for more of you."

Gently, he wiped the tear from my cheek. "Someday, I'll *show* you exactly what you mean to me—how I feel you."

His promise ran deep into my abdomen, making me shiver.

***

An hour later, we were on our way to the hospital. We entered through the main lobby and checked in with the front desk. Hand in hand, Lucas and I walked to Mike's new room.

"Play nice, okay?" I begged as we passed the nurses' station. "He's probably had a rough night."

"Of course. You won't even recognize me."

I paused and stared at him. I guessed it was better than his usual answer, *"I will if he does."* Ugh!

Mike's door was open, so we let ourselves in. Still in the same immobile position as the night before, Mike grunted when we—Lucas—came into his line of sight.

"How are you feeling?" I asked, ignoring the look he sent my boyfriend.

Mike's eyes flicked toward the morphine drip. "Buzzed."

"Good game last night, man," Lucas congratulated him.

Impressive. I didn't even have to prompt him.

"Hell yeah!" Mike answered. For some reason, they connected well when it came to sports and stupid guy movies. Sorry, "classics."

"Oh, Mr. Morrison said you won. Next game is Thursday. At home, again," I told him.

"Nice. I hope I'm outta here by then so I can go," Mike said.

"You're joking, right?"

Mike's brow furrowed. "No."

"I'll go with ya," Lucas offered unexpectedly. "Carrie probably won't be able to make it." He winked at me.

I hoped he caught some of the daggers I shot at him.

Mike caught on to our exchange, and his gaze drifted over me. "Isn't that your game night sweatshirt?"

"Um, yeah." I looked over my faded blue jeans and Blue Jays hoodie that he had bought me.

"So, same clothes as last night?" Disappointment clouded Mike's expression.

I cleared my throat. "Not that it's any of your business, but I slept on Lucas's sofa last night."

Suddenly a grin spread across his face. "And Rob and Renae were *okay* with this?" His pitch dripped with amusement now.

He knew the answer. He just wanted me to say it out loud.

I gave Lucas a sideways glare. Yeah, his flippant comment was why I was explaining myself to Mike. He leaned back against the wall, arms crossed with a smirk on his face that I kind of wanted to kiss off him. "Um, no. They don't know."

"Hmm." Mike crossed his arms, smug. "Well, I guess I won't see you until next year then. And neither will you, buddy," he added, full-out grinning at Lucas.

Ah, right.

Groaning, I lowered myself onto the chair against the wall. Mike had worked with my grandfather for a few years now and, in all honesty, knew them better than I did. Before my mother forced me up here last May, I hadn't seen my grandparents in a decade.

I crinkled up my nose, ignoring his comment to Lucas. "That bad?"

"If you're lucky, baby."

I crossed my legs and slumped lower in the seat. "Fantastic."

"They scheduled surgery on my collarbone for Monday morning, by the way," Mike said. "They're putting in metal screws and shit."

I made a face. "Ew. I'm sorry. What can I do?"

Mike laughed. "*You* won't be able to do anything except eat and sleep for months."

"Surely they'll let me come visit you." I paused. "You think?"

"Uh, no. I don't think. Renae will have you locked up. Although, I could use my assignments. Maybe I'll give Rob a call and see if you can drive by my place and throw the books out your car window."

"Funny," I said, narrowing my eyelids into small slits.

Beside me, Lucas held back a laugh. So. Not. Amusing.

"Well, when Carrie gets out of jail, we'll have to have a movie night," Lucas suggested, still trying to be nice. "Your choice." Under his breath, he added, "I guess."

"Yeah, there's a good ghost one coming out I wanna see."

A ghost movie? Really?

"Let me know when you feel up to it, and I'll take care of everything."

"Thanks, Luke," Mike said.

Luke?

We stayed for another hour, until Mike's parents showed up. Mandy wrapped her arms around me.

"Do you *have* to go?" she whined, her puppy-dog eyes bigger than ever.

"Yeah, I'd better," I said, hugging her. "You stay here and beat your brother in a game of Go Fish, okay?"

Her smile widened. "I always win that game. He really sucks at it."

"I'm counting on you then."

On our way back to Villisca, Lucas stopped at a pizza place and ordered a pepperoni pizza. We stayed in the Jeep, me eating, Lucas picking. After a few slices, I pushed the box aside and cuddled up beside him, my head pressed against his soundless chest. His steady breaths soothed me.

"Do I have to go back?" I asked, dreading the answer.

"Yeah," he said quietly, stroking his fingers through my hair.

"I'd rather just stay right here forever." I traced my fingers over his lips. Oh, how I longed for him to feel it! I stared at my hand as I circled the soft skin repeatedly. Silky smooth.

I barely had time to notice the sad glint in Lucas's eye. When I glanced up, it was gone, replaced by sheer contentment.

He cupped my face between his palms, lifting it to meet his own. His lips pressed against mine, the coolness of his touch sending a flurry of tingles through me.

"With you," he murmured, "forever isn't long enough."

Chapter 4

"Carrie Anne Reese!" Grandma burst out when she walked through the door. "You have a lot of explaining to do, young lady!"

It was just after 4:30, and I was sitting alone in the living room awaiting the fireworks.

The finale came first. Heat poured off of her, and I rose to face the flames.

"I'm so sorry," I said, frowning.

Grandma stood inside the doorframe, her hands on her hips in a lovely impression of my mother.

"Where were you last night?" she demanded.

"At the game, like I told you. But then Mike got hurt, and he was life-flighted to Omaha. So, I left the game and went to the hospital." I kept my tone even and matter-of-fact with just a hint of innocence. Direct eye-contact was a must.

"Have you heard of a phone?" Grandma asked without a trace of sarcasm.

"I forgot."

"We were worried sick! Then you weren't here this morning either!"

"Yeah, I, uh, left for the hospital again early this morning. I was worried about him." Yes! That was all true.

"You are grounded, missy! You go to school. You go to work. You come home. That is all. No Mike. No Lucas. Do you understand?"

Unfortunately, I did.

"Yes, Grandma." I took a deep breath, debating on whether to ask a possible damning question. "For how long?"

Laser beams shot out of her eyes and zapped me to pieces. I guess I shouldn't have asked. "Until. I. Tell. You," she growled through gritted teeth.

The hard lines on her face softened slightly when she changed the subject. "How's Mike? What room is he in? I should send flowers…or a football…or something."

Until now, I'd wondered if she'd even heard the part about Mike. Then again, she probably got wind of it from a customer at the store today.

Small town syndrome strikes again.

I gave her the information and collapsed back on the sofa. Mike was so wrong—I was going to be grounded for the rest of my life, even without them knowing I'd stayed most of last night at Lucas's house. If Grandma knew that little tidbit, I'd probably be dead right now.

Grandpa still wasn't in from the fields, so Grandma and I spent the quietest dinner on earth in the kitchen before she sent me directly to my room without passing 'Go' or collecting two hundred dollars. Since my grandparents never came in to check on me before bed, I figured it would be safe if

Lucas came over early. Grandma had taken away my cell, though, concluding that I didn't need it since I apparently didn't know how to use it anyway. I guess I'd have to wait until 9:30 when Lucas would appear.

Bummer.

In the meantime, I opted for homework. I skimmed through the assigned Literature short story, *A Rose for Emily* by William Faulkner. Somewhere on my laptop, I had the paper I'd written for my teacher back in Texas last year. I could just turn that in—I'd gotten an A.

I peeked at the clock. Two more hours until Lucas would be here. I decided to write a new paper to pass the time.

The Fine Line Between Love and Obsession

By Carrie Reese

A Rose for Emily portrays an older woman with a lust for love and acceptance. She falls for a man who eventually chooses to leave her. In her pain, she decides that she can't let him go. Her love for him is too strong, and her heart can't handle any more pain. To keep him, she kills him. Now, he'd stay with her forever. Her love turns quickly into selfish obsession.

I glanced up when I heard a soft knock on my bedroom door.

"Come in," I called out.

Grandpa Rob stepped inside, his face solemn but not angry. "You really upset your grandmother, kiddo."

He'd probably already spoken with Grandma and got all the necessary Mike info along with my excuses for not coming home.

I set my computer aside. "I know. I'm sorry."

Grandpa nodded. "She was worried 'bout you, Care Bear. And so was I."

"I'll remember to call next time. I don't know what I was thinking."

Grandpa scratched the whiskers on his chin. "Visitin' hours at the hospital start at eight," he said. His eyebrows rose, lines racing along his forehead. "Now, your grandmother might not know that, but I checked up here at 5:30 this mornin', and you weren't here. Omaha ain't that far away."

Uh-oh. He knew. Yep, I was dead with nowhere to hide.

The truth seemed like my best option now.

"I did come home," I explained. "But I was upset and lonely, so I left again and went to Lucas's. I didn't mean to fall asleep there."

I waited for Grandpa to blow a gasket. He didn't.

"Is that all, Care Bear?"

"Yes," I replied, looking him square in the eye. "I slept on the sofa. Nothing happened, I swear."

My grandpa studied me hesitantly. He wasn't stupid. He'd raised four children, one of them my father.

"I swear," I repeated, holding his stare.

Satisfied, he sighed. "All right. Don't let your grandmother know. She'd have a cow."

I'd always known my grandpa was the best!

I threw my arms around his neck. "Thank you."

He kissed the top of my head. "I love you, Care Bear. You need to call next time, okay?"

"Absolutely. I promise."

I seemed to be making a lot of promises lately. This one I knew I could keep, though.

Grandpa smiled and rose to his feet. "Good night, Care Bear."

"G'night."

Grandpa left my room, closing the door behind him. My gaze drifted to the clock.

8:31.

Rolling onto my stomach, I opened my Word doc again and read through what I'd written so far. I tapped on the keys. Love. Obsession.

8:39.

I couldn't concentrate. All I needed was two lousy pages. I re-read my one paragraph.

8:42.

Emily's love. Wait. No. She didn't love him. Not really. She only wanted to keep him for herself.

8:45.

Oh God! Am I *Emily*? Do I love Lucas enough to let *him* go? Was it right for me to stake a claim on him even if that meant his soul would be lost forever? Like Emily's obsession, would Lucas's soul rot while I cuddled up next to him?

8:58.

No. Never. Our souls were connected, and Lucas

loved me as much as I loved him. *"Forever isn't long enough,"* he'd said.

9:02.

However, Lucas had never hid the fact that his love for me was partly selfish. Even when danger loomed over us, he couldn't stay away.

9:12.

Can love be selfish? Is it wrong to love someone so much that no one else can fill you up? Is it selfish to want to live and die for that person? Does loving someone mean you have to let them go?

But Lucas *wants* to stay.

Doesn't he?

Doubt rolled in thick. *Is that what he'd said?* No, it wasn't. He said he didn't know what he'd do when he found his soul.

9:20.

I paced my room, my fingers entwined through my hair. From my nightstand, I lifted the crystal angel frame that held the picture of Lucas I'd taken under the weeping willows this summer. I swept my fingers over the glass. His green eyes gleamed back at me.

Slowly, I turned the frame over and slid the small metal rungs to the side. I read the words I'd written on the back.

Through Love and Devotion, we are spared a life of loneliness and despair. To have someone to love so greatly and have someone love back so deeply is the only way to live a life of Happiness and Joy. Even in death, you can still Love in

9:26.

I sat on the edge of the bed, still holding the open frame. Yes, there were worse things than death: Life without Lucas topped my list; him lost for eternity without his soul; the idea of Lucas never existing in any form, and, of course, him being tormented in the fires of Hell.

Selfish or not, Lucas was mine and I was his. Obsessive or not, I couldn't live without him. Love or not, I had to think of what was best for him.

Because sometimes, selfishness felt more like desire. Obsession felt more like need. Love felt more like pain. And sometimes, pain meant letting go.

I can't! There has to be a way. There just has to be.

I closed the flap, set the metal rungs, and placed the frame back on my nightstand.

A cold breeze circled the room, smelling like lilacs and springtime. I closed my laptop as Lucas appeared on my bed. He kissed me slowly, and my arms wrapped themselves around his neck on their own.

"How long are you in for?" he said against my mouth.

I pulled him closer. "Life."

Cautiously, I slid a leg over his lap, straddling him on the mattress. I hesitated, waiting for him to tense before I deepened the kiss. His hands slipped to my hips, pushing them against him.

My fingers worked their way into his dark hair, and my lips moved to his neck. I needed him while he was still here, needed him more than air. Like in his kitchen that morning, heat began to simmer under my skin. My heart sped up, and I got lost in his embrace, his lips, his body.

Unconsciously, I tugged on the back of his shirt, lifting it up. The world around me melted away. I ran my fingers up Lucas's back, his muscles tightening under the pressure—but suddenly, my thoughts returned.

He couldn't feel my touch. The warmth and waves he left all over me, he didn't feel himself. When he swept into my room, his scent filled my lungs, making me long for him. But he couldn't smell me. Couldn't…

"Carrie?"

The world slammed back into focus, and I hadn't realized I'd stopped kissing him. "Yeah?"

With my legs still folded around him, I sat back a little. I couldn't read the expression on his face, and it made me uncomfortable.

He didn't say anything about what just happened, though. He'd said enough earlier.

Carefully, he pulled me off his lap. "I spoke with Megan today."

The way he said it sent chills up my spine. Not good ones.

"God, there's so much to tell you," he said, pushing a hand through his hair. His gaze met mine. "She did another memory charm, and…"

For a second, my heart stopped.

And…?

"She saw something—someone—by my car after it crashed."

"You remember?"

Lucas shook his head. "No. It was all fuzzy. I couldn't make much out."

"But that's good, right? I mean, maybe your memories are coming back?"

"Care, the fuzz…it was black."

"Black? Like…"

"The person with me was a cambion of some sort. A half-demon."

Like at the park.

"Okay." I nodded, ignoring his somber tone. "We have a place to start. We know *what* we're looking for."

Lucas sighed. "That's just it, Care." He paused. "You can't help."

I shot up off the bed. "What? Why? You said you wanted me to help you."

"I know, but that was before I knew for sure what we were dealing with. Half-demons, Care." Lucas cocked his head to the side. "Cambion is the umbrella term for those creatures without souls. He could be a vampire. An incubus. A reaper. It's too dangerous. Cambions can't be trusted with humans. They're soul-stealers."

"They can't be worse than the demons from the house. Besides, Megan is human," I said, defending myself.

"Megan's a witch. She has powers to protect herself. They won't touch a witch. It would start a war in which they are vastly outnumbered and outpowered."

"But this cambion *helped* you." I remembered what Megan said about cambions not being prone to helpfulness. "This one's different."

"Maybe, but I'm not going to risk your life on it."

"Then Megan can protect me too." No way was I giving up. "You said we'd do this together. I'm holding you to it."

Lucas's eyes narrowed as he thought. "Compromise?"

I shrugged. "Depends."

"Let Megan and me look for him first. When we know what he wants, I'll come and get you. I want to make sure, though, that if I need to, I can get you out."

"What do you mean, 'get me out?'"

"I'll practice teleporting with Megan until I'm comfortable enough to do it with you," Lucas said, though his tone carried traces of uncertainty. "I need to know that I can protect you. I can't lose you, Carrie."

What if I *lose* you?

"Okay," I finally agreed. "I'll wait for you."

Lucas moved closer, nuzzling my neck. "Thank you."

Again, I circled my arms around him, but he pulled away and stood up. I watched his back as he went to stand by the window. Even though he didn't need to breathe, his shoulders rose and fell heavily.

I stayed glued on the bed, knowing there was more he wasn't telling me. Something else Megan had said.

And then I remembered.

"What did she say about me being able to see what you saw?"

Slipping both hands into the pockets of his jeans, Lucas kept his focus out the window.

"Lucas?" I prompted, sliding my legs over the edge of the mattress.

Slowly, he turned to face me. Glowing emerald eyes softened as they rolled over me and faded a little. "Carrie, Megan received a book from a warlock the other day. It's loaded with information about Incenamus."

All I could do was nod because his tone didn't sound right.

Lucas rolled his lips together, dropping his gaze for a split second before refocusing on me. "It says that Incenamus has the power to bring the dead back to life."

Chapter 5

I lay in Lucas's arms, feigning sleep. The possibilities of the gem he'd just handed us ran through my mind, making my whole body jittery with excitement. True, I'd been ready to sign-up immediately, but Lucas burst that bubble real fast.

"Megan can read the parts written in Latin, but most of the book is in Cumbric, a language that died out sometime in the twelfth century," he'd explained, again pushing his fingers through his hair. "And," he sat down next to me, "it can't be that easy. We shouldn't mess with fate."

I frowned. "If it can be done, we're not messing with it. Fate gave it to us. It's a gift."

Lucas rested his elbows on his knees, hunching forward. "I don't know, Care. We'll just have to wait and see what Megan can come up with. It could be dangerous if the whole book isn't translated before we use it."

Now, hours later, I still couldn't figure out why he'd been so squeamish. Didn't he want this? To have a body, spirit, *and* soul? To be alive and with me? To feel me?

"If I could figure out a way, I swear to you, I would. I'd do anything," he'd said.

I chewed on the inside of my cheek. No downsides came to my mind. This was it—our way to be together.

Why can't he see that?

Sometime during the night, I'd fallen asleep only to wake up alone as usual. My heart sank, realizing it would probably be days until I saw him again. He and Megan would start their "doubled efforts" to find the cambion today.

I readied myself for church and jumped into the backseat of Grandma's Impala. Usually, I listened to my grandparents jabber on their way into town— not today, though. This morning Grandma sat oddly quiet.

Probably still mad at me for not calling Friday night.

The news at church, all over town actually, was Mike's exit from the football field. Since everyone knew we were friends, all of the questions regarding the play and his injuries were directed at me. It made for a busy morning.

"We're going to visit Mike at the hospital today," Grandma said on the way home.

I took my chances. "We, as in me and you guys? Or just the two of you?"

"Grounding means you stay at home."

Of course it does.

She held out her hand to me, and I dug in my purse and set my car keys in her palm. I figured if I cooperated and didn't argue, maybe I'd be off the hook sooner. The strategy always worked with my mother.

"Thank you," she said as I slumped lower in my seat.

After lunch, my grandparents headed out, and I moseyed up to my bedroom to collect my homework. I changed into a pair of turquoise pajama pants and a white long-sleeve tee, and I pulled my hair into a ponytail, ready for the world's most boring afternoon. Downstairs, I dumped my homework on the floor and flipped on the television.

The Weather Channel, one of my grandparents' favorites, indicated it would be a beautiful day for November. Man, that sucked. If Mike wasn't injured, and I wasn't grounded, we'd be out horseback riding today, as was our Sunday afternoon tradition.

I shifted the curtain to the side and peered out to the barn. My horse, Goldie, was outside enjoying the fresh air. Glad one of us could.

The sound of the phone ringing made me jump. I debated for a second whether to answer. Technically, I was grounded from talking on the phone, but no one called *me* on the landline, so I picked it up.

"Hello?"

"Carrie?"

Oh crap!

Yeah, I knew that voice. Known it my whole life and it was a voice I was perfectly happy to avoid. I considered hanging up, but like a complete idiot, I didn't.

"Carrie?" my father repeated. "Are you there?"

I said nothing, choosing instead to bite my lips together and stare at the wall.

"How have you been, Princess?"

Heat raced to my cheeks. *How dare he call me that?* I assumed he could hear me breathing, and I hoped *he* assumed I was still pissed.

"I know you're angry, and you have every right to be."

Damn straight.

"Please give me a chance to explain."

He waited for an answer; I didn't give him one. No amount of explaining could fix what he'd done.

"Your mom and I were trying; we were," he started, "but it wasn't working. I knew I'd never be happy unless I went out on my own. I didn't want my unhappiness to drag down you or your mother."

Sure, I heard him speaking, but the only thing I understood was the screaming in my head. His words sounded like a bunch of self-centered teenage bull, and I didn't buy it. He left because he wanted to. For his barely-out-of-college secretary. Sick.

"Anyway, I just wanted to tell you that. No matter what happens, though, Carrie, I still love you. Nothing will change that. You're still my daughter, my princess."

I rolled my eyes. What a load of horse shit—no offense to Goldie.

"I know I've probably told you about Ami from the office. Um, I think you've met her before. She, uh, she was my assistant."

Secretary. The word is secretary.

"Well, I, uh, just wanted to tell you that she and I

are getting married."

Um...what?

If I wasn't gripping onto the phone so tightly, I'd have thrown it against the wall. The bomb had been dropped, and I waited for it to explode.

"We set a date for late September. And we, I mean, Ami would really like it if you'd be a bridesmaid."

Boom!

Three times I unsuccessfully tried to swallow the lump in my throat.

Un. Freaking. Believable.

The stretch of silence grew longer. I figured *Griffin* was waiting for me to cry, scream, yell, or just hang up. No, I was *not* going to give him the pleasure.

"Um. Well. You think about it, okay? And let me know." He paused again. "You enjoying Villisca?"

Lame.

"I always hated living there. Have you visited the Moore House yet?"

Oh, if I could breathe fire, I so would.

Griffin cleared his throat. "I heard you have a boyfriend. Is he treating you all right?"

Like you treated Mom and me? Nope, Lucas is awesome. You, however...

I remained silent, my gaze fixated on the wall behind my grandparents' recliners. This was the conversation from hell that wouldn't end.

"Hey, sweetie. I'm really trying here. Can you give me something, Princess?" he pleaded. Personally, I liked the unease in his tone.

I shook my head, knowing he couldn't see it.

"Okay. Um. Well, you have a good week at school, okay?" He paused, waiting again. "Okay. That's okay. I love you, Princess." He sighed, and I heard the phone click.

I hit end and laid the phone carefully back on the cradle. My knuckles white, I cracked them to relieve the tension.

Had I heard him right?

It felt like a dream. Unfortunately, it couldn't be; I remembered every syllable of the conversation more clearly than what I ate for breakfast. Yes, my father was getting re-married—engaged as soon as the divorce became final.

And his half-his-age bride-to-be wanted me to stand up with them? Was this some sort of sick joke? Dressing up and standing next to my soon-to-be-stepmom wasn't going to make us more of a family like *Griffin* alluded to.

I fell backward onto the sofa, wondering if Mom knew. What would she think?

I fumbled for my laptop—the one thing Grandma hadn't taken away since it was "for school." I started the email telling my mom about my grounding in case Grandma hadn't told her (*fat chance*), and I didn't leave out the part about sleeping over at Lucas's house. Then, I told her about, ugh…*Dad*.

Did you know about this? I mean, it's only been six months! How long has he been cheating on us?

Just so you know I will NOT be going.

On a more pleasant note, school is

```
good. Weird that's it's so small,
though. I think Jessica and Stacy are
still coming up over Christmas break—
if Grandma lifts my sentence by then.
   I've got homework to do, so I'd
better go.
   I love you, Mom. Take care of
yourself, okay?
   Carrie
```

I sat back for half a minute, analyzing the email. The last thing I wanted was to propel my mother overboard, but she needed to know, and I much rather she hear it from me.

Send.

Sighing, I opened a new message for Jess and Stacy. Maybe it would keep me from screaming. They'd be driving up in four short weeks, and I was so excited that I'd started X-ing off all the calendars in the house and the antique store with a red sharpie. Jess's parents had needed some convincing: a call from my grandmother, a long conversation with my mother, and Jess's state-of-the-art groveling. Stacy's parents, however, were spending Christmas in Costa Rica and told Stacy she could stay with a friend—me.

```
   Jess & Stacy,
   Hey! Everything ready for your
trip? I figured we'd go shopping on
Saturday after you arrive. I could
really use some mall time with my
besties. Oh, and you'd better bring
the warmest stuff you own. I swear
polar bears couldn't even survive
```

here.

Anyway, I wanted to tell you that Mike got hurt at the game last night. He's pretty banged up. After visiting him, I stopped by Lucas's and accidently fell asleep on his sofa. So, yeah, I'm grounded. I guess that means I'll have plenty of time to clean out the spare room for you, though. ☺

Griffin—I refuse to call him my father anymore—called me today. He's marrying her. Ditched us to marry her. And get this: she wants me to be a bridesmaid! Yeah, not happening.

Could one of you please go check on my mom?

See you soon!

<3 Carrie

Uninvited, thoughts of Griffin's call entered my mind. Instead of the emails being a distraction, they became a catalyst for the tears threatening to overflow. I wiped the moisture away before it had a chance to spill over.

Already, I hated Ami. She was nothing but a thief, stealing my dad, our family, and everything I cared about. Little Miss Home-Wrecker didn't belong in my life.

I closed my laptop and set it aside. Curling up on the sofa, I grabbed a pillow and squeezed it to my chest as hard as I could.

Oh, God! What did I do? Why did I have to tell my mom?

That did it. I sobbed into the pillow, allowing the

pain to win this battle.

In my mind, I pictured her sitting in the black office chair, all alone in her home office. It played out like a movie.

She has a tall glass of water on a coaster to her right. Her computer is on, its glow the only light in the room. A message pops up, alerting her that she received an email from me. She cracks a smile and opens it immediately. I can hear her soft laugh as she reads about my grounding, nodding slowly in agreement with Grandma's decision. Her eyes bug open in surprise at my staying over at Lucas's house, but she knows I'm telling the truth about nothing happening. If it had, she knew I'd tell her.

Then, her smile fades when she reads the last part. She reads it one more time just to make sure she read it correctly the first time. She did. Without closing out of her email, she shuts her laptop and reaches for her water. She takes a small sip, letting what I'd written sink in. Slowly, she stands up and walks to the kitchen, dumping the rest of the water down the drain. Now she pours herself a glass of red wine. She crawls onto the sofa, positions herself like me, draws the lavender blanket up to her chest, and breaks down.

All because I wanted her to hear it from me.

My jaw trembled when I realized I couldn't comfort her. My stomach hurt. With my arms wrapped around my waist, I slid off the sofa, ran upstairs to the bathroom, and threw up in the toilet.

***

Knock. Knock. Knock.

The soft raps at my bedroom door woke me. My head spun when I sat up. I rubbed the sleep from my eyes. I didn't remember crawling into bed, much less falling asleep.

Knock. Knock. Knock.

"Carrie?" Grandpa's voice carried through the door, concerned. "You okay, Care Bear?"

Suddenly remembering Griffin's phone call, the email to my mother, and my race upstairs, I nervously wound my long, brown hair around my hand, draping it over my shoulder. "Come in."

The door cracked open, and Grandpa Rob's head popped through. A sad smile graced his lips. He sighed and opened the door wider, stepping into my room. I wondered if the signs of my break down were still written all over my face.

Then I noticed the lines on his and the downcast angle of his eyes.

My stomach churned again as fear gnawed at me. *Mike's surgery!*

"What happened? Is Mike okay?"

Grandpa took a seat at the edge of my bed and patted my knee. He had farmer's hands: permanently stained in the creases, calloused, with dirt wedged under each fingernail.

"He's fine. In good spirits, actually," Grandpa assured me. "He's a tough kid."

Relief washed over me. "Oh, good," I said, still cautious. It was something else. "So, what's going on?"

Grandpa cleared his throat. "I came up here to apologize."

What did he have to apologize for?

"Renae didn't say anything to me until we were on the way home, and by then, it was too late," Grandpa continued.

I narrowed my eyes at him, not understanding.

"You father called here this mornin' and told your grandmother that he wanted to speak with you, but Renae knew you wouldn't want to talk. She told him to call while we were gone and that you'd probably answer the phone."

My grandma set me up?

She had been too quiet on the drive to church this morning. Great. Now I'd been betrayed by my grandmother.

True, it had never been a secret that she didn't agree with the silent treatment I was handing her son, but guess what? I didn't agree with how her son was treating his family!

Anger swirled around me until Grandpa Rob patted my knee again. My unwillingness to hear my father out had built some tension between my grandparents. Grandpa was the one who fought for me, reminding Grandma that I needed the space. Now he'd done it again.

"I wish I'd have been here for you, Care Bear."

I twirled the end of my hair through my fingers. "Did you know?" I asked. "Did you know what he wanted to tell me?"

Grandpa Rob nodded. "Yeah, he told us last week."

A tear dropped from my eye, sliding down to my chin. "Are you okay with it?"

He shifted on my bed. "He's a grown man,

capable of makin' his own choices."

"That's not really what I asked."

Grandpa sighed again. "Yeah, I know. I'm more concerned about how all of this is affectin' you."

"I'm fine," I lied, and from my leftover red, puffy eyes, he probably knew it.

"Well," he said, the makings of a grin beginning to appear on his face, "your grandmother feels horrible now."

"Yeah, I'll bet she does," I mumbled.

"So," Grandpa drawled out. "You're off the hook. Groundin' is over."

"What?" I studied him, but Grandpa was never one to joke around. "Seriously?"

He held out his hand, palm up, and opened his fingers. Inside laid my most coveted possessions: my car keys and cell phone.

I gaped at him. "How'd you do it? I've only been grounded for, like, a day."

"She owed you," Grandpa replied, standing up. "I'm sure Mike would like your company and his homework after school tomorrow. No staying over at Lucas's, though." He eyed me hard as he said the last part.

"Thanks, Grandpa. Lucas is out of town for a few days anyway."

"Well, I hope everythin' is okay." He walked to the door and turned around. "I know it doesn't mean much now, but for the record, I did tell Griffin he needed to rethink some things."

I nodded. "I love you, Grandpa."

"I love you too, Care Bear," Grandpa said, and closed the door behind him.

***

I avoided going downstairs for dinner, not wanting to face my grandmother yet. She didn't bother me about it, leaving a tray of food outside my door.

I tried to call my mom, but it went directly to voicemail. My heart sunk, reliving the earlier film clip of her I'd imagined.

After a lame attempt at homework, I packed the unfinished assignments into my backpack and crawled under the covers, calling it an early night.

A rush of cold air startled me, and I rolled into Lucas's arms as he materialized on top of the duvet. His lips pressed against my temple. "I'm so sorry I couldn't come sooner."

I snuggled into him, unbelievably happy he was there. His arms felt so safe. In them was the one place I could hide, the one place no one could hurt me. "What do you mean? I didn't expect you for a few days."

Lucas's head rested against mine. "You were hurting today. I felt you."

I peered up at him, his glowing green eyes staring back. "My dad called, and—"

"I know."

My brow furrowed. "How?"

"Incenamus." Lucas's fingers brushed down my cheek. "I spent the day translating some of the chapters in Megan's book."

My breath hitched. "Did you find out…"

"The chapters that are in Latin," he specified too quickly.

"Oh," I grumbled, sinking into the cradle of his elbow.

"It's mostly speculation, but I think when we get angry or upset, somehow we let our guard down. Like an inner barrier breaks apart, allowing the connection between us to fuse together. That's when I can sense what you're feeling." He paused. "And read your thoughts. It's a stronger connection than the dreams."

Yes, at the football game when Mike got hurt, he heard me. I took a deep breath, clearing my mind.

"Okay. What am I thinking?" I asked.

Kiss me.

Green eyes studied me. "I don't know. I don't hear anything."

I blinked, disappointed.

"I've only been able to hear you when you've been upset." He grinned, his dimple sinking deep. "I'd love to know all the time, though."

"I felt you once," I said. "That night I came over."

Lucas nodded. "Yeah, I was thinking about Becca and the implications it had."

"I didn't hear you, just felt you."

He puffed out a chuckle. "I guess that gives us something to work on."

"Wait, you want bad things to happen so you can read my thoughts?"

"I was kinda hoping we could figure it out without the bad stuff."

I sighed, looking away. "I have a feeling the bad stuff is here to stay."

Lucas turned my face back to him and kissed me

softly. "Everything will work itself out how it's supposed to be."

I pressed my forehead against his. "Oh, and how's that?"

His wintery breath rushed across my lips, and he pulled me closer, his jaw clenching. "I wish I knew."

Chapter 6

Lucas returned to Iowa City with Megan as soon as I fell asleep. He and I decided to try and break down the invisible barrier between our souls during his absence in order to test his theory. I had no idea where to start.

I lay awake in bed with my eyes closed, sunlight creeping through the window in warm beams over my face. *Breathe in. Breathe out.* I puckered my lips and blew out as I thought it. *Breathe in. Breathe out. Clear my mind.*

I zoned out, concentrating on fusing myself with Lucas's soul. In my mind, I pictured a massive wall crumbling, brick by brick, to the ground, and light filtering in through the crevices.

And then my alarm went off.

Beep. Beep. Beep.

My eyes flew open, and I slammed my hand on top of the snooze. I lay back and tried again, ditching the imagery this time.

I love you. I miss you, I thought and kept thinking it until the alarm went off again. It would be a few days before I knew if my message had gone through. I, however, felt no different.

Disappointed, I got ready for school.

***

The whole school buzzed over Friday night's game and Mike's less-than-spectacular exit. More than that, whispers of the team's unlikely chances of winning the second playoff game without their star captain seemed to have left everyone, including the players, with a shadow of pessimism lingering over their heads.

"A hundred bucks says we get forty-fived by Stanton," Logan said during lunch.

Even though Mike was absent, I still sat at our usual table with the rest of Mike's friends, who in the last months had become my friends as well.

Jesse shook his head. "No way. Odds are too good to take that bet."

"I'll take the under," Jeremy piped up. "I say we get beat by no more than three touchdowns."

Logan fist bumped his teammate. "Bold, dude."

Jeremy's girlfriend rolled her eyes. "Great attitude, guys. We'll lose for sure."

"We're not planning on losing." Jeremy shrugged. "With Mike out, we're just being realistic."

Logan shot me a nod. "You in, Carrie?"

I took one last look at my untouched lunch and stood up. "No. And I don't think Mike would be either."

Morons.

Picking up my tray, I walked away.

***

Lugging both my backpack and another bag filled with Mike's books through the hospital parking lot winded me. As soon as I made it inside the elevator, I dropped both bags on the floor and drug them down the hall to Mike's room when the doors opened to the second floor.

His door was cracked open, but I knocked anyway.

"Yeah?" Mike's groggy voice answered.

Using my hip, I widened the door and walked in backward, dragging the bags with me. Exhausted, I plopped in the chair beside Mike's head. He stared at me with the strangest expression.

"Um, are you supposed to be here?" he asked, eyeing me with one brow lowered, half concealing a hazel iris.

I shrugged innocently. "I'm off the hook."

Mike held the same face, waiting for more of an explanation.

"Grandma tricked me into speaking with my dad, and Grandpa put his foot down. Ungrounding me is her way of apologizing, I guess."

"I'd say you lucked out big time."

"And good thing for you too."

"For me?"

I grinned. "Yep. I brought your homework." I hoisted the bag up so he could see it. "No need to thank me."

"Please tell me you cleaned the garbage out my

locker, as I see you've managed to get everything else out of it."

"Nope." I set the bag back down. "I wanted to make sure you had something to come back to. Home sweet home and all that."

"I appreciate the thought." Mike turned up the corner of his lips, reminding me of the way Lucas smiled.

I sat down again. "You've been the talk of the town."

"So I've heard," he said. "I still hope to be outta here by Thursday. Stanton will be tough to beat."

Football. Always football.

"Yeah," I drew out the word. "About that. Logan's taking bets that we'll be forty-fived."

Anger blazed in my best friend's eyes. Yeah, I knew it would.

"Dickhead!" Mike grumbled. "So much for leadership."

"I don't think anyone took the over," I said, hoping to soften the blow.

It didn't work. Oh, if looks could kill…

"He needs to keep his damn mouth shut." Mike pounded his fist against the mattress. "I wish I could play! We had a shot at the championship this year!"

"Hey," I said, placing my hand carefully on his shoulder. His eyes rolled down to my touch. "You still have a shot."

He sighed, glancing up at me. "You're right." His irises darkened, and I wondered if we were still talking about football. Lightly, he brushed a lock of hair out of my face, and I sucked in a breath as I took a step back.

I gazed down at my feet. "Sorry," I muttered.

"Yeah, me too." Regret coated his tone.

Suddenly he snickered. "Everything works itself out in the end, right?"

"Sure." I nodded, remembering that Lucas had said the exact same words the night before.

But how?

***

Everyone in the bleachers rose to their feet as the assistant coach wheeled Mike out on the field before the game Thursday night. Since Lucas bailed on me to research a new lead with Megan, I sat with Mike's parents and little sister, Mandy. Mandy stuck her pinkie fingers in the corners of her mouth and whistled.

"How do you do that?" I asked, impressed.

She shrugged. "I dunno. Mike taught me." Sticking her fingers in her mouth, she did it again.

The assistant coach left the wheelchair at the end of the players' bench. Mike rotated his whole body to check out the crowd until he spotted me. He shot me a nod—sort of—and I offered my habitual thumbs up. Mandy waved at him like a lunatic, almost smacking me in the face with her mitten.

"Hey!" I cried out, laughing.

"Sorry." She smiled. "He saw us, didn't he?"

"You were hard to miss, squirt," I said, using Mike's new nickname for her. It fit.

The Villisca Blue Jays ran out onto the field to another round of thunderous applause and Mandy's whistling. I shivered. The wind had picked up, carrying small flurries of snow with it. When Mandy and I sat down, I quickly threw the blanket over us.

I wished I could say our team dominated from the first play, but I'd be lying. Most of the time, I found my gaze wandering to Mike, who was screaming angry-coach style from the sidelines.

Mandy saw it too. "He's got anger issues."

"I've noticed."

Good thing she can't hear him.

By half-time, Stanton led the Blue Jays twenty-one zip. Mandy slumped in her seat and leaned her head on my shoulder.

"This sucks," she pouted.

I looked down to the field at Mike. He was yelling at the team manager, pushing him over the track toward the press box.

"Sure does," I agreed.

Beside us, Mrs. Carson stood up. "You girls want some popcorn?"

Mandy's eyes widened. "With extra butter?"

Her mother laughed. "Extra butter. Got it." She slid past us, making her way down the bleachers. At the bottom, she turned toward the concession stand, and that's when I saw him. Standing with his hands in the pockets of his faded, ripped blue jeans, his gaze locked on me.

He sure wasn't from VHS. Too old to be a student, for one. College, maybe?

Orangish, red hair fell across his eyes, and he didn't bother brushing it away. His eyes narrowed as he stared at me. Goose bumps popped up over my skin, and my breath caught.

Oh crap. I knew this feeling. *Fear.*

I shuddered.

He took a step forward, the tip of his tongue seductively trailing over his bottom lip. I scanned the crowd; maybe he was looking at someone else? When I glanced back down at him, he shook his head and pointed directly at me.

This can't be good.

I stiffened, unable to take my eyes off him. Good God, he was gorgeous. Under the stadium lights, the gold of his irises seemed to sparkle. And his lips! Oh, how warm they'd feel pressed against mine.

My entire body relaxed as I drank him in. Broad shoulders, solid chest, hard abs, tight thighs—the things I wanted to do to him! I felt myself smile when he reached the bottom of the bleachers, finally shifting the wind-blown locks from his face. Heat filled me, even in the cold, pressing low into my abdomen. Yes, he was coming for me.

Mandy tugged on my coat sleeve. "Carrie? You like extra butter, right?"

I squeezed my eyes closed for a few seconds, pulling myself out of the trance.

"Carrie? Earth to Carrie," Mandy sang out.

I opened my eyes. The guy was gone.

"Uh, yeah. Yeah, I'm here," I said, slowly turning my attention back to Mike's sister.

"Are you okay? I asked if you liked extra butter. When I told Mom, I didn't think about you."

"Oh. Oh, yeah." I looked over the crowed walking below us, searching for…Wait, what was I doing? "Extra butter is fine." I spotted Mandy's mom on her way back to us and a sense of relief washed over me. Mrs. Carson. Right. I was waiting for Mrs. Carson.

She hurried up the stairs and placed the popcorn in my lap. "Share, little missy," she told her daughter.

Mandy puffed out her lower lip. "I share."

The third quarter began better than the first but steadily went downhill from there. Mike, on his feet most of the time, was barking out orders more than Coach Morrison. I made a mental note to steer clear of him for a few days if we lost. Until things settled down a bit.

By the end of the third quarter, Mandy and I had successfully reached the bottom of our large popcorn bucket.

"That didn't last long," I said, rolling my eyes at the little girl with butter breath.

She shrugged innocently. "I like popcorn."

"And extra butter." I doubled the blanket on top of her. "I'm going to get us some hot chocolate. I'll be right back." I stood up then twisted back around. "Without butter," I added, and Mandy giggled.

I swear everyone had the same idea at the same time—raid the concession stand. I waited in line, shivering and listening to the Stanton fans explode into cheers as another six points was added to their score. I fought the urge to peek in Mike's direction—I could easily imagine his response.

I stepped up to the counter, ordered, and the Booster Club mom handed me a large hot chocolate, filled to the top. Heat poured through the Styrofoam, warming my hands through my gloves. I inhaled the steam.

Heaven!

Taking a sip, I turned around and dumped the chocolatey goodness down my bubble coat and the black wool coat of the guy behind me.

Horrified, I clasped my hand over my mouth. "Ohmygod! I'm so sorry. I didn't—"

"Hey, don't worry about it," he said, examining himself before casting his caramel gaze on me. He brushed the ginger strands of hair off his face. "I think you got the worst of it."

I rubbed the hot liquid into my coat, not sure what else to do.

"I guess I'll be extra warm," I said, forcing a smile.

"Here," he reached behind me for a stack of napkins, "let me."

"No, it's okay, I—"

"I got it," he said, sparkling golden irises tilted up at me through thick lashes.

I paused, letting him wipe me down.

"I have a boyfriend," I blurted out.

He chuckled. "Does that mean I'm in trouble?"

"Uh, no," I stuttered. "I—"

"Hey, I'm just trying to save you from having to purchase a new coat. He won't have a problem with that, will he?" He took one last swipe with the napkins and tossed them into the garbage. "I'm Reid, by the way."

"Carrie," I said, stuffing my hands in my pockets. "And thanks."

"My pleasure, Carrie." Reid nodded, and for a split second something changed in his gaze. The hair at the back of my neck spiked up.

Reid craned his neck to the game behind him and balled his hands. Seconds later, he slowly returned his attention to me, relaxed. "I'd better go."

"Are you from Stanton?" I asked, unable to place him.

He sighed. "Nah. Just in town."

"And you came to a local football game?"

Reid's eyes flitted over me, narrowing a little. "Everyone seems to be here. I was looking for someone."

"It's a small town, maybe I can help," I offered against my better judgment.

Reid puffed a laugh. "He's not here. I'll find him some other time." He peered back out to the field, his attention landing on Mike. "If your boyfriend gives you any grief about the coat, let him know I was here and he wasn't."

"Mike's not my—"

Reid turned around, his gaze piercing me. A flicker of nostalgia fell across his face. "It was nice to meet you, Carrie."

Before I could answer, he walked away.

***

Out of habit, I took a final glance up at the scoreboard. Final score: Stanton 42, Villisca 10. I cringed.

"Can I stay with you tonight, Carrie?" Mandy begged.

My eyes settled on Mike, still on the field. He kicked a water jug before falling into his wheelchair. Yeah, he was pissed.

"School night, squirt," I apologized. "Sorry."

Her shoulders slumped, and she offered me her best puppy-dog eyes. Oh, she was good.

I gave her a hug. "It'll blow over soon. I promise."

I hope.

Before Mike could dig into me about the game, I darted through the gate and slid into my car. Out of the corner of my eye, through the mass of fans making their way to their vehicles, I caught a glimpse of Reid.

He was leaning up against a car, black wool coat, ripped faded blue jeans…and blond hair. Nope, not him. I sighed. Why did I even care?

I slipped through the back door of my grandparents' house and immediately jogged up to my room, successfully avoiding my grandmother.

Since I knew I wouldn't be seeing Lucas tonight, I decided to get a start on those college applications my mother had been hounding me about. I promised her one per week; I'd sent two in the last two months. I really needed to start making good on my promises.

Standing in front of the dresser mirror, I brushed my hair and gathered it up into a messy knot on top of my head. I fumbled through the bottom drawer and pulled out a pair of pajamas.

With only one leg through, I caught a shadow dashing by my second story window. Half falling over myself, I stuffed my other leg in and tossed the purple cami on as I made my way to the glass. I gently slid the curtain aside and peered out.

The wind rustled the upper branches of the tree,

and below me, leaves ran over the grass like tumbleweeds. Two farm cats with their heads cocked upward hissed at something at the top. A squirrel maybe?

I followed their gaze, easing up the trunk. Limbs jutted out, reaching their boney fingers into the night. Most of the leaves had fallen away, but the few that remained held on tightly as a gust threatened to yank them off.

The smaller branches at the top bent in together as if they were sharing a secret. Beside them, floating weightless, a cloud of smoke stretched out, vacillating in the breeze.

Clasping my hand over my mouth to stifle the scream, I stepped backward until I hit something solid, and cool arms wrapped around me.

For some reason, images of Reid flashed in my mind. The memory of the odd glint in his eye made me shudder. What the hell was Reid doing in my room?

Locked inside his arms, I rolled, ready to face him. Instead, I stared straight into the glowing green irises that took my breath away. Lucas laughed and removed my hand from over my mouth, replacing it with his lips.

Annoyed that he'd caught me off-guard, I tried to pull away, but he squeezed me tighter.

Transparent in his freaky, ghostly mist, he'd been sitting in the tree—moonbathing? Seeing him like that always made me uncomfortable—an awful reminder that he wasn't alive.

When he finally let go of me, I slugged him. "What the hell was that for? You scared me to death!"

With a sexy smirk, Lucas's eyes trailed over me. "Nope. Your heart's still beating. I'm no expert, but I'm pretty sure that means you're alive." He chuckled at his own joke.

So. Not. Funny.

"I saw something out there. Were you alone?" I sat on the edge of my bed.

"You're jumpy," Lucas said, getting serious. "Did something happen today?"

I shook my head too quickly. Reid was nothing, but...did something happen tonight? I couldn't remember.

I cleared my throat. "No. I...what were you doing outside my window?"

"Stargazing. And yes, alone." Lucas trailed the back of his hand down my cheek. "When I noticed you changing, I attempted to be a gentleman and backed off until you were finished."

"Attempted?"

Lucas offered a coy grin and shrugged.

A shiver ran up my spine, and I swallowed. "So, how was the view?"

Lucas curled his lower lip between his teeth. His eyes aflame, he ran his gaze slowly from my face, down my body, and back up again. Leaning in close enough for his breath to tickle my throat, he said, "Tempting."

Oh Lord!

"I meant the stars," I whispered, heat pouring off me like waves.

Yeah, that's what I meant.

His mouth pressed against my neck. "Beautiful

but not as intriguing as what was happening in here."

Holy buckets! Am I still breathing?

I felt my heart pounding in my ears. Surely Lucas heard it too.

"Wanna see?" he asked, taking my hand.

He paused and grinned, his lone dimple winking at me. "I'm talking about the stars," he murmured in my ear.

Yep. He heard all right.

"I can't. The branches won't hold me," I said, scooting closer to him.

"Not the tree. The roof."

I cocked my head up to him, confused. "I can't get up onto the roof."

Between two fingers, Lucas slid a loose strand of my hair down to the tip. "I think I can figure something out." He stood up and gathered the blankets off my bed. "Put a coat on, it's cold."

I looked at him in stunned dismay as he pulled more blankets from the top shelf of my closet. He tossed me an orange Longhorn hoodie, grinned, and disappeared.

Ghosts!

I slipped the sweatshirt over my head on my way downstairs to get my coat. By the time I got back to my room, Lucas was standing by the window, waiting for me.

"What's that on your coat?" he asked, nodding at the stain.

"Oh." Great. He noticed. "I accidently dumped hot chocolate on myself at the game."

Suddenly, Reid's words rushed through my

mind. *"If your boyfriend gives you any grief about the coat, let him know I was here and he wasn't."*

I shook it off. He'd looked at Mike when he said it. But…wait, how did he know about Mike? Lucas had so much on his mind, though, I wasn't about to add to it. It was probably nothing.

Lucas kissed the tip of my nose. "The one cup of hot chocolate you got yourself. I can't leave you alone for a second!"

"Nope, you can't. So don't."

Ignoring me, he wrapped his arms around me and held on tight. "Lean your head against me, and whatever you do, don't let go, okay?" he said.

I obeyed, clutching the back of his shirt into my fists.

"Um, and maybe close your eyes."

I peered up at him, suddenly worried. "Why?"

"I don't know. Just might be a good idea." He winked at me. "Ready?"

Pressing my cheek hard against his chest, I nodded.

"Here we go," Lucas muttered.

Pressure squeezed into me from all sides, and all of a sudden, the crisp November air stung my face. When Lucas's arms fell from around me, I opened my eyes. Overhead, the night sky glittered with stars.

I gasped out an amazed laugh.

How is this possible?

Slowly turning in a circle on the roof, my face pointed at the sky, I took it all in.

"Careful, there, baby," Lucas said, reaching out a hand I didn't take.

I feel so...free.

Stepping closer, Lucas cupped my face between his cool palms. He looked delighted with himself, beaming with a gorgeous glow.

"I—"

Quickly, Lucas's lips silenced me, moving over mine in slow, tantalizing motions. For a moment, the whole world evaporated into the night.

Without breaking the kiss, Lucas swept me up into his arms. He knelt down and laid me on the mass of blankets he'd spread out over the shingles. His tongue slipped into my mouth, deepening the kiss.

I folded my arms around his neck and entwined my fingers into his hair. Knowing the link between us, I forced myself to hold back. I didn't want him in my thoughts right now, not if that was what had stopped him before.

I held onto him tighter, concentrating on how his lips tasted like snow and vanilla. The kiss overwhelmed me, and I had to break away to breathe. Sure, I was still holding back, but for once, Lucas wasn't.

"I feel you, Care," he murmured, pressing my palm against his chest. "I feel you."

If I didn't know any better, I could have sworn I felt throbbing against his ribs.

Ever so slow, he moved to my neck. I craned my head to the side, allowing him better access. Heat stirred in my abdomen. A small hurricane of desire. When his hand glided out from under my knee and worked its way up my thigh to my hip, I fought to hold back the storm.

"Someday, I'll show *you exactly what you mean to me—how I feel you."*

Tonight?

Lucas found my mouth again, sucking on my lip as his fingers slipped under my three layers of clothing. His palms caressed my stomach, and the kiss changed. Tenderness turned to hunger; euphoria to distress. His grip on the back of my neck tightened, and my body began to shake with uncontrollable longing.

The spiral of need within me wanted to be unleashed.

Lucas let out a moan and intensified the kiss. More than craving, the noise sounded agonized, like the passion was trapped inside him, ever building but unable to be released. His fingers clenched against my stomach and pressed into the flesh at my ribs. His body stiffened over mine, making the pressure rise inside me. I pushed my hips into him, needing to be closer. So much closer.

Breaking through his own mental barrier, his hand moved to massage a breast. That did it. My body responded on its own, the hurricane freed and swirled throughout me.

I pulled him into me and dug my fingers into his back, raking up his shirt. I barely recognized myself; my limbs seemed to be moving on their own. My legs wrapped around his, my hands pushing deep into the taut muscles at his waist.

It wasn't until he sat up that I realized he'd dropped his arms to the side and stopped kissing me. Glowing emeralds bored into mine, his body flickering into transparency and back, losing concentration.

"Damn," he murmured as he solidified.

Panting, I couldn't peel my gaze away from him.

Lucas traced two fingers over my cheek, my lips, my chin, all the while keeping his eyes locked on me.

I swallowed, my breathing still coming fast. The invisible wall between us remained intact, at least from his end. I couldn't hear his thoughts, but I didn't have to. Frustration, pain, remorse radiated off him like steam.

He sighed, sinking his fingers through his hair. "It's unbelievable how much I want you."

"I'm right here," I whispered.

"It's not that," Lucas said. "Believe me, I would if I could, but I can't."

"You wavered into transparency, so what? You're back now."

"Oh, Carrie. I…" he trailed off, lifting his face to the sky for a moment. When he faced me again, his eyes wandered over my face. "I get so lost in you, so transfixed, that I lose all concentration to remain in corporeal form. This body isn't real, remember? It doesn't work like yours."

His gaze dropped to the blankets beneath me, and I understood. Not only could he not feel me physically, we'd never get to be together like regular couples. Without a body, Lucas had to live with the limitations of his death.

It was another unfair reminder of the vast difference that separated us. As I peered at Lucas with his head bowed, I realized this might be the first time he hated the reminder as much as I did.

***

"How did you do it? How did you get me up here?" I asked after Lucas had me tucked snuggly under a warm blanket and lying on his chest.

The stars lit up the sky above us, and I realized how small we really were.

Lucas unwound the elastic band. Letting my hair fall over him, he combed his fingers through it. "I teleported you. Because you have a physical body, I have to concentrate harder so that I don't run you into a wall."

"That's a possibility, huh?"

"A very real one. I took you out the window to avoid them."

"Well, I appreciate it."

Lucas snickered in my ear. "You are so very welcome, my love."

I shivered as his breath breezed over me. "Anything on the cambion?"

"Nothing. The lead was a dead end—an abandoned cabin in the mountains in Tennessee. Whoever lived there left years ago."

"Can't Megan do a spell or something to find out who it was?" I asked, rolling to look him in the eye.

"I wish it were that easy. We need a recog witch for that—someone who sees the past. Megan's making contacts; they're rare, though."

"Maybe you'll know something soon?"

Lucas studied my hopeful expression and sighed. "I doubt it."

Chapter 7

A week later, Lucas and I sat in Mike's bedroom with *The Dead Nightmare*, a carry-out pizza from the gas station (best pizza ever!), and a six pack of Pepsi. Mike lay on one side of his bed, propped up on pillows, neck still immobilized. Feet crossed at the ankles, I settled in on the other side of him, and Lucas sunk into an oversized mushroom chair next to me.

Mike blindly grabbed for an extra blanket on the floor. "Damn, it's cold in here."

My gaze shifted to Lucas.

"It is kind of chilly in your room," Lucas agreed. He shot me a sly grin and took a blanket from the foot of Mike's bed, folding it over me. Yeah, he probably didn't like the idea of me sliding myself under Mike's comforter with him.

Mike's bedroom door bolted open, and I jumped.

"The movie hasn't started yet, Carrie. Calm down," Mike said, stifling a laugh. Then he turned to the intruder. "What are you doing in here, squirt? You're not watching this movie."

She puffed out her lower lip. "I know, dorkface. I just wanted to see Carrie and give her a hug."

Mandy bobbed over to me, the curls in her blonde ponytail bouncing behind her. She wrapped her arms around my neck and whispered in my ear, "Do you wanna come play Barbies with me?"

"Oh, Mandy," I said, hugging her. "I promised your brother we'd watch this movie tonight."

"Okay." She elongated every syllable. Glaring across the bed at her brother, she stuck out her tongue. "I guess she's staying with you."

Mike shrugged. "Told you so."

"Bye, Carrie." She waved. "Bye, Lucas." At the door she spun around. "Bye, loser!" She slammed the door behind her.

"What was that about?" I asked.

"When she heard you were coming over, she got all excited. She thought Lucas would stay and watch the movie with me and you'd go play with her. I told her that probably wasn't going to happen, but she insisted on betting me a peanut butter and jelly sandwich that you'd pick her over me." Mike folded both hands behind his head. "I guess lunch is courtesy of the squirt, tomorrow."

"Peanut butter and jelly?" I asked, eyeing him.

"She's seven. It's all she can make by herself. Besides, I have a soft spot for them."

"I still wouldn't eat it if I were you," I warned.

"Why?"

"Hell hath no fury like a little sister scorned."

Mike grimaced. "Good point. Where's that pizza?"

Lucas tossed him the box. "Have at it, man."

The body count in the movie rounded double digits in the first five minutes. Seriously, the amount of gore, guts, and blood was enough to make me question my choice to stay instead of taking Ken and Barbie on a weekend cruise in their convertible around Mandy's room, a.k.a. Hollywood.

What mostly made me uneasy, though, weren't the pools of blood, but watching a ghost movie so far from the truth with the truth sitting beside me, holding my hand. Each time a ghost brutally murdered a person, a fresh layer of sweat coated my palms. I knew it didn't work that way.

I knew what really killed the necromancer, Susan Taylor. Demons.

I gave a side-long glance at Lucas. He squeezed my hand and offered a reassuring smile.

He turned his attention back to the movie, but I kept my focus locked on him, concentrating. Squinting, I tried to see through him, into his mind. It hadn't worked last time when I was in bed and he was in Iowa City, but maybe, with him so close, I could somehow break in.

After a while, Lucas's emerald irises flitted over to me. "What are you doing?" he whispered so only I could hear him.

"Listening."

"To what?"

"You're not breathing."

"How is that new?"

"Well, you know, with—" I flicked my eyes in Mike's direction.

"It's dark in here," he said.

"That's *it*?"

Lucas's brows furrowed. "Sorry, I don't speak female. What's it?"

"You're not, you know, *thinking* anything?"

"Should I be?"

"Do I need to pause it?" Mike asked loudly.

"Sorry," Lucas and I murmured at the same time. Beside me, I could feel Mike roll his eyes.

The movie ended with two guys, one good ghost and one human murderer, fighting for the same girl. To keep her from being killed by his best friend like he was, the ghost strangled her, forever sealing her to him. It didn't take long to form the connection between this movie, the essay I'd written on *A Rose for Emily*, and my own life. Love. Death. Obsession.

Damn, I was selfish.

No, Lucas would never kill me. Ever. However, in the end, the dead guy got the girl. Sure, Lucas had me now, but not for always. The girl in the movie willingly gave her life, at his hands even, to be with him. So simple, yet not.

"Don't even think about it," Lucas whispered in my ear.

I bit my lip, annoyed. If he heard, somehow I'd let down my guard. Or he knew me.

"You believe in ghosts, Lucas?" Mike asked, and I immediately held my breath.

Lucas thought for a second before answering, "Yeah, I do."

"Carrie wasn't a believer until I took her to the Moore House over the summer. Did she tell you about that?"

Yep. He was there, and I'd like to forget the whole thing, thankyouverymuch.

Only I couldn't. The vision of Hell still woke me up at night.

"I know enough to never go," Lucas said.

You can say that again.

Our connection, Incenamus, would create a disturbance in the force field Megan and her mother, Vanessa, conjured around the house, allowing the demons to be freed. Been there. Done that. Not interested in doing it again.

"It's not that bad," Mike said. "You scared?"

Lucas nodded once. "Terrified."

"I'm fairly certain the ghosts won't kill you. Mmm, okay, maybe fifty-fifty." Mike shifted his whole body on his bed so he could look at Lucas. "You should go sometime."

I narrowed my gaze at him. "You are *so* lucky you're injured right now."

Mike smirked at me. The gleam in his eye said more than words.

My boyfriend caught his meaning loud and clear.

"Thank you for the…hospitality," Lucas said, standing up and reaching for me. "But I think you need your rest."

Boys!

"I'll see you at school on Monday." I patted Mike's arm. "Call if you need help with your homework."

"Count on it," he murmured as Lucas and I let ourselves out.

***

I hopped into the black Jeep Compass. Without Lucas beside me, the vehicle was warm enough, but as soon as he slid behind the wheel, I had to flip on the heat.

He drove down the highway, and I peered out the window, watching the trees, fields, and farms fly by. The movie forced its way back into my thoughts.

What was I willing to give up to be with Lucas? The rest of my life? His soul?

One of those options would have to give, and I didn't want to choose between either of them. But I didn't want to lose him either. He meant everything to me.

If I died then…

"I told you to not even think about it," Lucas interrupted my thoughts.

Before, it was kinda cool. Now, though, I felt invaded. "You can't just jump into my mind uninvited."

"I didn't. You were loud." He grinned. "Besides, I know you, and it's not like it's something we haven't discussed before. Answer's still the same—no."

"Lucas—"

"Pretend that every time that thought crosses your mind, a piece of me dies, because it does. We're not talking about it again."

I crossed my arms over my chest. "Translated the Incenamus book yet?"

He tensed—I could feel it. Glancing at him, I noticed his jaw clench. Yeah, definitely hiding something.

"Well?" I prompted.

"We don't get something for nothing."

What does that mean?

"You didn't answer the question."

Lucas's irises seemed to darken. "No. Not yet."

We drove in silence for awhile, listening to the drone of the tires on the pavement. Not comforting.

"There's still time, Care," Lucas said, taking my hand in his. "We don't have to decide anything right now."

I nodded, still unconvinced. "Not now." I gazed out the window and under my breath, I added, "But not never either."

I knew Lucas heard me. He said nothing.

***

"I was freezing all night, yesterday, and as soon as you guys left, my room warmed up. It was strange," Mike said.

I flipped to the next page of our Government text and switched the phone to my other ear. "Yeah, well, maybe the heat in your room isn't working right. The answer's on page 142, under the picture of FDR."

I heard paper crinkling on the other end. "Maybe, but if it's broken here, it's broken in your living room too. Well, that's stupid. Who reads the freaking captions?"

"How's it broken here? I read the captions, and everyone who's going to pass the test will have read the captions. The page was assigned reading and that means the *whole* page."

"It's broken there because every time I'm there for Sunday night movies, it's just as cold as it was here. If that's true, you're the only one passing the exam. No one reads the captions," Mike grumbled.

I switched the phone to my other ear again. "It's your imagination. It's always cold here." I couldn't let Mike put the pieces together. "The pictures and captions are there for a reason—for you to look at and read."

"How about number eight? You're delusional. It hasn't always been cold there. Pictures and captions are nothing more than placeholders to make it seem like we aren't reading as much as we actually are. It's a conspiracy."

Shuffling through my finished review packet, I found number eight. *In what three New York newspapers were the Federalist Papers originally published, and in what year?* Seriously, did Mike pay *any* attention in class?

"I think you're a cold-blooded reptile. Besides, it is winter. And, no, captions hold necessary information, and the pictures enhance the text so we can actually see what's being talked about." I flipped back a chapter. "You know, for visual learners."

"Did you find number eight?"

"Looking."

Two seconds of silence passed before Mike said, "What's your answer?"

"Cheater."

"I call it good time management skills. Why should I look it up when you can just tell me? Both of us shouldn't have to waste this time."

"Well, I call it 'check-the-caption-on-page-119,' and I won't even comment on the last part."

Mike groaned, but I heard him move pages. "I'm gonna fail this test."

"Agreed, if you don't study the captions."

I tapped my nails on the cover of the textbook, waiting for his next question. To answer, I'd conveniently find the page number in the index, which would inevitably lead me to a caption he hadn't bothered to read. Major. Eye. Roll.

"Have you ever considered that it's your boyfriend?" Mike asked.

"My boyfriend is not in our Government text," I said, buying some time.

"That's not what I meant," Mike said. "Have you ever considered that he's the one who makes rooms cold?"

I swallowed. "Like he's a robot with a built-in air conditioner?"

"Something like that."

Good thing he couldn't see me fidgeting with my notebook. Dead giveaway. "How's that concussion of yours?"

Mike sighed into my ear. Well, through the receiver. "Yeah, you're right."

"Can I write that down?"

He laughed. "No. Unless it's the answer to number nine."

"Can be. I'll write it in a caption for you under a picture of today's date."

***

My uncle and his family came over for Thanksgiving. I helped Grandma in the kitchen all morning. We'd spoken so little since the Griffin incident that I felt slightly uncomfortable. Sure, she'd apologized to me a few days after, but it still stung. Baking pies and a fifteen-pound turkey together, I hoped, would lessen the tension between us.

"Will Lucas be joining us today?" she asked me, wiping her palms on her apron.

I shook my head. "No, he's uh, spending the day with…family."

In Iowa City with Megan's family.

"Good for him."

Yeah. For him.

I stared at the knife in my hand, not really seeing it chop the walnuts. His time away kept growing longer, and whenever he returned, he seemed more distant, yet never had any more information. If I thought about it too long, it made me angry.

I shook the thought away, determined to not let it get to me.

***

After dinner, Grandma brought out the main event: pie.

Oh, yeah. Then the pie-bickering fest between my grandparents ensued. God, I loved them!

"Those look amazin', Renae!" Grandpa Rob said, ogling the pies.

My mouth watered at the sight of the Dutch apple she'd baked especially for me.

"Don't lie to me, Rob! I know they don't. The top of the pumpkin isn't smooth, I think the brown sugar got too old. The crust on the chocolate mousse is soggy, and don't you dare get me started on that apple one. Sorry, Carrie." When she swiveled to me, the lines on her face softened a little.

"How they look don't affect the taste anyhow," Grandpa assured her.

"Nonsense! If it looks bad, no one's going to eat it!" She put her hands on her hips, and I stifled a giggle.

The rest of the family knew better than to say anything if we wanted to keep our heads. Grandpa would bring her down eventually. The rest of us sat back and waited for him to work his magic.

"Don't be ridiculous, Renae. Everything is fine." He stood up and pulled her into his arms.

I smiled. Grandpa was her Lucas. Right then, I wished I had mine.

Grandma relaxed in his embrace. "They could have been better, that's all I'm sayin'."

***

I didn't expect Lucas that night, so when I walked into my bedroom and saw him in the chair in the corner, legs out and arms behind his head, I almost screamed.

In a flash, he stood beside me, a hand clamped over my mouth. When my heart rate slowed, he let go.

"What are you doing here?" I demanded, a little

irritated that he'd scared me.

"I can go if you'd prefer?" He curved up one side of his mouth, the side that exposed his dimple.

I studied him, suspicious. Something was off. The gleam in his eye seemed darker. His skin paler than normal. Worry lines stretched over his skin. And his smile didn't feel as genuine. He looked…tired.

He held me against his chest, resting his chin on the top of my head. "I missed you," he whispered.

I said nothing. There was no logical reason for him to miss me or be away so long. He could easily have appeared in my room anytime and went back to Megan's in under a minute.

The more I thought about it, the more worried I became.

He must have felt it, because he pulled away and refused to meet my gaze.

Lucas raked a hand through his dark hair. "Megan got another lead."

"Really?" That made me perk up. "A connection with the cabin?"

"Maybe. We don't know yet. All we have is a name," Lucas said. "Carver."

He slumped down on the edge of my bed, fading a little into transparency like a flickering light bulb before regaining his concentration.

That's not like him. What's going on?

I plopped down beside him. Seeing him so exhausted made my irritation fizzle out some.

"A cambion?" I asked, leaning my head on his shoulder.

"An incubus, actually. He probably isn't *the*

cambion, though. Who knows how long it will take to find him." Lucas put an arm around me, fatigue heavy in his voice. "Cambions don't like to be sought out."

"I get to come with you, right?"

For the first time since our conversation began, he looked at me. "Carrie—"

Oh no. Not that tone.

I shot to my feet, agitated again. "No, we had a deal, remember?"

"I remember," he said, his voice deepening but still too calm. "Our compromise was when we found *him*. This isn't him. It's only a possible lead *to* him."

I shook my head. "That's not fair!"

Inhaling deeply, Lucas let out a long breath. He rubbed his face and leaned back on his palms. Why was he so tired? "Carrie, this…this Carver, he's…" My boyfriend's once bright emerald eyes, now so light in color they no longer qualified as green, flitted to me. "I don't want you anywhere near him. From the information we've gathered, this one's different from other cambions, other incubi." Slowly, he took my hand in his, and a calm instantly flowed through me. "Listen, Care, this Carver doesn't just kill to stay alive himself; he does it for the thrill. For the adrenaline rush. The list of warnings we received is a mile long. If things go awry, and he somehow catches your scent, he may not stop hunting you until he's killed you. I can't let that happen."

"But…" I trailed off since I didn't know the rest of my sentence anyway.

"No compromise. You're not going." A swirl of green filled his irises as he trained his stare on me.

The conversation was over; no amount of arguing would make a difference.

Lucas stood up and pulled me against him. "I love you so much. I can't lose you."

Longing and sadness coated his voice, making my stomach drop. "I'm sorry I got mad."

"I know."

I don't know how long we stayed like that, holding each other in the middle of my bedroom floor. It wasn't long enough.

Lucas let go first, taking my face between his cold palms. "I've gotta go."

"Why? You just got here." I frowned.

He bit the inside of his cheek, the dimple pinching inward.

"Stay, please," I begged.

"I'll be back soon." He pressed his lips against my forehead and kept them there.

"What's going on with you?" I murmured, not expecting an answer.

And I didn't get one.

"Lucas?" I whispered, my body shaking with fear. "Are you fading away?" I barely heard the words myself.

"No, baby. It's not that," he said, his mouth not leaving my forehead.

"Then what? Are you sick or something?"

He finally stepped back and lifted my chin to meet his gaze. A grin appeared on his face, and for a moment he seemed normal again. "No."

I wanted to ask again, beg for an answer, but he

leaned over me and kissed me with the same fervor as the night on the rooftop, silencing me before he disappeared.

Chapter 8

Three days before my BFF's, Jessica and Stacy, were due to arrive from Texas, the UPS guy came to Renae's Antiques and dropped off a large box for me. I signed for it, noting the return address label, and threw it in the backseat of my car.

No thanks, Griffin.

I lugged it to my room when I got home and tossed it in the back of the closet, unopened. Good riddance.

Two days before, it snowed. White fluff coated the ground, and suddenly, I was a child again, running outside to romp through it and make snow angels. I'd never had a white Christmas before. To celebrate, Lucas, Mandy, and I built a snowman right outside of Mike's bedroom window, using Mike's actual clothing. Kudos to the squirt for thieving a pair of her brother's boxers: Iowa Hawkeye football. Nice touch.

Not surprisingly, I had to talk Lucas out of having our creation flip Mike the bird with its stick fingers.

"He'd find the humor in it," Lucas mumbled, grinning at me.

Now, two hours before my friends were due to pull into the driveway, I sat on my bed with Lucas across from me. In the last few weeks, he'd started looking and acting more like himself again. The exhaustion seemed to have lifted, but he still refused to talk about it.

"Let's practice. Close your eyes," he said, the sound of his voice swirling flutters in my stomach.

My eyelids fell shut. I inhaled through my nose and let it out slowly from my mouth. After another two breaths, I nodded, ready.

"Okay, relax," he instructed.

Air filled my lungs again, and I exhaled. In my mind, I pictured my hand reaching out to him and our fingertips touching. I laced my fingers through his—connected.

Breathe in. Breathe out.

I concentrated on fusing my soul with Lucas's lost one. Minutes passed, and I didn't feel or hear anything from him.

Come on! Work!

When Lucas's hand actually touched mine, I opened my eyes. He looked at me, brows arched high in question. I shook my head.

"Nothing," I said, disappointed. "You?"

"I wasn't trying. I've been hearing and feeling you quite a bit lately."

"Well, isn't that fantastic." The sarcasm in my voice made Lucas laugh.

He reached for me, and I twisted around so my back leaned against him. His arms folded around me, and I settled against him, sighing.

"Don't worry about Mike. He won't find out," he said.

I chewed on my lip. Yeah, he'd definitely been listening in on my thoughts during the last few weeks.

"You're gonna have a great time with Jessica and Stacy. You've heard from your mother, and she said she was fine—trust that. The incubus, Carver, is none of your concern, so get him out of your mind—let Megan and me worry about that. Yes, some college is going to love you and want you, so yeah, it's worth it. Keep sending them out."

I stuck my tongue out at him, and he kissed the top of my head before he continued.

"I'm perfectly fine, not fading away. And no, silly, nothing is going on with Megan and me—and I'm seriously surprised you've even thought that. There's nothing you can do about your dad, and who knows, maybe Ami's a nice person."

I tilted my head up to glare at him.

Traitor.

Lucas chuckled. "I'll pretend I didn't hear that."

"Maybe I need to be practicing how to block you," I grumbled.

"Hush," he said and kissed me. "I'd better go so I can be back for real when Jessica and Stacy get here."

Stacy had been adamant that Lucas and Mike both be here upon their arrival. Mike, unfortunately, was out of town for the weekend. I promised she'd meet him as soon as he returned.

I kissed Lucas again before he disappeared.

***

Stacy's red Mustang convertible parked next to Lucas's Jeep. I threw on my coat and boots and darted out to meet them. Jessica jumped out of the car, springing toward me.

"Carrie!"

"Jess!" I squealed, bouncing into her arms. "How was your trip?"

"Great, although Stacy's driving leaves something to be desired."

"My driving is amazing," Stacy said in a perfect Texan twang. She pushed the white oversized sunglasses on top of her head. "Jessica only recently got her license in backseat driving. We'll have to give her some time to get used to her new position then maybe she won't freak out so much."

"I didn't freak out!"

Stacy nodded. "Sure you didn't." Quietly she said to me, "She so did."

I laughed and pulled Stacy into our group hug. "I've missed you both so much!"

"Ugh, how do you stand this cold?" Stacy whined. "Let's get inside, like, pronto. There's heat in there, right?"

"No, Stace. They don't believe in heating houses up north," Jessica said while grabbing her bags out of the backseat.

Stacy didn't miss a beat. "Well, that's dumb. Someone should tell them about the miracle of fire." She popped the trunk to gather more stuff. "So, where's that hottie of a boyfriend of yours?"

I peered up at the house and froze. Lucas was

leaning against the door staring at Jessica, his fingers massaging his chin like he recognized her from *America's Most Wanted.*

What's that about?

When he caught me looking, he snapped out of it and grinned. He pushed off the door and sauntered toward us.

Stacy flipped her long, golden locks out of her face and gaped at him. She stepped closer to me and hissed in my ear. "Is *that* him? Oh. My. God, Carrie! You've been holding out on me. Freaking A, he's gorgeous!"

Oh yeah, he totally heard her, but judging from his expression, no one would know. I laughed to myself. Same old Stacy!

"Has he got any brothers?"

"Sorry, no," I said.

That we know of.

"Why the hell not? That's a disservice to the universe."

When Lucas got to the car, Stacy stuck out her hand before I had a chance to say anything. "I'm Stacy, and it's an absolute pleasure, Lucas." She thickened her accent as she said it. Geesh.

"Pleasure's all mine."

Stacy cocked her head toward me. "I wish."

Oh. Good. Lord.

"That's Jessica," I said, nodding in her direction.

Jess turned and smiled, her arms too overloaded to shake hands. "Nice to meet you."

"Here," Lucas offered, "let me take some of that."

His gaze stayed molded to her as he shifted some

of the bags and pillows from her arms to his. The exchange made me uncomfortable.

My grandparents were waiting for us inside the mudroom. "I hope you girls didn't have any trouble drivin'," Grandpa said, taking some bags from Stacy.

"Nope. All clear and spectacularly flat," she told him.

Jessica rolled her eyes. She was good at that.

"Thanks for letting us stay here," Jess said.

"We're happy to have you, dear," Grandma replied. "Why don't you girls get your things upstairs and come back down. Dinner's about ready."

"Oh, thank you so much, Mrs. Reese. I am starving," Stacy drawled.

"Call me Renae, dear."

I led the way to the upstairs guest bedroom where my besties would be staying.

"I'll wait in the living room," Lucas said, kissing me before he left.

"Carrie, he's a gem!" Stacy swooned, fanning herself in her southern belle rendition.

Drama queen to the core.

Jessica dumped her stuff on the floor and collapsed on the bed.

"Would it be rude to skip dinner and just fall asleep?" Jess flopped her arms above her head. "I'm exhausted."

"She dozed off in the car and had a nightmare or something," Stacey informed me. "I had to wake her up. She was screaming."

"Same old, same old," Jess moaned.

"Still?" I asked. She'd been having these for months now. In most of them, I die. Yay me.

"They're getting worse," she said, resting an arm over her forehead. "And more frequent."

A conversation we had over the summer made me pause. *"I've been having all sorts of strange dreams, and all of them have started coming true. I think there may be something wrong with me."*

Stacy's giddiness interrupted my thoughts. "Ohmygod, Carrie!" She clutched her hand over her heart. "Did you get us flowers?"

Taking one of the roses out of the vase, she inhaled the perfume and smiled. "They're even white, my favorite! And this black vase—holy frick! Love it! You're awesome, you know that?" She put it back on the dresser and offered Jessica her hand. "Come on. Eat then sleep, darlin'."

Jess groaned, but clasped Stacy's hand anyway, yawning. "Yes, Mom."

Ten minutes later, all six of us were seated around the table in the kitchen, eating chicken and wild rice.

"This is delish, Mrs. Reese—I mean, Renae," Stacy caught herself.

Jess nodded and took another bite of chicken. "Yes, really good." She gave Lucas a sideways glance. "Don't you like it?"

Lucas put his fork down and wiped his mouth with a napkin. "I do, it's wonderful as always. Mrs. Reese is an amazing cook."

"Lucas doesn't eat much," Renae answered. "I don't know how he stays so sturdy on so little. You should be wasting away by now, young man."

His gaze settled on me for a second. "Yeah, I should be." Slowly, his eyes moved toward Jessica again.

I sat back in my chair, my appetite gone. What the hell was going on?

After dinner, I cornered Lucas in the mudroom. "Have I missed something? Ever since Jessica got here, you've been having an awfully hard time keeping your eyes to yourself."

His brow furrowed, deep lines spreading across his forehead. "I need to go see Megan," he said. "I'll be back in awhile."

"That's not good enough—"

"I love you." He kissed me and walked out to his Jeep Compass without an explanation.

This sucks!

I sulked my way upstairs to where Jess and Stacy were unpacking.

"Where's Lucas?" Stacy inquired.

"Um, he'll be back. He had to run out." It ticked me off that I didn't have to lie—that was everything he'd said.

"Too much action on that front porch, huh?" Stacy dumped her clothes into the drawer.

"I'm too tired to unpack," Jessica droned. "I'll just live out of my suitcase tonight."

I plopped on the bed beside her.

"I checked up on your mom before we left," Jess said, sweeping her hair into a ponytail. "She's doing all right. She said to tell you not to worry about her."

"Thanks," I muttered.

Not so easy in practice, Mom.

My head was chock-full of worry right now. Thank God for Stacy.

"Oh!" Stacy danced across the room to her pile—yes, *pile*—of matching luggage. Had she seriously brought six bags? "Your mom sent us goodies."

"Goodies?"

"Yep. Snacks for the trip for us and Christmas presents for you." Stacy held up a couple of packages wrapped in blue and silver snowflake paper. "Open them now!"

"No. That's cheating," I said without conviction. I scrunched up my face, my lips puffing out. "Okay, gimme!"

Stacy giggled and pranced over to me. She handed me the smallest box first. The goofy grin on her face made me pause before I ripped it open.

"I helped her pick it out," Stacy said proudly.

A sticky note attached to a new iPhone read: *With unlimited text and data. Merry Christmas, sweetheart. Love, Mom*

"See?" Stacy squealed, holding up her identical cell phone. "We match!"

"Well, I sure hope whatever is in box number two isn't a matching case," I teased, but inwardly I was praying. No way did I want a pink rhinestone cell phone cover.

Stacy dumped the last gift in my lap. "Judging by the size and weight of this box, I doubt it."

Inside, I found two new pairs of jeans, a couple shirts, a designer scarf, and new pair of jammies. Perfect.

"Cute." Jess nodded her approval.

"Your mom has spectacular taste," Stacy said, picking up each piece of clothing and examining it. She wrapped the scarf around her neck. "I hate this stupid cold. Please tell me we're still going to the mall tomorrow," she said. "I'm desperate for a new one of these since I'm in Polar Hell."

"Polar Hell? Really?" I made a face, and Stacy smirked.

"I think we should get something for Carrie's grandparents for letting us stay here," Jess suggested.

"Yeah, that too." Stacy agreed. "Why are you always so practical?"

"Because you're so not."

We talked and laughed, and soon the clock read midnight. I had no clue where the time went. Like old times!

When Stacy finally stopped talking and Jess's soft snores filled the room, I ducked out. I closed my bedroom door quietly and tucked myself in bed fully dressed.

Lucas hadn't returned, but I was too tired to be upset. Instead, I easily drifted to sleep.

***

"Oh, come on, Carrie. Wake up."

I grabbed a pillow and put it over my head to drown him out. "Go away."

Okay, so maybe I wasn't tired enough to calm the anger. Still.

I heard the lamp beside my head click on.

"Seriously?" I groaned, cramming the pillow

tighter over my head. "It's not my problem you didn't come back earlier like you said."

He lifted the corner slightly, his lips right next to my ear.

Gently, he brushed my hair away from my face. "Forgive me?" Stupid electrifying shudders, I wanted to be mad!

I peered up at him through hooded eyelids. "I've been doing a lot of that lately."

"Not lately."

"Earlier…lately…whatever."

His cool breath blew against my ear and forgiving him became way too easy. "Shut off the light and come here," I said, eager to have his arms around me. God, I missed them.

"Now might not be the best time for that."

"It's always the best time for that."

He chuckled. "Not when we're not alone."

I could almost feel my pupils dilate. "What?"

Lucas sat down beside my head. "Ready?" he asked, taking a hold of the pillow still covering my head.

"Ugh."

"I'll take that as a 'yes,'" he said and peeled it off me.

I squinted to see the person in Lucas's usual spot. Megan sat cross-legged in the chair, long black boots over skinny jeans. Her dark auburn hair flowed down her shoulders in layers.

"Nice haircut," I mumbled, none too excited to see her in my room at—I peeked at the clock—2:30 a.m.

"Good morning to you too." She smiled, amused.

Clearly, I wasn't.

"How did you get in my room?" I glanced at Lucas, who had his brows raised. Oh. "Never mind. So…what's this all about?"

Megan uncrossed her legs and leaned forward. "Your friend, Jessica."

I blinked, still straining to see through the bright light. "Jess? What about her?"

The air around me suddenly thickened. To cut some tension, I scooted closer to Lucas and leaned my head on his shoulder.

"She's a witch, Carrie," he said. "Her green aura is faint, but it's there."

I rubbed my temples, letting it sink in. Yeah, I heard him. I was just having trouble believing him.

"Jessica?" I repeated.

"Has she ever said anything to you? About things she may have done or seen that were out of the ordinary?" Megan asked as if this was a business meeting. Typical.

"Um." I shook my head. "I'm not sure. I mean, she's the one who told me something about Lucas seemed off. She chocked it up to intuition."

"Clairvoyant?" Lucas asked Megan.

She frowned. "Maybe. Alone, though, that's not a strong enough indication. No matter our specialty, we're all intuitive." Megan flipped her attention back to me. "Does she have dreams? Or know things about people or objects without ever being told? Has she ever gotten sick then better suddenly?"

The fog lifted from my mind and everything became clear.

"The nightmares are getting worse. And more frequent."

"I already knew that you'd stay in Villisca. I dreamt it last week."

"There are people with ESP that can see the future, but...Carrie, I'm scared."

"Dreams," I said. "She's been having dreams, and they're all coming true."

Megan's sat up straight, realization dawning on her. "She's a precog." She stood up and paced the room, a soft smile playing at her lips. "Jessica's a precog. Unbelievable."

My eyes teetered from her to Lucas and back to Megan again. "A precog? What's that?"

Megan faced me. "Precognitive. It's suppressed, but Jessica has the ability to see the future."

My mind raced, rolling over everything she'd predicted that had come true. Snow storm in Dallas five years back. Her aunt's house fire last year. Her brother breaking his arm at school. Me running into a tree in Lucas's car. And...

"Your death, Carrie. At the mercy of a vampire, I think."

If Megan was right, I was going to die.

As soon as I thought it, Lucas yanked me onto his lap, arms wrapped protectively around me. "Not gonna happen. I won't let it."

Megan cocked her head to the side, confused. "What's wrong, Carrie?"

"Jess," I said, focusing on my comforter. Saying it out loud would make it real. "She, uh, she foresaw my death."

Yellow-blond hair. Turquoise eyes. Vampire.

I swallowed.

"No. That's it. I'm done. Search is off," Lucas said, his voice rising.

"There's no need to jump to conclusions." Megan sat back down, crossing her legs again. "She's untrained. For all we know, she hasn't figured out how to tell the difference between a vision and a regular dream. It could mean nothing."

"Or it could mean everything." Lucas clutched me closer. "I'm done taking foolish risks, Megan. It's not worth it."

Foolish risks? What foolish risks?

"We need to talk to her, know exactly what she's seen," Megan said, the all-business tone back in her voice.

"She's asleep in the guest room." I unlocked Lucas's arms from around my waist. "I can get her."

Reluctantly, he let go of me. I felt his stare on my back even out in the hallway, never breaking its hold.

I reached for the doorknob of the spare room. If Jess had seen my death happen, it was inevitable, right? Everything else had happened exactly how she'd predicted.

Not long ago she'd said that her nightmares were getting worse and more frequent. Did that mean my death was coming sooner rather than later?

I pushed the door open. Thankfully Stacy could sleep through a hurricane. Jessica, however, not so much. Her head lifted as soon as the door creaked.

"Carrie?"

Light from my room spilled into hallway. I

beckoned to her without saying anything.

Jess tossed the covers off and tip-toed to me.

"Come on," I whispered.

"Where?"

"My room."

"What's wrong?"

Everything.

I closed the door to the guest room. "Nothing."

We padded toward my room, my gaze locked on Lucas's. Now he saw only me.

When we walked through the door, Jessica grabbed my hand and all but glued herself to my back.

"Why is it colder in your room than anywhere else in this house?" she muttered to herself. Well, herself because I wasn't going to answer.

"Hi," she muttered to Megan as we walked past. "There's a strange person in your room, Carrie," she whispered into my back.

"Hello," Megan said, grinning and nodding toward Lucas. She must see what Lucas saw: green.

Lucas leaned back against the headboard, legs straight out on top of the comforter. I slipped back under my blankets and snuggled close to him. Jess slid in on the other side of me, shivering.

"What's going on, Carrie?" Jess nudged me. "This is weird."

"You're telling me," I murmured. "Jess, this is Megan. Megan, Jessica."

"It's really great to meet you, Jessica," Megan said, standing up and plopping back down at the foot of my mattress.

"Megan has something to tell you."

Jess's brown irises seemed larger than usual as she scanned the room and landed on Megan.

Megan sighed. "I'll get straight to the point," she said. "You're a witch."

Yep, straight to the point exactly.

Jess blinked, opened her mouth then shut it. She sat perfectly still, pursing her lips.

Then she leaned into me, her voice low. "Did that girl just call me a bitch?"

"Uh, no. She said you're a witch."

"How is that better?"

I thought for a second, mulling over her question. "It's really not."

"Well, that's enlightening, Carrie. Thanks."

"Anytime."

Beside me, I could hear Jess breathing. She stuck a fingernail between her teeth, her gaze not wavering from Megan.

Finally, she sighed. "A witch?"

Megan nodded eagerly.

"Like magical powers?"

"Yep."

"Are you…?"

"Yes."

Jess leaned forward. "Are you one of those Harry Potter crazies who keeps a wand in your back pocket at all times in case a Death Eater crosses your path?"

Megan's face went blank. "What's a Death Eater?"

"Never mind." Jessica sank into the mattress. "So, if I'm going accept your assertion—which I don't, by the way—how would it even be possible that I'm a witch?"

"It's inherited," Megan explained. "Someone in your family, at some time, possessed magical abilities. While the magic continued to be passed down each generation, the information and training did not. It happens sometimes."

"Cool…what does that mean?"

"It means you have two souls inside you. They give you the capacity and responsibility to protect the living and assist the helpless." Megan paused. "You see some people differently, don't you?"

"Differently? I don't understand."

"Look at me," Megan said. "What do you see?"

Jess's studied her, clearly confused. "Uh, reddish hair. Hazely eyes. I don't know."

"It's dark auburn, but…anyway, no. Not on the surface. Look deeper." Megan nodded to me. "Compare me to Carrie."

Oh, great.

Jess concentrated on me for a minute. I sat still, knowing what she would see. She'd find nothing around me. Plain and human.

Satisfied with me, she scrutinized Megan. "You have a glowing light circling you. All over you. It's…green."

"Believe me now?" Megan smiled.

"Maybe," she said, and I could see on her face that she did.

"Now Lucas. What do you see?"

As Jessica studied Lucas, I grabbed his hand. How would Jess react once she knew the truth? Even more, that I didn't tell her said truth? My heart pounded, waiting for Jess to figure it out.

"Silver," she said. "Silver light."

Megan nodded. "Yes. It's how Lucas knew what you are. Like me, you have a green aura radiating off you. It identifies you as a witch in the supernatural world."

"I'm green?"

"Witches and warlocks, both."

Jess stared over the bed as she began to piece things together. She looked over at Lucas. "Yours isn't green."

Lucas shook his head. "I'm not a warlock."

"What are you?"

"Each being in our world has a different color aura. Angels, gold. Demons, red. Cambions, uh, vamps, incubi, succubae, reapers—black. Ghosts, silver. Werewolves and Shifters, blue, and so on," Megan said.

Jessica faced me, and I sucked in a breath. She hadn't missed Megan's description. I knew that expression: hurt.

"I wanted to tell you," I said, rushing to explain. "But it wasn't my secret to tell."

She held my gaze for only a second before she passed onto Lucas. "You're dead?"

"Yes," Lucas answered.

"Jess, I'm so sorry I didn't say anything. I—"

"It's fine." Jess held up a hand. "I'm a little shocked is all. Really, it's fine."

"You can only see him and his aura when he's corporeal, though," Megan explained, keeping the conversation on track. "We're wholly human, so we can't see angels or demons without bodies either, but that doesn't mean we can't sense them when they're close."

Jessica gnawed off her fingernail, a habit I thought she'd outgrown two years ago. "You said 'special abilities.' What abilities do I have?"

"I think you know."

Jess studied my duvet intently. Yes, she knew.

"Most witches are clairvoyants, like me. Others are telepaths, healers, precogs, and recogs. The last two, especially, are extremely rare." Megan said the last part slower than necessary. "We think you're precognitive. That you see the future."

Beside me, Jess bowed her head and fidgeted with the blanket.

"Carrie said you've had dreams that later came true," Megan said.

Jessica nodded. "Not usually good things, and always about those I love."

"That's how it works; your connection with them is stronger than with anyone else. It makes them easier to see."

Jess nodded again.

"Jessica," Lucas said softly, "I need to know what you've seen about Carrie."

Her heavy eyes washed over me. They narrowed, and she sighed. "She dies. Sometimes the visions change, but this one hasn't, and now, it's coming more often. Every day."

"Can you give me details? No matter how small and seemingly insignificant," Lucas said, his voice low.

"I never get a whole picture. Only fragments." She closed her eyes as she concentrated. "It's, um, dark. Behind her is a wall of bricks—a building, I think. I see hands; pale, large. They slam into the bricks by Carrie's head. He's angry. There's a puddle of water on the ground. Something Carrie is holding falls into it—a slip of paper?"

"That's okay," Megan assures her. "What else?"

"Um, I can see *him*. He has bleached blond hair, bright blue eyes, unnatural looking. Then his pupils start to grow, they overtake his irises until they're covered in black. He grabs Carrie's hair, yanking her head to the side. He leans over her neck, and suddenly she's lying on the ground." Jess's eyelids fly open. "That's when I wake up. It's all I see."

"Vamp, Megan. No mistake," Lucas said, squeezing me too tight. "I'm not putting Carrie in that situation. We're done."

"It doesn't work like that, Lucas." Megan stood up, her hands on her hips. "Sometimes the future changes. Sometimes it doesn't."

"What do you mean the future doesn't change? Of course it does. It's always changing," I interjected.

"How long have you been having these dreams, Jessica?" Megan asked.

"Um, since summer."

Megan turned to Lucas. "Months with the same dream. It's not changing."

"No. I'll *make* it change."

"Some things are inevitable, Lucas. No matter what we do, fate will find a way."

Chapter 9

"Ohmygod, Carrie!" Stacy exclaimed, her eyes bulging. "Are we seriously taking *his* car? Like, without him?"

Jess slid into the backseat, letting Stacy have shotgun. The whites of Jess's eyes were bloodshot, and I wondered how late she'd stayed up talking with Megan.

I shrugged. "It has four-wheel drive, and I'm not exactly used to driving in the snow."

"You realize this is huge, right? So, like, how serious are you two?" I swear Stacy's pupils dilated in an instant as the thought formed in her head. "OMG! Do I hear wedding bells?"

I clicked the seatbelt and adjusted the strap unnecessarily. Sure, Stacy was only being herself, but her words sliced through me more than I wanted. Marriage, children, a real future—no, that stuff would never happen for us. How could it?

"I love him, but—"

"Well, duh! That's sickeningly obvious," she said, playing with the blonde braid she'd draped over her shoulder. "Okay, I'm dying to know…how's he in bed?"

I could feel the blood rushing to my face. "Did you seriously just ask me that?"

I shouldn't have been *that* surprised. It was Stacy after all, the queen of *Cosmo*.

My eyes flashed to the rearview mirror when Jess snickered. "Yeah, Carrie, how does *that* work?"

I leered at her. "I don't kiss and tell," I said, drawing my attention back to the road. As besties since forever, we tell each other everything. I was going to go down for this.

"Since when?" Stacy asked, annoyed.

"Since now."

"Not." Stacy puffed out her lip. "You're dishing girl, so spill it."

Catching a glimpse of Jessica's reflection, I cocked my head once toward Stacy. "Has she?" I mouthed.

Jess nodded, smirking.

I thought so.

"Apparently some of us in this Jeep exhibit more self-control than others." I batted my lashes at Stacy.

She twisted in her seat and glared at Jess. "Did you tell her?"

"Not exactly. Sort of. Maybe?"

"Who?" I asked, happy to have the spotlight off myself.

Stacy slumped back around. "Andrew."

"Ah! Eww." I contorted my face. "Really?"

"Yeah," she muttered. "So not spectacular."

"I could have told you that," Jess said. "It's *Andrew*."

"You could *not* have told me! With your track record, you're going to die a virgin." Stacy crossed her arms and Jessica laughed.

"At least I didn't give my V card up to Andrew-the-man-whore."

Stacy ignored her. "You really haven't"—she waggled her eyebrows—"you know, with Lucas?"

I shook my head. "Sorry to disappoint you."

...and myself.

No marriage. No children. No sex. Did any of that matter when you love someone so much?

Lucas's words came back to me. Incenamus had the power to bring the dead back to life. That book could give us everything we ever wanted. He needed to get it translated—and pronto.

Stacy knocked her sunglasses down over her eyes. "God, I was so sure."

"How?" I asked. "Is it written on my forehead?"

"No, it's just the amount of tension between the two of you. It's thicker than ice, girl."

I scrunched my nose, confused. "Before you said—and I quote—that our love is 'sickeningly obvious.'"

"It is. And the two go together like mascara and eyeliner."

"That makes no sense," Jess said from the back.

"Trust me, it does."

***

After Stacy dragged us into half a dozen stores

where she bought enough scarves for life, I dove into the bookstore before she could protest. I hadn't bought anything for Lucas yet, and the only thing I came up with was a book of constellations. While I was there, I picked up a new Farmer's Almanac for my grandpa. It looked boring, but apparently a new edition of it came out every year. Weird.

On the way past, Stacy ducked into Victoria's Secret. Jess rolled her eyes and followed suit, grabbing my hand and yanking me along. Stacy's obsession with this store meant only one thing: two hours—minimum—of her trying on bras while Jess and I acted as her personal shoppers. Fun! (Insert Jess's famous eye roll, again.)

"There's a five item maximum in the dressing room," the attendant told Stacy.

"Bummer." Stacey handed off half of her items to me and half to Jess, keeping five for herself. "They've never told me that in Dallas."

"That's because you're on a first name basis with everyone there." Jess almost dropped a pink polka-dot bra, but caught it by the strap at the last minute.

"It's a stupid rule," she said, flipping her blonde curls over her shoulder. "Be right back, biatches!"

As soon as the dressing room door closed behind her, Jessica dumped her armload on the floor.

"Biatch is right," she muttered.

"Consider it community service," I suggested. "If it wasn't us, it would be some other lackeys."

"Go us!" Jess raised her hand above her head to shake a fake pom pom. "Now that we're alone, tell me, how *does* it work?"

"How does what work? We give Stacy new bras

to try on when she knocks twice on the door, like it's always worked."

"*Worked* is a debatable term, but that's not what I meant. I mean you and Lucas."

Knock. Knock.

I stood up and walked to room number four. "How many?"

"Three," Stacy said through the door and tossed three rejects over the top. Jess, standing behind me, caught them and created a new "no thanks" pile the poor attendant would have to put away later.

We sat back down on the bench, and I sighed. "If I don't think about it, it works great. It's when the little reminders roll in that I start to have my doubts. Sometimes I wonder why he was even allowed into my life—why Incenamus even exists—if I can't have him. It's so unfair." I shook my head and scanned what Jess and I affectionately call "the waiting room." "Now we've had all this time together, and I can't imagine my life without him."

"What happens when he finds his soul?" Jess asked.

I toyed with the price tag of one of the bras on my lap. "He has to choose—me or it."

"Carrie," Jess said, patting my arm. "That sucks, but a person's soul was never meant to be separated from them."

With my head bowed, I nodded. Of course she was right. Still, I didn't want to believe it. Somehow, there had to be a way. Something in that book would tell us how to bring him back to life, and everything would be okay. If only we could find someone who spoke Cumbric and could translate it, but no luck yet.

"There's still time," I said. Hell, I couldn't even convince myself of that.

Knock. Knock.

Sluggish, I stood up and leaned against the dressing room door. "How many?"

"Five." She tossed all five over at the same time. Jess caught them all like the bra-catching pro she was. "Give me the blue lacy one."

I handed her four random bras from my arms, and Jess dug through her pile. When she found the requested bra, she tossed it over the door instead of under.

"Ouch!"

"It's a bra, Stacy," Jess grumbled. "Not a basketball."

"Still!"

Snickering, I sat back down.

"How much time?" Jess asked in her worried tone, the same one she used when I originally told her about Lucas.

Can we drop it already?

My gaze flitted to her. "To find his soul? My lifetime, I hope." I didn't want to let him go, and Jess knew it.

"That's a long time for him to be separated—"

"I know, Jess. I know. I…I don't want to think about it."

Jessica pursed her lips and held my stare. "It's not going to go away just because you don't want to think about it."

I swallowed back a retort. I hated that she was right.

Knock. Knock.

This time I didn't bother getting up. "How many?"

"How many are left?"

My stack had depleted to two, leaving Jessica's pile with the most. "Twelve," Jess told her.

Stacy's voice lowered a little. "Is the attendant still there?"

My eyes swept the waiting room. "No."

"Give me the rest. Hurry."

Jess scrambled to get her load under the dressing room door, and I tossed in my remaining two.

I sat with my back to Jessica. I should have asked her about what she and Megan discussed and how she felt about finding out she was a witch. Sure, I wanted to know all that stuff, but my mind spun with thoughts of Lucas, reminding me of how selfish I was.

In a reverse situation, I'd pick him over my soul…wouldn't I?

Stacy emerged from the dressing room holding up two bras in the same style. "Black or pink?"

"Black," Jessica said the same time I said, "Pink."

She lowered her arms and puffed out her lip. "You two are no help." One at a time, she lifted them up and studied them. "I think I'll get both."

Jess shot me a wide-eyed look.

Of course she'll get both!

"Okay, biatches, let's go find some matching panties!"

***

Jessica and Stacy slinked into bed with me the next morning sometime after eleven. It was Sunday, and apparently Grandma and Grandpa had gone to church without me. Odd, since it would be one of the two Sundays a year my parents would have attended church.

"I majorly need a shower," Stacy whined.

"We're baking pies and stuff today…" Jessica yawned mid-sentence, "you're gonna get dirty anyway."

Stacy examined her perfectly manicured nails. "Can I just watch y'all?"

"Sure," I told her. "But if you don't help make them, you can't help eat them."

"God, Carrie, you're so cranky in the morning." She tossed off the blankets and got up. "I'm taking a shower."

Jess rolled on her side to face me. "It's her time of the month."

I laughed. "Hey, I'm sorry for being so short with you at the mall yesterday."

"It's okay. I figured you and Stacy were cycling together."

I grabbed a decorative pillow and hit her with it.

Since I still didn't want to talk about it, I dove in to her and Megan's convo. "Is it weird to know?"

Jess shifted her hair to the other side, thinking. "Actually, I'm relieved. For so long, I've wondered if something was happening to me, and the CIA was going to find out and haul me in for testing."

"'Cause that's not paranoid," I said, grinning.

"You should talk."

"Touché."

"Megan's contacting a coven in the Dallas area. Hopefully I can begin training as soon as I get back, but…"

"But what?"

"I don't know. Megan said Precogs are rare, and I really need one of them to train me to get the full benefits. She doesn't know if there's one in the Dallas coven or not." She studied my comforter harder than necessary. "Now that I know what I am, I want to help you. I want to help Lucas."

I shifted on my bed, uncomfortable. She wanted to help Lucas find his soul so he could reunite with it. I still hung on to the idea that it might not need to come to that.

Instead, I said, "I'm sure he'd appreciate it."

"What about you? I don't want to hurt you, Carrie."

"I'll be fine." My voice cracked, and I barely got the words out. I cleared my throat and tried again. "I'll be fine. Let's go downstairs."

***

After lunch, Grandma Renae handed each of us an apron. She mixed up the pie crust dough, and I rolled it out into flat circles. Stacy volunteered to use the star cookie cutters, thinking it would be the least messy thing she could do. Jessica mixed up the pie fillings: apple, cherry tort, pumpkin, and Grandpa's favorite, mincemeat.

"How many people are coming tomorrow for dinner?" Stacy asked, carefully topping the pumpkin pie with stars.

131

Grandma set the oven timer. "You girls, us, and is Lucas coming?"

"I think so," I said, handing her the finished apple pie.

"That's it?" Stacy eyed the table. "There are five pies here, that's like six slices each."

"I see your math skills have improved," I teased her, and she stuck her tongue out at me.

"One of the pumpkins is for the Carsons; they'll be back in town the day after Christmas." Grandma wiped her hands on her apron on her way to the pantry. "Carrie, grab the almond bark in the cupboard up there, will you, please?"

"Carsons? As in Mike Carson?" Stacy whispered in my ear.

"Correct."

She waggled her eyebrows. "You're going to introduce us, right?"

Jessica snickered at my expression. "You mean you?"

Stacy furrowed her brow, puffing out her lips in confusion.

"Introduce you, not us," Jess clarified.

"Huh?"

"Blonde," Jessica pointed out.

"Stereotype…person," Stacy spat out through her giggles.

I put the almond and chocolate barks on the table. "Yes, we're going over that evening."

Stacy sat down. "I'm wearing my new blue lacy bra."

"And a shirt, I hope." Jess grabbed some mixing bowls off the drying rack.

"That bra makes my boobs look good," Stacy said, shaking her chest a little.

"What makes you think he'll even notice?" I asked, a small pang of jealousy nipping me.

Settle down, sparky.

Stacy gave me a slide-long look. "Trust me, Care, if he's alive, he'll notice."

I peered down at my own chest, sighing.

My dead boyfriend notices, but...

Grandma came back up from the pantry and tossed two bags of pretzels, a package of Snickers bars, and an oversized bag of apples on the counter.

Stacy's mouth dropped open. "There's more?"

***

We woke up to five inches of snow blanketing the landscape. Like me, Stacy never had a white Christmas.

"I probably have," Jessica said, staring out my bedroom window. "But I don't remember it. My grandma used to live Colorado. I wonder if she was the one..." Jess trailed off, realizing Stacy was there.

Who passed down her powers.

"The one who what?" Stacy asked.

"Um, who taught my mom and me to ski," Jess said, shooting me an awkward glance.

"You wonder if she taught you how to ski? What?" Stacy followed Jess's gaze, and I cleared my throat.

"Super cute skirt, Stace," I said, nodding my approval.

Stacy hesitated, the sudden change in conversation not escaping her. "If your grandma plans on fattening us up today, I plan on letting her. I pulled my weight yesterday, and I want pie, damn it!" She stretched out the elastic waist of her black and white skirt and let it snap back into place.

"Then pie you shall have!" I linked my arm through hers, and she smiled. We skipped downstairs, giggling the whole way.

***

Bellies full, especially Stacy, who downed almost three slices of pie, we gathered in the living room. Stacy slumped onto the sofa, and I was sure she made a wise wardrobe decision. The top of my jeans were digging into my stomach.

Lucas sat beside me and took my hand, bringing it to his lips. "I've missed you." He leaned closer, his breath tickling my neck. "I hate sleeping alone."

Shivers raced up my spine, and I fought the urge to not fling myself on him in front of everyone.

Grandpa Rob handed out the gifts from under the tree. He and Grandma had even gotten something for my friends.

I watched Lucas as he unwrapped the silver package from me. When he lifted the lid, his puffed out laugh made me smile. He turned the constellation book over in his hands and flipped through the pages.

"Thank you." He pecked me quickly on the cheek. "I love it."

I opened the small box from Lucas last. Slipping

off the light blue ribbon, I set it aside. Lucas slid his arm around my waist and pulled me closer. In that moment, we were alone. Inside lay a silver necklace with two intertwining hearts that were molded together like the infinity symbol.

"Oh, Lucas," I murmured, lifting it out of the box.

"Turn it over."

On the back, Lucas had inscribed the word *forever*.

"I'll love you forever," he whispered so only I could hear him.

The world stopped spinning, and I didn't care that six sets of eyes were plastered on me. The only ones I cared about were Lucas's.

Gently, he took the necklace from my hands and wrapped it around my neck. I pulled my hair to the side, and he hooked the ends of the chain together. His cool fingers against my skin sent waves of warmth through me.

I touched the charm lying against my chest, the symbol of our love. Two hearts, like souls, interlocked until the end of time—Incenamus. Forever.

Chapter 10

"Oh, come on, dude!" Mike swiveled around on the desk chair. "Alabama?"

Lucas shrugged. "They've got something to prove."

The five of us were in the den at Mike's house, and no matter how great Stacy's new push-up bra was, Mike seemed interested in only football today. As usual.

"I think Ohio State has more to prove, being Big Ten and not SEC," Mike noted, his eyebrows raised. "I mean, how often has a Big Ten team made it to the National Championship lately?"

Lucas threw up his hands. "Exactly. 'Bama has the experience out there, and they won't want to lose to a Big Ten team. More to prove."

When they talked sports, they always seemed to get along, so I didn't interrupt.

Stacy leaned on my shoulder, pouting. "You think my boobs look good in this bra, don't you?"

"Perfectly perky, Stace. Mike is…well, Mike."

On the other side of me, Jessica yawned, and her

eyelids drooped further and further until they closed completely. I nudged her.

"Sorry. I didn't sleep well again," she said, yawning again.

"That's the understatement of the century," Stacy muttered. "I woke up screaming because you were clawing me in your sleep." She shoved up the sleeve of her shirt. "See?"

Red nail marks, some deep enough to draw blood, slithered up Stacy's arm like something out of a horror movie.

"They go all the way to my shoulder," she said.

"I said I was sorry." Jess rubbed her eyes, undoubtedly trying to keep them open. "I really am."

"When we get back home, I think we need to find you a sleep study or something. This is crazy." Stacy slid her sleeve back down to her wrist. "You definitely need some help."

"I plan on it, Stace," Jess assured her. She didn't tell Stacy who she would be getting the help from, though.

"Me dying again?" I whispered to Jess so only she could hear.

Jessica bit her lip. "It's different."

"What's different?"

"I don't want to talk about it. Not now." She shot a glance at Stacy. Without ever discussing it, Jess and I had apparently come to the same conclusion: excluding Stacy for her own safety seemed best.

"What are you two gossiping about?" Stacy asked, smearing another layer of lip gloss over her cherry lips then sticking the tube between her breasts. "I want in!"

"Nothing," Jess grumbled. "Just my stupid dreams."

Lucas's gaze cut to me then back to Mike. With his perfect ghostly hearing, he'd heard the conversation, and I had no doubt he'd report it to Megan. The two of them seemed to share everything these days.

"Carrie," Mike hollered from across the room. "You care to add your two cents?"

"Um, Alabama," I said, forgetting who was rooting for whom. This year's bowl games didn't matter much to me—Dad and I used to watch them all together. Too many bad memories.

"Traitor." Mike sulked.

Yeah, there seems to be a lot of that going around.

***

My alarm began to buzz at one in the morning. I slapped it off, and then I remembered why I'd set it in the first place.

"What time is it?" Lucas groaned, his body filling out beside me.

"When did you get here?" I asked him.

"After you fell asleep. I didn't want to wake you." He propped up on his elbow and kissed the tip of my nose. "You're too cute when you sleep."

God, he was gorgeous lying there, and the desire to press myself up against him and kiss him until I forgot how to breathe almost overwhelmed me.

No, not tonight. I needed to talk to Jess.

"It's still the middle of the night," I said, toying with the dark hair lapping over his forehead. "Jess's dream, she said it's different."

"Maybe the future changed. Maybe Megan's wrong."

"Only one way to find out." I let my hand fall from his face. "I've got to talk to Jess."

Lucas sat up, brushing a finger down my cheek. "Remember, she's untrained. It may not mean anything."

I peered up at him. "And it might mean everything."

***

I snuck into the guest bedroom as quietly as possible. From the bed on the opposite wall, Stacy's back faced me. I kept my gaze trained on her, trying to think of a killer excuse if she happened to wake up.

Sleepwalking…then she'll rush Jess and I both to a sleep clinic.

Okay, not so killer.

I quickened my pace to Jessica's bed. She slept on her stomach, her hair swept to one side, and with her arms folded under the pillow. Last time I'd summoned her in the middle of the night, she'd woken right up. Tonight, though, she seemed to sleep peacefully. I hated to bother her.

"Jess." I shook her a little. "Jess, wake up."

She stirred, rolled her head toward me, and then sunk back into steady breaths.

I peeked over my shoulder to check on Stacy.

Thankfully, she hadn't moved.

"Come on, Jess," I whispered louder. "Get up."

"If the sun's not awake, go away," she mumbled.

I groaned to myself and lied. "The sun's up. Come on. And be quiet."

Jessica grumbled something unintelligible and flung her legs over the side of the bed. She stretched her arms over her head, yawning.

I grabbed her arm. "We don't have time for that. Let's go."

"Stacy's right; you *are* cranky in the morning." She shuffled her way down the hallway to my room.

Quietly, I closed the door behind her and spun around.

Jess's eyes were half-open as she dropped down on my bed, the mattress bouncing with her. "What do you want at this ungodly hour? You realize I was actually sleeping for once, right?"

"Sorry, but we needed to talk without the possibility of Stacy overhearing us. Tell me about your dream last night. What was different about it?"

"I don't know, Carrie." She shook her head. "It's…It's almost like it's telling more, but maybe it's not. Maybe it's something completely unrelated."

I sat beside her, crossing my legs. "We can't figure it out if it only stays in your head."

"I know what you're thinking, and Megan said—"

"I know what Megan said! What if she's wrong? What if the future changed the second Lucas decided to call off his search?" I paused, taking a deep breath. "Am I in the dream?"

Jess nodded.

"Am I still going to die?"

Jess sighed, hesitating. "Yes."

I bowed my head. "Then what's different?"

"I only see glimpses, like the electricity is flashing on and off in my brain. It was raining this time, and I saw a kitchen and a cemetery with a large green tree." She closed her eyes, sinking into the memory of the dream. "There's a wooden chair shattered into pieces on the floor. A window breaking. People—I can't make out who—are fighting."

I stared at her, and she swallowed, her eyelids squeezed tighter together. "Uh, there's a number: 314. A bouquet of flowers. I don't...I don't know what they mean. I hear screaming, and I see blood. Someone is cut, I think."

"From the broken window?" I interjected.

"Maybe. I don't know." She shook her head. "I—"

"Is there anything else?"

"Um, yeah. There's a table. Nails scrape over someone's arm, and a body is thrown through the air. It lands on the table, splitting the wood down the middle. The person, they're not moving. I think...I think they're dead."

Her eyes shot open, tears streaking down her cheeks. "They're dead. They're..."

I put my arm around her shoulders and pulled her into me. "It's okay, Jess. It's okay."

"No. No, it's not. I...people are going to die, Carrie. How is that okay?" she sobbed.

I didn't have an answer.

***

"Uh, why wasn't I invited to the sleepover?" Stacy's hands rested on her hips as she stood in the doorway. "What, did you two wait until I fell asleep to continue the little gossipfest you left me out of this afternoon?"

"No, Stace, of course not," I said, wiping the sleep from my eyes.

"I woke up from another dream last night, and I didn't want to bother you." Lying was never Jessica's forte. Now, she combed her fingers through her hair and swiped it up into a messy knot on top of her head.

Stacy's pale blue irises shifted from me to Jess. Me to Jess. Me to Jess. "So you came to bother *her* instead?"

"She only has two more days to put up with me. You, however, are in for the long haul." Jess grinned too big, and I knew we were doomed. "Come on. Come sit with us." Jessica patted the duvet.

Stacy's eyes narrowed. "You two are hiding something."

"No, we're not," I said quickly and bit my lip to shut myself up. Like Jess, I wasn't a good liar either. Stacy, however...

Stacy stared at me for a few seconds before she relaxed. "Sure. Whatever. Keep your secrets; you know I'll find out eventually. I always do."

***

Over the next two days, we included Stacy in everything, and I mean *everything*. It was strange to have her sitting on the toilet seat talking to me while I showered, but the happier Jessica and I kept her, the more we hoped she'd forget about the late night pow-wow that hadn't included her. I vaguely remembered the strategy had worked in the past—like when we were eight.

After hauling down the last of the suitcases and bedding out to Stacy's convertible, I hugged Jess first.

"Check in on my mom, will you?" I asked.

"She already moved. We're not neighbors anymore."

"Yeah, I know. Could you still?"

"You know I will."

"And let me know if anything changes." This wasn't about my mom, and Jessica knew what I meant.

"Definitely." She hugged me tighter. "Stay safe, okay?" she murmured in my ear.

I nodded.

"Hurry up, you two. I'm freezing my ass off here!" Stacy bounced on her toes, her teeth chattering.

I let go of Jess, and she smiled.

"Now, I've personally checked Jess's backseat driver's license, Stace, and it's perfectly legit," I teased and wrapped my arms around her neck.

"Yeah, well, I checked it too, and it expired when she was six."

"Thank you for coming, Stacy."

"It was fun," she said. "Even without Mike."

"Give him a break, he's a gimp right now."

"Maybe next time then." A sob made her words slur a little.

I pulled back. "Are you crying?"

With her index finger, she wiped tears from under her lashes, careful not to smudge her eyeliner. "It's so weird, you know? You being up here and not back home."

"Trust me, I know."

"When are you coming home?"

My gaze dropped to the snow under our feet. Honestly I hadn't thought about it yet. "I'm not sure."

"Am I ever going to see you again? I mean, it's not like the three of us are all going to the same college next fall."

"We'll see each other before college, for sure." I swallowed, wondering when exactly I was supposed to die. "This summer, definitely."

Or at a funeral before then.

"Okay," she said, satisfied, a small smile creeping onto her face. "I've really missed you, Carrie."

I was her go-to when her parents up and left on one of their lavish business trips, and I could tell Stacy had been lonely cooped-up in that empty mansion of hers.

"Hey, make Jess stay with you a few times until your parents get back. Maybe that will make you miss me less."

She shrugged. "Maybe."

"Yo! Why so glum?" Jess chided, trying to suppress a smirk. "I'm the life of the party, girl!"

"Oh really?" Stacy drawled out. "Okay, Miss Life of the Party, whatcha doing Friday night?"

"I have no plans…yet. You'd better reserve me soon, though, my phone will be ringing constantly anytime now."

Stacy giggled, and I loved Jess for cheering her up. "Well, schedule it in your little black book then."

"Ha! Black? Mine's red." She winked.

"Of course it is," Stacy snickered.

"Have a safe drive." I hugged Stace again, and stepping back, I watched her convertible make a U-turn in the driveway.

I waved until I could no longer see the car.

***

It snowed almost every day during the month of January. It comforted me a little, knowing that I probably wasn't fated to die until after winter since, according to Jessica's vision, rain was supposed to be falling that night.

Jess emailed me on a regular basis, saying her dreams had become a nightly occurrence, though her scope hadn't widened and nothing had changed. Death would be knocking on my door soon.

Because of this, Lucas became overly protective. He picked me up each morning and drove me to school, using the snow-and-ice-covered roads as an excuse. During the day, I could feel him next to me, floating down the halls and close by as I sat in class. Then he'd magically appear in his Jeep and take me back home.

The biggest highlight to his bodyguard routine was that he stayed the whole night with me most nights instead of leaving after I fell asleep. Still, nothing ever happened between us. I had to ignore the ripples in my stomach and the fire in his eyes when he kissed me. Man, it sucked, but at least we were burning together.

Slowly, winter faded into spring, and the blanket of white that covered the country fields melted into a mud bath. Instead of jeans and sweaters, my wardrobe changed to short-sleeved tops and capris.

Grandma started to buzz about graduation and the three college acceptance letters I hadn't responded to yet. Heck, I hadn't even opened them yet. It was hard to think about the future when I couldn't stop thinking about how I might not have one.

Chapter 11

I flipped the sign to 'closed' on Renae's Antiques' glass door. "Bye, Grandma!"

At the sound of my voice, she poked her head out of the back room. "Be home by ten o'clock."

"Ten!" I whined. "Spring break started today—midnight?"

Grandma tapped her nails on the door, considering my slight tweak in curfew. "Eleven."

"Deal," I muttered. "I guess."

"Have fun."

I opened the glass door and hollered back. "I'd have more fun if I could stay out until midnight."

"Nice try," she called, and closed the back door, enclosing herself inside her workroom away from further discussion.

I groaned to myself, stepping out into the sunshine. As I turned the key in the lock, arms folded themselves around me.

"I can't wait to have you all to myself tonight." Lucas kissed my neck, and I giggled.

"What did you have in mind?"

Staying all night with me pushed his limits for sure. His frustration grew, seeping into me so that I could feel it too. Even though we knew it could only go so far, we tested the waters anyway. Problem was we'd be so wrapped up in each other that he'd lose concentration and fade into transparency. Yeah, it totally sucked.

Lucas spun me around, his fingers weaving themselves in my hair. His nose touched mine, his lips teasing me. "Guess you'll have to find out."

I rose up on my tip-toes and sucked on his lip. "Sounds promising."

Lucas curved up the corner of his mouth. The way his dimple sunk into his cheek made my stomach sizzle.

Heat rose to my face, flushing my cheeks. "Eleven o'clock curfew tonight—we're running out of time. Let's go." I grabbed his hand, pulling him toward his Jeep waiting across the street.

"You hungry? We can—"

"Nope. I'm good." My stomach growled.

"—order some pizza," he finished, snickering.

I reached for the door handle. "You heard that, huh?"

"Pizza it is."

I slid into the Jeep, my imagination running wild at Lucas's words. Since he'd called off the search for the incubus, Carver, he hadn't been going off to Iowa City to see Megan. I also noticed that without those visits, he was completely back to normal—no pale skin, no exhaustion, no anything. He still refused to talk about it, though, and I stopped asking because it didn't seem like a big deal now.

Before Lucas had the door closed behind me, we heard "Hey!" Mike's rusty truck pulled into the spot next to us. Without the neck brace, Mike had rushed full-speed into life again—well, without the football part.

Good as new.

I smiled, thinking about my mostly fulfilled promise to Mike's squirt-sister.

"Fantastic," Lucas muttered under his breath. He leaned up against the open Jeep door, arms crossed like he was ready for a fight.

"Play nice," I reminded him.

"I will if he does."

Typical.

Mike jumped out of his truck, slamming the door behind him. "What are you two up to?" He only looked at me.

"*We* were—"

"Off to get pizza," I interrupted Lucas. The ego trip could wait for another day. "What's going on? You weren't at school today."

"Doctor's appointment. They approved baseball for the summer, so I'm gonna go talk to the coach."

"I'm sure you'll be amazing, as always." I ignored the way Lucas's eyes shifted to me in a jealous stare. "We'll be at your first game."

Mike shot me a half-grin, and I felt a punch in my gut, probably from Lucas's and my soul connection.

"I hope so." Mike paused, holding my gaze a second too long. "Um, by the way, Lucas, I overheard some guy in town asking about you."

Lucas knit his brows together. "About me?"

"Yeah, described you to a T, man," Mike said. "Had to be you."

"What did he want?" Lucas dropped his arms and straightened.

Mike shrugged. "To know if you lived in town."

"Do you remember what he looked like?" Lucas asked, his hand grabbing mine and squeezing. "Blond?"

"Sorry, I didn't notice. Why do you ask?" Mike glanced at me then back at Lucas. "You in some sort of trouble?"

When Lucas didn't answer, Mike continued. "What's going on? Why's this guy looking for you?"

"I'll take care of it, thanks." The roughness in Lucas's tone worried me a little. Mike didn't seem to like it either.

Suddenly the hair on the back of my neck perked up. My eyes roamed over the park, and that's when I saw someone's head swing back behind a tree.

"Um, Lucas?"

He ignored me.

"Someone's watching us," I said to myself, my fingers gliding across the heart-shaped infinity necklace Lucas gave me for Christmas.

"Why don't you let me take Carrie home, and you can do whatever you gotta do." Mike took a step forward, but Lucas blocked him.

"I said I'll take care of everything, *including* Carrie."

Still focused on the tree in the distance, I started to slip out of the Jeep, but Lucas held me back.

"I…there's…I—" I mumbled, unsure of what I

was saying.

Mike's eyes flitted to me, his jaw clenching. "Don't drag her into your shit, man. She doesn't deserve that."

Lucas's lips pulled tight, and I wished I could hear what he was thinking.

The head poked around the tree again and jerked back when they caught me watching.

"Lucas," I repeated softly.

"I know," he said, backing down, though I wasn't sure if he was talking to me or Mike. "I'll let you know if I need anything."

Mike's gaze flitted over me, skeptical.

"It's okay," I mouthed to him.

"Yeah, Luke, you do that," he said and hopped back in his truck. Mike's tires skidded over the cement, and he sped off.

Lucas shut my door and rounded the Jeep to the driver's side. When he crawled in behind the steering wheel, he flickered into transparency.

"Lucas?"

Regaining his concentration, he materialized and started the engine. "Buckle up."

"Who is it? Who's looking for you?"

Lucas shook his head. "I don't know."

"Carver?"

Lucas's attention snapped in my direction. "Let's hope not."

I swallowed, gearing up the courage to ask my next question. "Is Carver blond? Is he the one that…" I couldn't finish out loud.

Kills me?

"No. He can't be; he's not a vamp, Care.

Besides, it's not going to happen. I'm not leaving you for a second."

"Jess's dreams, Lucas, they're not changing, and—"

Lucas cut me off. "When's she coming?"

"Megan is picking her up in Omaha on Saturday."

Sherman's spring break aligned with Villisca's, and Megan wanted my best witch-friend to come up and meet her family. Last time I had spoken with her, she said the coven in Dallas really helped, and her powers were progressing abnormally quickly, even without the help of another precog. I'd run out of reasons to doubt her now.

My palms began to sweat, and I wiped them on my capris.

How much time do I have left? Weeks? Days? Hours?

I lifted my eyes to the sky, wondering when it would rain next.

Sure, I'd considered that possibility before, but now that it stared me down, I didn't want to die. My death would destroy Lucas, and since I still hadn't forgiven my father for tearing our family apart, I could end up between worlds, forgetting my life— forgetting Lucas. Unfortunately, forgiving someone wasn't always as easy as it sounded. At this point, bringing Lucas back from the dead seemed more plausible.

"Um, at the park, did you see someone watching us?"

"I heard you. It was just a person, Care, a human. Probably waiting for someone."

"No colored auras then?"

Lucas snickered, clearly amused by my paranoia. "No, you're fine. No one's going to hurt you, not as long as I'm around."

I sunk deeper into the seat, trying to block my mind so he couldn't hear my doubts, my fears. It may have worked; he didn't say anything else.

Lucas pulled into his driveway and shifted into park. "We'll have the pizza delivered," he said, his sensual tone from earlier completely gone.

"Yeah, sure." I unbuckled myself and followed Lucas to his front porch.

Lucas slid his key into the lock and opened the door. "Pepperoni?" he asked, flipping on the light.

"I wouldn't eat it if it—" Lucas threw his arm out, pushing me backward over the threshold. "Hey!"

"Who are you? What are you doing here?" he growled into the house.

I moved to peer around Lucas's body, but he blocked me again.

"Nice to see you too, Lucas."

Why did that voice sound so familiar?

"How do you know my name?" Lucas asked, keeping a hand firmly pressed against my stomach.

"Let's just say we knew each other in another life," the man answered.

Lucas hesitated. "So, why are you here?"

"I heard you've been searching for me," he said. "Here I am."

"Carver?" Lucas took a step backward, taking me with him, hooking his arms around the small of my back and welding me against him. "No, it can't be. You're human."

"You do *not* want Carver anywhere near here. Neither of us do," the stranger said. "Trust me, I'm who you've been seeking out. It's me you want."

Lucas loosened his grip for only a second, but I took the opportunity. I couldn't stand not knowing, especially when the stranger's voice rung out oddly familiar in my head. I sprung around Lucas in a play Mike would have been proud of. At the sight of the man lounging on the arm of the chair, I gasped, wide-eyed.

"Reid?"

Chapter 12

The ginger who wiped hot chocolate from my coat at Mike's last football game jumped to his feet.

"She's here with you?" He sounded horrified, as if we'd broken into *his* house instead of the other way around.

Lucas gripped my shoulder. "You know him? Who is he?"

"She needs to leave, Lucas," Reid demanded, eyes drilling into me as if he loathed the sight of me. "Now. Before I—"

"I met him at a football game, the one you didn't go to," I interrupted, my gaze staying locked on Reid. His expression gave me the creeps.

"Lucas, take her—" Reid ground out.

"Just shut up, will you? This is *my* house—*you're* the intruder here. Don't tell me what to do!"

"Wait," I said, squinting at Reid. "At the game, you said you were looking for someone. Then in Villisca today—you were trying to find Lucas, weren't you?"

The muscles in his jaw tensed as he lowered

himself back into the chair. He clutched at the armrests until his knuckles paled. "Lucas, and *only* Lucas."

"Why? What do you want with me?" Lucas asked.

"I already told you. *You're* the one who wants something from *me*." Reid leaned forward, not loosening his grip on the chair. "Tell me, and I'll be on my way."

Lucas shook his head. "Something from you? I don't even know you."

"Sure you do, Luke," Reid said. "You just don't remember."

Thick silence fell in around us until all I heard was the sound of my own heart thumping. Lucas studied Reid, scrutinizing him with narrowed eyes, as if he was trying to place Reid in his past.

I concentrated on Lucas. Maybe he'd let his guard down, let me in. Something connected these two men. Something bigger than what was happening right now.

Giving up, Lucas shook his head. "I can't remember."

Golden irises peeked through dark red locks, landing on Lucas. "Almost five years ago, I stood in the rain, watching your spirit leave your body."

"That's...that's not possible." Lucas's brows knit together. "You're human, you couldn't have seen that."

"I'll prove it. Close your eyes." Reid sat back in his chair and crossed his legs.

"I don't think so," Lucas said, still wary of the trespasser. "My eyes stay open."

"Your choice," Reid replied, shooting a glance at me. The corner of his mouth twitched upward.

Icy tingles raced up my spine, making the hair at the back of my neck stand on end. The sudden hiss in Reid's tone sent ripples under my skin. I didn't know why he had this effect on me. I had a strange sensation that he'd made me feel like this before somehow.

Doing a quick sweep of the room, I saw that nothing had changed. Even so, it *felt* different. The energy surrounding me had morphed into something oddly familiar. Oddly terrifying. Oddly…sweet.

It scared me. Enticed me. Sent shockwaves of desire through me.

Is it getting warm in here?

Shifting his gaze back to Lucas, Reid continued as if he and Lucas were best pals. "It was only me and you that night, so no one else would know what happened."

Lucas nodded once in confirmation, and I sucked in a breath. If Reid was telling the truth then he might hold the answers that Lucas so desperately wanted. If not…

Who is this guy?

Reid continued, "You were driving a black Grand Prix down a windy asphalt road. Dude, you were taking those corners close to a hundred miles per hour; it was hard to keep up with you. I called your cell, but you must have shut it off."

Reid's sudden mood shift to Lucas's best buddy made me even more uneasy. Slowly, Lucas's eyelids closed as he immersed himself in the story. I pressed myself against his back, arms circled around his waist. Partly because I needed to be close to him, and partly to use his body as a shield against Reid. The odd mix of lust and fear stirring in my gut had only grown.

"It was about three in the morning, and the road was deserted. Thank God, because you stayed on the center line the whole time. You rounded a curve, lost traction, and slammed into an oak tree on the right side of the road," Reid explained. "Your spirit rose out of your body, and by the time I got to you, you were standing on the other side of the street, staring back at yourself. For a while, I stood quiet beside you. Then, I said your name, but you didn't answer me."

Lucas must have been concentrating intently on what Reid was describing because he faded into transparency. Instantly, my arms fell off him. Cool air surrounded me, making me shiver in its wake. Standing in front of Reid without Lucas's body between us, I felt exposed. Too exposed.

Reid's gaze flicked in my direction again. A hardness filled those caramel irises, and they seemed to darken as his pupils dilated. My stomach twisted at the sensation he exuded. I wanted to cling to Lucas, but only his vaporous outline floated in front of me.

Come back to me.

"When you finally noticed me, Lucas, I knew right away you didn't recognize me," Reid said as if his malicious stare hadn't just ripped into me.

Now focused on Lucas, his eyes softened. "I'm not sure if you even realized I could see you, at first. I explained who I was and what had happened, but as soon as I told you that you were dead, you took off. I tried to go after you, but I no longer had the power to see through the forest." Reid paused. "It was like you disappeared. I never saw you again."

When Lucas opened his eyes, he immediately solidified, and I wrapped my arms around him. Feeling his body against mine eased some of the tension flooding my muscles.

"Believe me now?" Reid asked, his brows raised.

Lucas's cool breath floated down over me. He hadn't reached for me yet, and I wished he would.

"Where?" Lucas said. "Where were we?"

"Blue Ridge Mountains, North Carolina."

North Carolina. That's where Lucas died. Did that also mean that's where he lived?

For a moment, Lucas focused on Reid, probably rolling what I'd just thought around in his head. Lost in his thoughts, he looked at Reid without really seeing him.

The intensity of Reid's gaze hardened, and I could feel the pressure begin to creep into the corners of my boyfriend's small house. Even though Reid was careful to keep his eyes pinned on Lucas, I had the odd feeling he was actually watching me. The sparks slinking into my veins nipped at me as Reid's mood shifted once more. It was almost like he was a different person…again.

I pressed into Lucas and laced my fingers with his. It took too long for his to tighten the hold on my hand.

Does he not sense the change in the air?

Like a predator gearing to assault its prey, Reid

waited patiently in the armchair, preparing for the perfect moment to attack. Something brewed in the back of his mind, I could feel it.

"Lucas," I mumbled without moving my lips. "Lucas?"

My attention teetered back and forth between the two of them. Neither moved.

Then, Lucas blinked. "You were following me through the mountains?"

Reid nodded once.

"We knew each other before I died. You being there wasn't an accident."

Reid uncrossed his legs and leaned back. "You can say that." Frigidity had sliced back into his voice, and I held back the apprehension clawing at me. Lucas would notice if something seemed off, wouldn't he?

"I don't get it. Who *are* you, and how did you see me that night?" The muscles in Lucas's jaw cinched.

Reid smirked, rolling his gaze over me instead of meeting Lucas's stare. Unable to peel my eyes off Reid, I let go of Lucas's hand. Reid captivated me, triggered a seductive stir in my abdomen. A voice in my head urged me to run, to be afraid, but the part of me that feared him only strengthened the sudden need I had for him.

No longer was the room filled with tension. Instead, alluring warmth surrounded me, drawing me in, and I wanted to melt into it. My heart raced and heat pooled low in my stomach. I ached for him.

"I'm not who you think I am, Lucas. Not *what*

you think I am," Reid said through gritted teeth, as if he were holding back.

The sound turned me on even more, my nipples hardening. Blood rushed through my veins harder, faster, flushing my skin in all the right places.

Reid balled his hands into fists over the arm of the chair. The muscles under his black t-shirt pulsed, making me want to rip the material off him.

"It's coming," he growled to Lucas. "You might want to get her out of here now!" Panting, he leaped off the chair and plastered himself against a door.

Reid's irises dug into me, his pupils dilating, covering the whole of his eyes like delicious dark pits. Reid caged me with his gaze, and I was utterly lost in him.

From somewhere in the room, a voice from a guy I didn't remember floated to me. "What the hell is happening?"

I ignored him. There were only two people in the room that mattered. Reid and me. Hungry to have him devour me, I bit my lower lip in anticipation. He could have me any way he wanted.

I took a step toward him, combing my fingers through my hair and letting it fall over my shoulder. My skin crawled with an overwhelming burn only Reid could satisfy.

His lips curved up into an enticing smile. With one finger, he beckoned me to him.

"Oh, yes," I heard myself say.

I crossed my arms around my stomach and grabbed ahold of the hem of my shirt, lifting it over my head. I couldn't wait another second to—

Then I was suddenly being squeezed like a tube

of toothpaste. I tried to suck in a breath, but I couldn't breathe.

Cool, fresh air washed over me, and I inhaled deeply, almost choking on it. I doubled over with my hands across my stomach, dropping to my knees.

"What. Was. That?" I asked, out of breath.

"Incubus," Lucas said as he lowered himself to the ground and lifted my chin.

His fingers rippled against my skin as his body flashed several times before fading into transparency.

"Damn," he muttered, exhausted. "You okay?"

I nodded, though honestly, I wasn't sure. Hell, I didn't even know what had just happened, or why I was…

My eyes tick-tocked from side to side: a cornfield to the left, cows on the right. I looked down at my feet: pavement.

"Why are we outside in the middle of the nowhere?"

Solidifying for a moment, Lucas handed me my shirt.

Huh?

I glanced down at my chest, seeing only my bra. "What's going on here? Why do you have my clothes?" I paused, studying him. "Did we…?"

Lucas chuckled, amused. I, on the other hand, was more confused than ever.

"The cows are staring, better put it on," he said, his eyes wandering over me in appreciation. I stood up and slipped the shirt over my head, and he continued, "What's the last thing you remember?"

I puckered my lips to the side. "Um, when we got your house, Reid was there, sitting in your living room. He acted as if he's known you for years. Then he started acting odd then normal then odd…and…and that's it. I ended up here, shirtless."

His body re-formed next to me, but he looked pale and tired.

The corner of Lucas's lips curved up, exposing his dimple. He took a step toward me, reaching behind my head and lowering his mouth over mine. Out on some road in Nowhereville, I sunk into his kiss.

"What was that about?" I puffed out, wanting more.

"Oh, baby. Someday, I hope you act exactly like that for me." The deep seduction of his voice sent shivers through me.

"Like what?"

"Reid's an incubus, a half-demon."

"A cambion?"

"Yeah." He took my hand, and we started down the road. "Like other cambions, he has to feed off humans to stay alive. But unlike vamps, he doesn't need blood; he needs a soul, energy and, uh, desire."

"Desire?"

In the light of the moon, the smirk on Lucas's face was even sexier than usual. "Drive. Will power. Need. And the best time to get the bulk of that energy is when you're turned on."

I made a face. "Please don't tell me…did I…with Reid?"

Lucas laughed. "You think I'd let that happen?

No. He put you under a trance, compelling you to want him then he doesn't have to work as hard. You go straight to him, and you won't remember anything. Incubi will take what they need from you and a little treat for fun before they suck out your soul."

"But you said he was human."

"Um, yeah. That's the weird part, he was—until he wasn't."

"I don't understand. Is he human or an incubus?"

"Both. When he shot up out of the chair, his black aura began to emerge. It wasn't there before. I don't know how that's possible."

"So, when I was under this trance, what did I do?" I swallowed, scared of the answer.

Lucas stopped walking and faced me, a grin spreading on his face. "If it was just you and me, it would have been one helluva show."

I stepped back, horrified. Had I done some sort of strip-tease for some other guy in front of my boyfriend?

"Trust me, it didn't get far. I got you out of there as soon as I understood what was happening."

"Thank you," I mouthed, embarrassed.

But I still got far enough to get my shirt off.

Lucas held back a chuckle at my thought. "Maybe part of that was for me."

True or not, I blushed at little. I had a hard time thinking he'd allow Reid to see too.

"I was too preoccupied with Reid to know what he was doing to you and how you were reacting. I'm sorry. Still..." He grinned, and we started walking again. "The view was nice."

My heart fluttered, and I sighed inwardly. "Where are we anyway?"

Lucas shrugged. "We can't be too far from Red Oak. I can't teleport for long distances with someone else, yet."

"You don't know, do you?"

"No clue." He pulled me to his side. "Got your phone?"

I dug in the back pocket of my jeans. "Yeah."

"You'd better call Megan to pick us up. Your phone has GPS, so she can track us." He sighed, his voice lowering. "I've got the feeling that Reid's not done with us yet."

Chapter 13

It didn't take Megan long to find us on a county highway, ten miles south of Red Oak. By the time she picked us up, Lucas's energy had returned, and I leaned on his fully-solidified shoulder as we drove.

"Drop Carrie off at the farm, first," Lucas instructed.

"What? No!"

The green in Lucas's irises intensified. "You can't seriously want to go back after that."

"Uh, yeah. I do. Besides, you promised—"

"—Contingent on—"

"Oh, hell no!" I jerked away, bumping into Megan. I really hated her truck right now, with all three of us crammed into the front seat. "You are not backing out this time. If you need to get me away from him, you just proved you could. I'm coming with you."

My tone and volume made Megan cringe. She cleared her throat, obviously uncomfortable with our fight.

"We don't even know if he's still there. I mean, why he would be?" she reasoned, but both of us ignored her.

"Reid is an incubus, Care. As soon as he transformed, he had you in that trance in under a second!"

Megan and I spoke at the same time: "Hang on a sec. What?" "You'll be right there this time too."

Megan sighed. "Let her come, Lucas," she said as if I was a sassy four-year-old throwing a tantrum. They'd left me out of the loop last time, and I'd be damned if they did it again.

Lucas's gaze swept over me. His feelings stirred within my soul—fear for me mixed with guilt over not getting me out of the house faster.

He slipped my hand in his, gently scooting me to him. "Stay close to me, okay?"

I nodded.

"I'm confused," Megan continued. "What do you mean by 'transformed?' Incubi are born—they're not Changers."

"I know, but that's what happened. Sitting in my living room, he was completely human, no aura, nothing. Then, so slowly, gray fuzz emerged all around him. Within seconds, it was pitch black, and he had Carrie hypnotized."

Megan shook her head. "That's…impossible."

"Not anymore."

Megan focused back on the road. "How?"

"You'll have to ask him."

I frowned. "Okay, you guys just lost me. What's impossible?"

Megan didn't answer. I'm not sure she even

heard me. A moment passed before Lucas finally replied. "Unlike Changers—werewolves, vamps, ghosts, shifters, even some demons—incubi and succubi are born, like witches and necros. They're not turned, or changed."

"Half-demons are born?"

Lucas grinned, his dimple winking at me. "Yeah, uh," he swept his hand through his hair. "They're the offspring of demons and humans."

It took a few seconds for that to sink in. When it did, I wanted to vomit.

"You mean humans actually have sex with demons?" I'd seen demons, felt them. Gross.

"In human form, they're almost indistinguishable from the living. Incubi and succubae children are also completely normal, that is, until they reach puberty. That's when the demon inside of them begins to take over, killing off their soul."

I scrunched up my face. "Reid's a little old for that, isn't he? He's got to be at least twenty."

Lucas puffed out a chuckle. "Should be, but—"

"But he's exhibiting the same behaviors as an adolescent incubus," Megan said, letting her thoughts mingle with our conversation. "Cycling incubi continue to weave in and out of their human and demon sides until they reach adulthood, when they become full-fledged incubi and can only survive by drawing out the life force of the living."

"Through seduction," Lucas clarified.

"Putting me in a trance before taking my soul," I said, remembering what Lucas had told me earlier that night.

"Pretty much."

"What would have happened if I'd have gone to him? Would I have become an incubus?" For some reason, I still hadn't been able to shake the feeling that Reid had drawn me in before. Had he succeeded then? How often had it happened?

"A succubus? No," Lucas said. "At least, not traditionally. Incubi and succubae—females—can't create more of their own kind, or any kind."

"They'd just kill me then."

When Lucas didn't answer, Megan did. "They'll suck most of your soul out of your body and poison what little remains until it dies off. Taking the souls of the living is the only way to ensure their own survival, like blood for the vampire."

Well, that settled half a question. If Reid had hypnotized me before, he hadn't succeeded. Still, I didn't feel much better. Incubus Reid was as dangerous as Lucas had said.

Megan pulled into Lucas's driveway and cut the engine. The house was dark, and I hoped Reid had decided to leave as soon Lucas disappeared with me. Thankfully, the incubus had no clue where we'd gone, so he couldn't follow, and I couldn't think of any reason for him to have stayed. I slid out of the truck, and Lucas instantly pulled me to him.

"I think he's gone," I said through my uncertainty. Regardless, Lucas didn't loosen his grip.

The three of us peered up at Lucas's little one-bedroom home.

"Can you feel him, Megan? Is he still here?" Lucas asked.

"I can't feel anything."

"Is there a spell or something you could do?" I said softly.

"Yeah, but I don't think it would do us any good. My senses are better than the spell…usually," she answered. "He's either gone, or he's human right now."

Lucas sighed. "I guess we'd better go in."

Megan led the way, followed by Lucas and me. Lucas's hand squeezed mine, and I almost gasped from the firmness. Megan opened the front door cautiously, standing back as it swung open. I wondered if Reid's power of seduction worked on witches too.

"Yes, but he'd be stupid to try," Lucas answered my thought.

I was about to ask why when Megan flipped on the light and I saw Reid, lounging in the same armchair as before, quite comfortable. He had his legs draped over one arm and both of his hands behind his head.

Human or incubus?

"At the moment, human," Lucas said to me. Then to Reid, he asked, "Why are you still here? What do you want?"

"Nothing you can give me," Reid said, not moving.

"Nothing but the girl?"

Uh, let's not patronize him.

The corner of Reid's lips rose. "The girl is of no interest to me."

"No interest? You don't really expect me to believe that, do you?"

"Believe what you want. I'm not leaving until I

finish what I came here to do." Reid rolled his hazel eyes over Megan, who stood to the side, studying him. "Who's the other chick?"

"How long have you two been gone?" Megan asked Lucas.

"Uh, about three hours."

"Huh." Megan nodded once at Reid. "Look at him."

"Gray fuzz," Lucas muttered.

"He's cycling again."

Lucas spun around, reaching for me. "Let's go."

"Hang on." Megan grabbed Lucas's arm. "Carrie, whatever you do, don't make eye-contact, okay? That's how he snags you."

I nodded and turned my head, staring at the floor. Lucas's body pressed me up against the wall, blocking my view of most of the living room. Even with those precautions, warmth began to caress my skin as if it radiated from Reid himself, and my body began to respond to its temptations.

"When was the last time you fed?" Megan asked.

Reid laughed. "I'm not a vamp."

"Would you rather me ask how long it's been since you've killed someone?"

"You're quite the nosy little witch, aren't you? What's it to you?" The coldness of his voice sent shivers up my spine, and I fought to keep my head down. I wanted to look at him. Wanted to touch him. This time though, I didn't. The desire was there, sure, but it wasn't as strong as when I met his gaze. Whatever hold he had on me didn't seem to have the same effect on Megan. My guess was that his aura was black by now.

"You're an anomaly to your kind, and I need to know why."

"An anomaly." He paused. "I guess you could say that. Why do you care?"

"It's my job. I can't have you disrupting the balance."

"The balance, the balance," Reid mocked. "'Can't have you disrupting the balance.' Oh, honey, I'm not the one disrupting your precious balance."

"Explain."

A few seconds passed, neither spoke. I wished I could see something. See Reid. Wait—no. I may not have been making eye contact, still I felt my resolve slowly deteriorating.

Yes, I want to see him.

At my thought, Lucas stepped back into me, blocking my view further, and strengthening my resolve not to sneak a peek.

"No," Reid said firmly. "I don't have to answer to you."

Out of the corner of my eye, I watched Megan walk around the sofa before she disappeared from my line of sight. "True, true," she said sweetly. "Hey Lucas, how far is the Moore House from here? Twenty miles?"

"Give or take," he said, and I could hear the amusement in his voice.

"I may not have the power to make you talk, but I do have the power to get you into Villisca," Megan taunted. "Your choice."

"Sneaky bitch," he muttered. "What information do you require, Your Majesty?"

"How old are you, Reid?" Megan asked.

Odd first question.

"Twenty-three."

"Why are you cycling? You should be permanent by now."

"Like you said, I'm an anomaly."

"How?"

Something about the energy in the room began to shift, becoming less…intense?

"I was forced into this position; I haven't always been demonic."

"Uh-uh. No, that's not how it works."

Reid snickered. "It seems you need some enlightening, Princess. Take a seat. You too, Luke."

"I'm good," Lucas answered.

"Of course you are. You're dead; it doesn't get much better than that." Reid's tone softened some. "Come on, old buddy. Let me tell you a story. I won't hurt your girl."

"His cycle's almost over," Megan said. That must mean his aura was fading and he would be human again soon.

Lucas reluctantly took a step away from me, leading me by the hand to the end of the sofa furthest from Reid. I felt Reid's gaze dig into my back as I walked past him. I didn't trust Reid to not put me under again.

After we sat down and the tension lifted, I stole a peek at Reid. He looked tired and weak, as if the demon inside exhausted him when it was loose. Reid flung his legs off the arm of the chair and slumped into the seat. I almost felt sorry for him.

"I was fifteen at the time," Reid started, his voice

low with a hint of a Southern drawl. "A friend and I played JV basketball together, and we stayed after the game to watch my older brother, Parker, on the varsity team." Reid's eyes, half hidden behind thick lashes, were tuned on the edge of the coffee table as if he was concentrating on trying to move it with his mind. His expression clouded over as he continued. "Parker was our ride home after the game, so we met up with him in the parking lot, which was empty other than his Bronco and some Sunbird convertible. Parker was always the last one out of the locker room.

"He opened the car door and was immediately lifted off his feet from behind and thrown onto the hood of the Sunbird. My friend and I tried to run to him, but the attacker grabbed my buddy next, tossing him away like a bag of garbage. He landed on the asphalt, face-down in a pool of blood. I thought they were both dead. I tried to run, but the guy blocked me, laughing hysterically. 'What comes around goes around,' he said then he knocked me out."

Lucas watched Reid intently, flinching once. A flash erupted in my mind, and I caught a glimpse of the parking lot in Reid's story. Or maybe some other parking lot from my own memory, I wasn't sure.

"I woke up in a cabin in the mountains, feeling strange. Sort of empty, like I wasn't myself anymore. Like someone, or something, had taken control of a part of me. My heart raced so fast I wanted to throw up, and I think I did, but my heart rate didn't slow; it sped up, and I couldn't breathe.

My whole body shook, and the room began to blur.

"Then a hand hit my shoulder. It was Parker's attacker, smiling at me. I'll never forget the look on his face, the amusement and pride he exuded. And it seemed directed at me; I didn't understand why.

"He told me I was going to die. That he'd make sure of it, unless I had enough will power to want to live. He stepped aside and nodded to a body lying on a bed behind him, covered in a sheet to the neck. The guy's bald head stuck out, gagged and blindfolded. My kidnapper informed me that he'd taken something vital from me, and if I wanted to live, I had to take life from the bald guy.

"I could barely stand, I was so dizzy. Then something screamed inside my head. It sounded like me, but the things it was saying," he shook his head, "couldn't have been my thoughts. And my stomach, it felt like it had been set on fire, and blackness closed into the edges of my vision, darkening everything. Parker's attacker held me up and led me to the other bed. He told me all I needed to do was want it; the rest of me would take over.

"Part of me wanted to say no, tell the guy to go screw himself, but the voice in my head had more power over me. So I leaned over the body, and my own body took over, controlling me, just like he said it would. I breathed him in, sucked out his soul. As soon as I did, the body began to convulse until it finally stilled. Suddenly, my vision cleared, my heart rate slowed, and I felt normal. Better than normal."

Reid swallowed, pausing. "The dude patted me on the back as if we were buddies. It wasn't until then that I wondered where my friend and my brother were. The guy laughed as he crossed the room to the body. He threw back the sheet and took off the blindfold, showing me Parker. I'll never forget what he said to me. 'I hope you take better care of your brother's soul than your own. Good luck out there, Reid.' The last thing I remember was his laughter as he left me and Parker alone in the cabin."

Lucas and Megan exchanged glances, and I remembered them mentioning an old abandoned cabin that had turned out to be a dead end. Was Reid's cabin the same one they'd scoped out?

Reid closed his eyes. "The police reports deemed it a kidnapping; they couldn't determine why I'd been left alive, and I didn't tell them. How could I explain that I killed my own brother?" His nostrils flared as if he was trying to hold back a sob.

"What about your friend?" I asked, surprising myself.

"He had a concussion and lost a lot of blood, but he survived. He was the lucky one." Reid shifted his gaze to Lucas then Megan. I pitied him, this heartbroken half-demon. "I was an experiment, the first successful one. Exactly how it worked, I don't know. The cycling didn't begin for three years after I took Par…my first soul," Reid concluded.

Reid shifted uncomfortably in the chair, and I realized that I was actually feeling sorry for this demonic creature. Or, at least, when he was human instead of incubus.

Megan tapped her fingers against her lip. "Most incubi cycle for five to seven years; you're almost finished."

And he becomes a full-fledged incubus.

"I know."

"So, back to my first question: When was the last time you fed?" she asked again.

The muscles in Reid's jaw pulsed. "About a year ago."

Megan sat up straighter. "That's not good—it's why your cycles are so fast right now."

"I don't want to kill anyone else."

"Yeah, well, I think that ship has sailed. The demon inside you won't be giving you that option. Either you do it by choice, or the demon overtakes you and forces it."

Reid peered out the window.

"Carrie's not safe with you around. I'll see if I can find a potion to slow the cycles, but it'll only be a temporary fix." Megan stood up. "I'm sorry, Reid."

"Yeah, me too," he mumbled.

Lucas studied Reid for a moment. "You didn't tell us who did this to you."

Slowly, the incubus faced Lucas. "You haven't figured it out?"

I sucked in a breath, hoping the name that came to mind was the wrong one. It wasn't.

"Carver."

Chapter 14

The name itself made me cringe.

If Carver could do what he did to Reid and Parker, what else was he capable of?

"I fear that if you were searching for him, he might have already found you. Word gets around, and Carver doesn't like to be summoned." Reid stood up, and Lucas's hand shot out in front of me, holding me back.

I threw a look at my over-protective boyfriend. "Seriously? He's human right now."

Lucas didn't answer me. Nor did he lower his arm.

Reid pulled back the curtain and peered outside. "Don't underestimate him, Lucas. Everything you've heard about him is true. He made me kill Parker for the sheer joy of watching me suffer afterward." Reid shot a glance over his shoulder at Megan. "He feeds daily."

Megan's lips parted in disgust. "Once a year should be enough to keep your kind alive if the soul is young enough."

"It's not about surviving for him. Taking a human soul is his high; it's what drives him." Reid turned back to the window. "If he's here, we're all dead."

"You? Why are *you* dead?" I asked.

"Because I'm here—with you."

"I don't understand. If he's out of control, why doesn't the Cambion Council eliminate him? His creating you goes against the Code," Megan said.

Huh?

I had a hard time picturing a group of soulless creatures in suits having a board meeting. Well then again…

I pursed my lips to contain the smile.

"Yes, and all of them are vamps right now," she answered in a sullen sigh. From last summer, I remembered that Megan didn't exactly have an affinity for vampires. In fact on numerous occasions I'd heard her call them "blood-sucking ego-maniacs."

Reid scoffed. "The Council's a joke. They fear him. If they make a move against him, they believe Carver may come back and take one of them—or all of them—out, and as you know, if a cambion kills a council member, they get the vacant seat."

"Really?" I blurted out. It made sense, though, them being demonic and all. "I guess, with all the cambions milling about, there's a lot of turnover then."

Lucas chuckled.

"But Carver is only one cambion," he said, his arm finally lowering to my lap. "He can't kill all of them."

"Connections, Lucas. Carver has spent years building his name and reputation. Keeping his secrets. For all anyone knows, he's got some sort of army behind him. Whoever has the gold makes the rules, and the information on how to create incubi out of humans is better than gold. You see where that can lead, right?"

"World domination by cambions," I concluded, and Reid pointed a finger at me.

"You got it, babe. And if he ever decides to share that knowledge—"

"Hell on earth," Megan finished. "Sounds fun."

"Well, has he?" Lucas asked.

Reid shrugged. "Not that I know of, but it's what makes the council so scared of him. It's like a nuclear bomb in the hands of Hitler. Carver has his peeps, and screw everyone else. Psychopaths don't share power."

Wow, that's a lot to digest.

Lucas slapped his palms on his thighs. "So he's gotta be wiped out. How're we gonna do that?"

"*We* can't," Reid said, taking inventory of those of us in the room. I did as well—one ghost, one witch in training (albeit, the end of it), a part-time incubus, and a human. That didn't bode well, especially if Carver, even by himself, was as powerful as Reid described. "Not alone," he finished.

Megan tossed her head back, groaning. "I hate that we ran full circle back to the Cambion Council."

"It seems like we don't have much of a choice." Lucas rubbed his temples as if the thought gave him a headache—which he'd once told me was impossible.

It seemed the three supernaturals had all reached the same conclusion at the same time. I, on the other hand, was completely clueless. Like *Twilight Zone* clueless.

"Um, so why do we need them, exactly?"

"Because we're not strong enough, not against a fully matured cambion who doesn't give a damn," Megan explained. "Made up of five vampires, the Cambion Council is sheer brute force. Together, they possess enough strength and speed to do anything they set their minds on."

"Okay, so if the council hasn't intervened yet, what will make them now? How can we convince them?"

Megan sighed, contemplating my freaking awesome question. "Well, I guess we'll need to wield Jessica's talents as soon as she arrives tomorrow. She'll need to convince one of them that Carver is after their throne."

"And how would this Jessica person do that?" The corner of Reid's lips arched up in a sly grin.

"She's a precog. She'll have to tell them she saw it in a vision."

"She'll have to be pretty damn persuasive." Reid's hand massaged the stubble on his chin, and I wondered how long he'd thought about taking Carver down. Since Parker, probably.

"All right, so who do we have?" Lucas said, grabbing a pen and paper from the end table and sticking the end of the pen in his mouth.

"Lucretia," Megan piped up. "The bitch landed

her spot because she's fearless."

Even as Megan spoke, Reid shook his head. An amused grin lit his face. "Lucretia was defeated, didn't you know? A vamp from South Africa, Tavian, did quite a work-up on her and her daughter for good measure. Sliced them into pieces before burning them. He's got strength, but he's not quick enough to take down Carver."

Megan heaved a sigh. "Fine. Sorin? He's the Code Keeper. I can speak with him, get him to—I don't know—form a committee and go after Carver."

"A committee?" Reid leaned up against the wall, his eyes wandering over Megan. "Truly a witch, aren't you? The only reason Sorin is still on the council is because the Sisters want him there. He's in their pocket, where they want him. I'll bet what's left of my soul the hags won't risk losing him—not for this. It's witch politics, my dear, as you know."

Great, just when I thought I was following them, they threw in something else.

While Reid and Megan hashed out who still had their seats, I nudged Lucas. "What sisters?"

His lips dipped close to my ear, cool breath wafting across my neck. "The Sisters of the Seven Stars are the seven witches who preside over witches, warlocks, and necros. If you really want to know who rules the world, it's them. When this is over, remind me to show you their constellation."

I loved the lightness of his tone, even if it only lasted a few seconds. I imagined us up on the rooftop, stargazing—among other things. In that moment, only the two of us existed in our own little world. With Reid here and Carver on the loose, I wondered if we'd ever get back to that.

"How about Julianna?" Megan tried again, bringing me back to reality.

Reality sucks.

For a second, the impish glint in Reid's eye made him look charming. "You've officially run out of Council members now."

"Answer the question."

"She may be the best chance we've got. As the youngest member, she's out to prove herself."

"How young?" I asked, thinking somewhere around a thousand. Vampires were immortal, right?

Reid's brows perked up. "Vamp years, ten. Human years, thirteen."

I literally felt my eyes bug out. "Julianna is stuck at the age of thirteen and can challenge Carver?" *Thirteen?*

"In this case, her age will work for you. I've seen her in action, and she's a cocky know-it-all, but she's strong and quick. Feed her the right story to spark her pride, and you can mold her. That is, if she doesn't kill you first."

"She sounds nice," I murmured.

Megan rose to her feet, hands resting on her waist. Pursing her lips, she paced back and forth behind the sofa.

"Great, we've got a plan," Reid said.

"We have *part* of a plan," Megan corrected. "I need to contact my aunts, see if they can track Carver, find out for sure when he's coming."

"So, tell me, Megan, what happens if he shows up tonight?"

I sat back a little. A slight edge crept into Reid's voice, stirring me in an all too familiar way. Warmth glided over my skin, and I had to lean onto Lucas's shoulder and breathe him in to remind myself who my heart belonged to.

Megan's gaze narrowed at Reid, lingering on him for a few seconds. The hint of a gray aura that would eventually darken to pitch black was probably beginning to glow around him. "There's nothing we can do tonight, Reid. Sure, I can try to cast some spells on Lucas's house, but they don't usually work to keep cambions out. Let's hope he has better things to do for a few days."

Reid swore and muttered, "Snowball's chance in hell," before he turned back to the window.

"Lucas, you need to get Carrie home before Reid begins a new cycle. Then hurry back." She swept her gaze in Reid's direction. "We need to find him a soul."

***

During the ride back home, I tried not to think about how they'd procure a soul for Reid. Lucas wouldn't kill anyone, and as a witch, I thought, it would be Megan's duty to protect the living. How could she help Reid and still stay true to her calling?

"It's Megan's job to maintain balance," Lucas answered, reading my thoughts. "She's not going to take someone's life, if that's what you're worried about—Reid will have to do it."

"Doesn't that make her" —I grimaced— "and you, accomplices?"

When Lucas didn't answer, I peered out the passenger window, watching the world pass by in a blur. How had it come to this? That Lucas and Megan were willing to help Reid murder an innocent human being?

My stomach twisted, and I fought to hold back the bile rising in my throat.

"No one deserves to die like that, Lucas," I said without looking at him. "There has to be another way."

"There's not."

"How do you know that?" I asked, irritation forcing my gaze in his direction. "You said that before about death being permanent, and now we have that book telling that it might not be."

"Carrie, I don't know what the book says about it. Or even if any of it is true."

"You're still trying to translate it, right? You've had it since before Christmas." I was accusing him now, but damn it, what was taking so long?

"Of course, I am," he said, enunciating each word and silencing me.

I bit my lips together to keep from saying anything else. With everything going on—Reid putting me under his seductive spell, Carver likely after us, my boyfriend leaving tonight to help pick out Reid's next victim—the stress was getting to me. Honestly, I didn't know how much more I could handle.

Lucas pulled into my grandparents' driveway. The front porch light was already off as if I were already tucked into bed. The clock on the dash read eleven-thirty—thirty minutes past the earlier compromised time.

Well, that's fantastic. Grounded for spring break.

"Megan did a memory charm," Lucas answered my thoughts again.

That's all it took for me to snap. Lucas's words struck me like a bolt of lightning, setting me on fire. "Excuse me? A memory charm?" The anger seeping out of me made my voice crack. I cleared my throat before I continued. "Who do the two of you think you are? You can't play God!"

In a hurry, I grabbed the handle, shoving the door open, but Lucas was instantly outside, standing in front of me.

"Carrie." Lucas's voice lowered as he took my hand. "We won't—we'd never—" He sighed and cupped my face between his palms. "Taking the soul of a child will satisfy an incubus's desire the longest—about a year. But the older the soul, the shorter amount of time it lives to keep the demon within at bay. Do you understand?"

A child? They want Reid to kill a child?

I tried to jerk away, but Lucas's grip was too tight. "That's disgusting. Get the hell away from me!" I screamed.

"We won't do that, Carrie!" He wrapped me into his arms, squeezing me so I couldn't move. His voice lowered into a soothing murmur. "We won't do that. Ever."

I stopped struggling; I wouldn't be able to break free anyway.

"I'm trying to tell you how it works. You know us, Care. You know *me*. I'd never, ever... We'll take him to the hospital, someone who's on their death bed. It will only stop the cycling temporarily, but it'll be better than nothing."

"Yeah, how long?"

"Twenty-four hours if we're lucky."

"One day?" *That's no time at all!*

"A child's soul is brand new—pure—so it lasts longer. Souls are immortal inside a human, but inside a demon, they don't live long."

"What about the potion Megan mentioned?"

"It takes time to make. And even then, it's a short fix."

Why do you have to help him at all?

"Because if we let him go, the demon will eventually take over, and it will feast on a new soul. A little soul." Lucas cradled my face again, but I kept my head down. "Look at me."

Slowly, I lifted my eyes to him.

Lucas glided his thumbs over my cheeks. "They're piss-poor options, I know, but it's all we've got right now."

"What if Carver's not coming for us?"

Lucas's lips pressed against my forehead. "Then I think we may be the luckiest people on the face of the planet."

I circled my arms around him. "What're the odds of that?"

Resting his chin on the top of my head, he held me closer. When he answered my rhetorical question, my heart dropped into my stomach.

"Not good. Not good at all."

***

The first thing I noticed when I flipped on my bedroom light was the clean bedding Grandma had washed sitting on the end of my bed. The second thing was the slip of paper sticking out between two of the blankets on the stack. For some reason, I already had a bad taste in my mouth. Even so, I picked it up and flipped it over.

Grandma's curly handwriting jumped off the paper, and I knew I should have burnt the message instead of reading it. It probably had fallen out of her pocket when she'd brought up the laundry.

Griffin and Amy have set a wedding date: September 8th.

Well, this day just keeps getting better and better.

***

Megan picked Jessica up from the airport early the next morning, and they headed straight to Iowa City to see Megan's aunts. That left Lucas to babysit Reid. I'd hoped to get some sort of premonition about what the two guys discussed all alone, but I got nothing. Not even the hint of a tickle in the back of my mind.

Stupid Incenamus that only works for Lucas.

I tapped my fingers on the counter, oblivious to the customer standing in front of me.

"Excuse me?" she said loudly, and I snapped back to reality.

"Oh, I'm so sorry! Of course, can I help you?" Good thing Grandma was busy in the workroom, or I'd be toast for spacing off with a customer.

The lady frowned. "That's why I'm standing here. I saw on your website that you have silver plated trays. Are they still available?"

I forced a smile. "Um, yeah. Over here." I led her to the far corner of the room where Grandma had set up a display on a hutch. "I think we only have a few left, though. Feel free to take your time."

As soon as I left her, another person walked in, followed by two more. The steadiness of customers helped to clear my mind of everything that had happened in the last thirty-six hours. I hadn't realized I needed the mental vacay.

Spring break shouldn't be this difficult.

At noon, Mike breezed through the door, wiping sweat from his forehead and adjusting his Villisca Blue Jays baseball cap on his head. Unbidden, he plopped down on a stool behind the counter, next to me.

"Um, I don't think you're supposed to be back here," I told him. "By the way, you stink."

Mike pulled at his shirt and sniffed, unfazed. "I was kinda hoping you'd come riding with me tonight. I promise I'll shower first."

"I can't. Je—I mean, I already made plans." For some reason Megan hadn't explained, she'd asked me to keep Jessica's arrival hush-hush. I assumed the new Reid/Carver situation had a lot to do with it.

"With Lucas?"

"Yeah."

Mike's lips curved up into his famous half-grin. "Okay, how about tomorrow night?"

I opened my mouth to agree, but then decided

against it. What if Carver showed up? Or worse, what if I was dead by then? "I'm not sure."

"Tomorrow is Sunday, Carrie. Our *riding* day."

"Yeah, yeah. I know, I—" had no excuse. I stared down at the counter.

He puffed out a long sigh. "Lucas?"

Slowly, I nodded. "I'm sorry, Mike."

He slid off the stool and took a step toward me. "No, you're not."

My eyes flitted up to him, catching his gaze and holding it.

He tucked a loose strand of hair behind my ear, a smile tugging at his lips again. "I'm not giving up, though."

I swallowed, realizing he wasn't talking about horseback riding anymore. How could I tell him that giving up would be in his best interest? That I'd never leave Lucas?

Unless he leaves me *by reuniting with his soul.*

I squeezed my eyelids shut and pulled away from his touch. "I can't."

I stared at the floor, listening to Mike's footfalls cross the store and the little gold bell above the door ring as he left.

When did things become so complicated? Not to mention, I still had a death sentence hanging over my head.

Spring break sucks.

***

When I arrived at Lucas's house after work, Jessica and Megan were already there. I avoided meeting Reid's eyes, but sadly he appeared a little healthier. His skin seemed less pale, and his golden irises had deepened in color, brightening into a lively glow. I tried not to think about the circumstances that brought him to this point. If I did, I'd probably throw up.

Lucas hugged me lightly, kissing my cheek. I let go of him, expecting a hug from Jessica like over Christmas vacation, but Jessica didn't budge from her spot at the table. Heck, she didn't even acknowledge my presence. That and two large pizzas sat untouched with four people around. Yeah, something was up.

"What's going on?" I asked.

"You hungry?" Lucas led me to the empty seat beside Jess.

"Oh, we were just talking," Megan said, as if I'd interrupted a lame conversation about napkin origami. Uh-huh, right.

I sat down, expecting Jessica to at least say something. She didn't. Instead, she nursed her ice water like I wasn't even there.

Lucas laced his fingers through mine. Silence dropped around us so thick that all I could hear was Lucas's refrigerator humming.

Reid scratched at the stubble on his chin and studied the slice of cold pizza on his plate while Megan stared at the cell phone lying in front of her.

Then it rang.

"Hello? Yep. Yeah, okay. No, he's here with us right now." Her eyes snapped to Reid for a second. "Yeah, I know…I understand. Okay, I will. Thank you so much for all of your help. *Vale*."

She set her phone down and flashed a peek at Jessica in an unspoken conversation. Jess nodded solemnly, folding her arms in front of her. She straightened, still avoiding me.

"He's coming, isn't he?" Reid asked. "Carver's on his way here."

"If he's not here already. And I learned another little tidbit. Apparently, he knows the *both* of you." Megan's eyes shifted between Reid and Lucas. "Want to elaborate, Reid, since Lucas can't remember?"

The muscles in Reid's jaw clenched. "Yeah, they've met before," he said, his voice low. "Lucas and Carver."

Huh?

"You didn't think that was important to tell us earlier?" Megan asked.

"It's complicated."

"And now it's about to get even more complicated," Megan groaned to herself.

As the shock of Reid's announcement wore off me, I stared open-mouthed at him. If he were in incubus mode, I'd say he was lying, except he was fully human right now, and the expression he wore made it clear that he was telling the truth.

"We met before I died, you mean?" Lucas scrutinized Reid, waiting.

"The night he took me and Parker, the night of the basketball game—"

"Your friend from the story—that was Lucas, wasn't it?" I said as Reid's story pieced itself together in my mind.

Reid bobbed his head, his gaze flicking to Lucas.

"Carver took me and Parker and left you there, alone. I don't know, I guess he thought you were already dead."

In a wordless stare, Lucas locked onto Reid before closing his eyes. He wavered in and out of transparency a few times then he remained in his silver ghostly haze. Both of his hands raked through his hair, his face contorted in concentration. Even though I couldn't feel it, I knew he was trying to recall that night. Trying to place Reid...and Carver.

Last summer, Susan Taylor had told us that Lucas regaining his memories was a possibility, but so far, he hadn't remembered anything.

Soft murmurs reached my ear, and I swiveled to see Megan and Jessica's heads bowed, a Latin spell spilling out of their mouths in unison. A memory charm in reverse, maybe?

When Lucas solidified completely, his gaze landed on Reid.

"Carver jumped you from behind. I was on the ground, but I saw him. It's blurry; I think I was losing consciousness. There's something more, though. I can't see it." Lucas paused, his brow furrowing as a new picture formed in his thoughts. Suddenly, his eyes widened, and he faced Jessica. "It's not a vampire."

"What?" she said, confused.

"Your vision. Yellow-blond hair. Turquoise eyes..."

"It's not," Jess whispered, and her hand flew to her mouth.

She stared at Lucas, rolling the implications around in her mind.

And I was pretty sure I knew why.

I crossed my arms over my chest, fighting to breathe. The time had come much quicker than I expected, but I guess it always did when you looked death in the face. Lucas's greatest fear was coming true, the reason he'd stopped his search, hoping it would change my fate.

Finally, Lucas completed Jessica's sentence. "It's not a vampire who kills Carrie. It's Carver."

Chapter 15

We all felt the pressure squeezing in on us as if the walls of Lucas's house moved in on their own. Suffocating us.

Jess's lips pursed into a hard line, and I noticed her hands shaking slightly at her sides. It was a subtle tremble, but I'd known Jessica since we were toddlers. She'd seen more of her vision than she was letting on, and something about it freaked her out. Surely, it couldn't be about me, though. We'd known my fate for months.

Megan seemed level-headed, as if the news hadn't surprised her. She combed her fingers through her hair and twisted it around the back before piling it on top of her head. With her other hand, she tapped her fingers against her lips, probably considering the implications of the phone call and my crappy date with destiny.

But no one's expression bothered me as much as Reid's. Of course, he'd expected this whole charade to go down exactly like it did; it's why he'd come here in the first place. No, it was the slight grin on his face that worried me. When he caught me staring, he frowned and crossed his arms over his chest.

Then there was me. No one looked at me, not even Lucas. It was like if they did, Carver's coming here would become true, and I'd be dead by the end of the week.

"What do we do now?" Lucas said, focusing on Megan.

In a sudden move, Reid jetted out of his chair. "We go after the son of a bitch. Screw waiting around here for him to come to us."

Wide-eyed, Jessica stared at him. His over-the-top reaction was totally unnecessary.

"I agree," Lucas said, calmly studying him, probably for the emergence of a black aura. "We need to go after him before he can get to Carrie. I'm not taking any chances."

Reid grabbed his chair and scooted it back against the table. He folded his hands on the table in front of him, but the tension in his shoulders was still evident.

Megan let go of her hair. "What are you two going to do, huh? Go out there in opposite directions, hoping you'll run into him? Then what?" Her gaze shifted between the two guys. "Reid, you don't have enough strength to do much of anything with a dying soul inside you, and Lucas, you lose concentration, and your fist will go straight through him! We need to come up with a plan."

"And how long will that take, Megan?" Frustration darkened Lucas's irises. "Reid is right, we need to move now. We don't have a week to argue about how to destroy him!"

"Well, we can't fly by the seat of our pants either. We go after him now, he'll crush us. So what do you propose we do?"

Beside me, Jess started to shake, her breathing shooting out in short gasps. Her eyelids were closed, and I could see her eyes dancing behind them. Until now, I thought she only had premonitions while she was asleep, but Jessica definitely wasn't sleeping.

If she's getting premonitions during the day, did that mean our discussion right now was changing the course of the future?

I reached out to her, but Megan stopped me. "No! Don't bring her out of it."

I snapped my hand back and watched helpless as tears streamed down my best friend's face. Then she screamed, pushing herself away from the table and bending over with her arms covering her head. Hushed sobs filled the room.

"Jess?" I murmured too afraid to touch her. "Jess, are you okay?"

I heard her sniffle before she lifted herself up, wiping her cheeks dry.

"Yeah, yeah, I'm fine." She pushed her chair back to the table, slipping into business mode as if nothing had happened. "We're going to need some help. The vision is hazy in places, meaning that those events have yet to be determined, but to even stand a chance to take out Carver, we can't do this alone."

"Who's there? Who do you see?" Megan asked.

"Um, some girl. Long black hair, black eyes,

young. Maybe, I dunno, thirteen?"

"That's Julianna," Megan said. "I'm sure of it. You sure we need her? She won't be easy to procure."

A shadow passed over Jess's face, and she hesitated for a second. I'd known her since we were little, and I knew that look. "Yeah, her presence is necessary. She's the only one strong enough to hold him."

Megan stood up. "I guess then, we need to plan a trip to Corvin Castle, Transylvania, and pay the Cambion Council a little visit. I don't think they'll be happy to see the three of us." She nodded at Lucas and Jessica.

The Cambion Council meets in Transylvania? Well, isn't that a shocker.

We'd known of this possibility since the other night, but now it was no longer optional. Something recently had shifted that changed the future, and we needed the vampire to take down Carver. Good thing we'd sort of planned for this. Jessica would have to feed Julianna a false vision about Carver gunning for her seat on the council to convince her to help. I sure hoped Jessica's lying skills had improved.

"No," Jess said. "It won't be a warm welcome, but we will be successful."

"Good to know," Megan said.

"Exactly how long will that take?" Reid asked, irritated. "What if Carver shows up while y'all are traipsing halfway around the world?"

Megan motioned to Jess for the answer.

Jess cleared her throat. "I, uh, I haven't seen

anything indicating that Carver will launch an attack before we return."

"What the hell does that mean?" Reid asked.

"It means I don't know."

"You're a precog, you see the future, and you don't know? Did you see me coming?" Reid's nails flicked the edge of his paper plate, the popping noise steady.

"It doesn't work that way. I only get glimpses. Some are clear, distinct, others are not. The clear ones will most definitely come to pass, the fuzzy ones either become clearer, or they change. I don't see everything, and no, I didn't see you."

I couldn't help myself. "Has there been anything else? Anything"—I swallowed—"new?"

"Um, yeah." She paused. "There's silverware falling from a drawer. Numbers, 314. A cemetery with a large weeping willow tree. And a bouquet of white roses in a black vase, like what you bought us over Christmas."

"But that already happened. Why are you still seeing it?" I asked.

Jess shook her head and mumbled, "I don't know. The details of the flowers showed up *after* Christmas."

"That's not much to go on," Reid muttered.

"I'll get more as the future unfolds," she replied softly.

A chill raced down my spine at the tremor in Jessica's voice. She was definitely keeping something to herself, and I didn't like it. We used to tell each other everything.

"Right now, we need to secure the area. Jessica

and I will place barrier spells around Lucas's house. They're weak for Cambions, but they may slow him down. Lucas, would you please create us a map of the inside of Corvin Castle. Reid—"

"It's not worth it," Jess mumbled, emerging from a trance I hadn't noticed her go into.

"What's not worth it? The map?" Lucas asked, studying her.

"No, the map is a must. The barrier spells, however…" she trailed off, focusing on the front door. "The barrier spells won't do anything; Carver's already been here."

Megan cocked her head to the side. "Jess, did you just get a glimpse of the past?"

"Here? As in *at* my house?" Lucas broke in.

"I'm not sure. I guess," Jess answered. "I mean, there was snow on the ground at the time, and the vision is different—darker. If it's true, barrier spells won't work to keep him out now."

"Well, that's great." Reid got up and leaned against the wall. "Carver is a master at hiding. His self-control is unparalleled. He'll wait for the most opportune time to attack."

"Judging by the story you told us when he changed you, I think he'll play with his food for awhile first," Megan mused. "We've got some time. So far, that we know of, he hasn't waged an attack, but we need to stay alert."

"Looks like you'll be heading to Romania by yourselves," Lucas said to the witches. "I'm not leaving Carrie here to be an appetizer."

"Don't worry, Lucas. She won't be alone. Reid's staying with her," Megan assured him.

That did it. Lucas's chair flew back, skidded across the hardwood floor and crashed into the wall on the opposite side of the room.

"Like *hell* he is. She is not staying here alone with that monster!"

Reid bowed his head before walking out of the room.

"It's *Carver* that's after Carrie. Not Reid. *NOT* Reid! Of all of us in this room, Reid has the best chance against him. Incubus against incubus, they know how each other thinks." Megan walked over and stood behind Jessica's chair. "We won't be gone long. We need you, Lucas. Otherwise, it'll take a week to book a flight, fly there and back, and by then..."

"Besides, you can be back here in a flash if she needs you, right?" Jessica asked.

"Not if I used up all my energy transporting the three of us to Transylvania." Lucas raked a hand through his hair. "Reid barely has enough soul to last the night. He'll cycle again soon."

Megan's eyes wandered over the incubus standing at the living room window. "We'll be back before that." She sighed. "And then we'll have to figure something out."

"I'm not killing anyone else," Reid said, turning around. "I'm done with this. After we take out Carver, I need your word that you'll kill me next."

Even with Reid being fully human, this outburst rattled me; I wasn't sure why. Lucas didn't seem surprised, though. He leaned back into his chair and crossed his arms, eyeing Reid with a distrustful gaze.

Megan didn't flinch at his request, keeping a straight face. "I can't give that to you."

Reid shot her a smug look and shrugged. "Then I'm not helping you."

Jessica shook her head in quick succession. "We can't fight Carver without you, Reid," she insisted. "I'm not sure how yet, but I've seen it. You're a vital part."

Reid huffed and peered out the window again. "Whatever."

"Good, it's settled. Jessica, Lucas, and I will leave for Corvin Castle tonight. Reid, you stay here and protect Carrie."

Lucas finally looked at me, his glowing irises filled with everything I didn't want to see: fear, anxiety, pain. All of it flowed out of him like air. This was what his search for his soul had come down to: I was going to die, and he was powerless to stop it.

I slid off my chair, needing to be closer to him. Climbing onto his lap, I laid my head on his shoulder, wrapping both of my arms around his neck. His arms folded around me and pressed me into him.

"We'll be in vamp territory, so we'll need to play by their rules. It's still daylight in Transylvania right now. We have to leave as soon as the sun goes down there, which doesn't give us much time to figure out what we're gonna do when we get there." Megan sat down at the computer, bringing up a map of Corvin Castle.

"But you can't teleport that far. Especially with other people," I murmured into Lucas's ear.

"We'll need to make a lot of pit stops. I need to rest."

"I don't want you to go."

Lucas shot Reid a scathing glare. "I don't want to leave you either, but I don't think we have a choice. It seems we need Julianna and pronto."

Maybe…

"What if destiny has slated me to die regardless of Carver's fate? Remember what Susan said? Some things are meant to be." I squeezed my eyes shut as soon as I said it. "What if this only postpones my death?"

We can run away together, let them handle this alone.

I swallowed back the guilt of my thought. These were my friends.

Lucas's fingers traced small circles on my back. "I'm not going to let you die, now or later."

"Everyone dies, Lucas."

Lucas breathed into my hair.

"Lucas," I whispered against the soft skin on his neck when he didn't say anything.

"Incenamus, remember? We'll pull through this," he answered.

I wanted to believe him. God, I wanted to so badly. But that naggy voice in the back of my head reminded me of Jessica's vision of Carver killing me. At this point, that was hard to argue with.

"Yeah, okay," I said, glancing at the cambion by the window.

This may be bigger than us, though.

Lucas followed my gaze, locking onto Reid's back. "You need to be careful, Care."

I will.

"Reid will protect me, don't worry." I said, even though I wasn't convinced.

"From Carver, yes, but can he protect you from himself?"

"Jessica said—"

"I know what Jessica saw. I'm just not that confident in her abilities yet."

I love you.

I slid my fingers down his face. "I'll be safe. At least for tonight. Megan and Jessica need you more right now."

Lucas pressed a palm over my heart. "Keep the lines of communication open, okay?"

I smiled. "I don't know how."

He flashed me his gorgeous dimple. "Exactly the way you do now. I love you too."

I laughed, unsure of what I was doing to allow him in my head. Transylvania was halfway around the world, though. Could we still connect at that distance?

Lucas cradled my face between his palms and brought my lips to his. Tonight, I didn't care that he couldn't feel the kiss the same way I did. He felt it somehow, and that was enough.

"Lucas?" Megan stood beside us, holding a map she'd printed off. "We need to do this."

"Yeah." He let go of me, and I slipped off his lap, returning to my earlier seat.

I nibbled on a slice of cold pizza as Lucas, Jessica, and Megan made their plans.

"Got it?" Megan asked when they'd finished. "Everyone clear?"

"I'd better try to get some sleep." Lucas stood up and shot a quick glance at me.

"Um, guys," Jess said before everyone left the table. "Earlier, when I said we couldn't defeat Carver alone, that we needed help?" She paused, biting her lip. "I saw two people. Not just Julianna."

"Okay," Megan said, unfazed. "Who else was there?"

Slowly, Jess turned her attention to me. "I'm so sorry, Carrie. We need Mike."

Chapter 16

The words knocked the wind out of me.

Did I hear her right?

Mike was such a common name. Maybe she meant a different Mike. Mike…somebody else.

"He, uh…he appeared in the vision not long ago," Jessica explained, her tone apologetic. "At first, I wasn't sure it was him. I mean, I've only met him once, but…"

"Mike?" I repeated, catching my breath. "As in Mike Carson?"

Jessica frowned. "I'm sorry. I know you never wanted to involve him."

"Mike is fully human, Jess. How can he help us?" From Megan's tone, she didn't like the idea of Mike's involvement either.

"I'm not sure yet. Right now, all I know is that he's with us—wherever we are."

"Wait," I said, holding a palm up to stop her. "You said that your visions are only definite if the image is clear. Is Mike…is he fuzzy? Can this be changed?"

Gingerly, Jess shook her head. "As soon as he entered the vision, his image was perfect."

This couldn't be happening. Reid, Carver, my foreseen death, vampires—this was dangerous. How could I risk Mike's life for something he shouldn't even be involved in? Besides, if I told him about this messed-up world, he'd probably think I was crazy.

Confusion set in, and I rose from my chair and placed my hands on the table, leaning forward. "What happened that brought him into this mess, and how do we reverse it?"

Jessica's brow furrowed in pity for me. "From what the coven taught me, it could have been anything, Carrie. Our lives are all inter-linked; the reason might not even be directly related to him." She sighed, pinching her lips together. "It could have been something as stupid as Stacy choosing the pink bra over the black one."

I blinked then narrowed my gaze. "You're telling me Mike was brought into this craziness because of someone else's decision?"

Jess shrugged. "Maybe. Or his own. There's no way to know. The future is complicated."

I twisted around, succumbing to the delusion that if I couldn't see them, they couldn't see me, and I was alone. I had to think about this. Find a way around Jess's vision. The threat of tears stung my eyes, but I fought them back. Mike couldn't be involved.

"Hey." Lucas appeared in front of me, his voice dipping low as he spoke. "One step at a time. We'll figure it out," he said, reading my thoughts. He ran a hand through the back of my hair, pressing my head onto his chest. Needing him, I circled my arms around his waist.

"What if Mike ends up like…" I swallowed the lump in my throat, but another immediately took its place. "Like Susan?" I finished, thinking of our late town necromancer who died helping me.

Lucas squeezed me against him. "We know nothing solid, Care. Jess only saw that he's somehow involved. To what extent has yet to be seen."

"Whatever it is, it's too much." I lifted my head, resting my chin in the middle of his chest. "Will Mike have to know about you? About all of this?"

"I don't think Jess knows what we'll need to tell him."

I paused, wondering if there was *anything* we knew. "So, what? We just ride this wave and see what happens? We control nothing?"

Lucas lowered his head until our foreheads touched, the tip of his nose brushing mine. "We can't control everything in life, Care. If we did, it would end up exactly how we planned it."

"Uh, yeah. I think that's the point."

He chuckled, his lips sealing over mine. The wintery temperature lingered on my skin. "We'd miss out on so much. Sometimes the best things in life happen when we don't have control. Like us."

"Incenamus says we would have found each other even if you'd survived," I retorted.

"Eventually. Maybe it wouldn't have been for another fifty years, who knows? The point is, we didn't plan for each other, and yet, you're the best thing that ever happened to me." He kissed me again, letting his words sink into me. "It'll all work out like it's supposed to."

He'd said those words to me before, but I was still slated to die soon. I wondered how that fit into his plans of "working out."

"Lucas," Megan hollered from the door. "We need to go."

Lucas swept his fingers through my hair a last time. "We'll talk when I get back. Don't. Leave. This house. For any reason." His eyes searched mine, drinking me in. "We'll be back by midnight." Without moving his head, he flicked his gaze at Reid sitting in the armchair. "Even though he has a soul for now, stay on your guard."

"Nothing is going to happen," I assured him, rolling a finger over his beautiful lips.

Something about the shadowy glint in his eye told me he wasn't so sure. "Be careful, okay? I can't lose you."

"You won't."

"Lucas," Megan prompted again. "We're running out of time. Daylight in Romania will end soon."

"Go," I urged. "They need you. I'll be safe here. Besides," I grinned, "death is no match for us."

Lucas's brow furrowed. "Given the circumstances, that's not funny."

"Lighten up. I'll be fine."

He pressed his palm over my heart. "Keep it open, okay?"

"I'll do what I can."

He kissed me again, holding me too tight. When

he let go, he sighed and joined Megan and Jessica by the front door. As he passed Reid, he pointed at him. "Don't you *dare* lay a finger on her."

"Chillax, Luke. I won't hurt her. She'll be here waiting for you, safe and sound, I swear."

Even from where I stood, I could see Lucas's irises darken into an unnatural shade of green. Obviously, he still didn't trust Reid.

"Keep her inside, Reid," Megan reminded him, placing a small vial into Jessica's hand. Without looking at it, Jess looped the leather strand around her neck, the glass bottle hanging low under the neckline of her shirt. "It's Liquid—"

"I know what it is," Jess said.

"In case we need it."

I wanted to give Jess a hug, tell her good luck, but she walked out of the house before I could move. Jess never acted this way, and I couldn't help taking it personally. What had I done to offend her?

Megan followed her out, and Lucas held my stare before he disappeared, leaving me alone with Reid.

"Bye," I murmured to the closed door, wondering what they might be getting themselves into. Something that possibly required a red potion, now in Jessica's possession. And I doubted that it was a peace offering.

I took a final glance at the closed door and sighed, fidgeting with the infinity charm hanging from my neck. Already, I was counting down the hours to midnight.

Too freaking many.

Reid grabbed a pillow and tucked it behind his

head. He settled in, a small smile grazing his lips. Stretching his arms behind his head, he groaned and closed his eyes.

Some bodyguard.

With nothing else to do, I headed for the kitchen. No one ate the pizzas, so I closed the lids, sliding the boxes onto the lowest shelf in the refrigerator. At first, the abundance of food in Lucas's fridge surprised me. Then I remembered he had a new roommate who had a body and needed food, regardless of what form he was in. Apparently, incubi ate normal stuff.

I grabbed a can of Pepsi and plopped down on the sofa. Tonight, I was stuck in a house with a sleeping half-Cambion.

How weird is my life? Seriously!

I tucked my legs under me, sitting crisscross on the cushion. One of Reid's eyelids squinted open, stealing a quick peek at me before closing it again.

"Still here," I said in a sing-song voice.

"Just checking," he sang back, mimicking my pitch.

I tapped my nails on the can and took a sip of the carbonated goodness. "Carver may be out there. I'm not leaving. Besides, I promised Lucas I'd stay in the house."

"Yeah, because no one breaks promises, right?"

"I can't speak for you, but I try not to."

Reid swung his legs off the arm of his chair, straightening up. "You're right. You can't speak for me."

The coldness in his tone caught me off guard, and I back-tracked. Pissing off the cambion would be a really dumb idea. "I didn't…that's not what I meant."

He rolled his head in a circle over his shoulders, his neck cracking then he seemed to relax a little. "So, what are we going to do? Sit here and stare at each other for the next several hours?"

I shrugged. "I guess."

"Fantastic."

I took another drink, slurping on the soda that caught below the rim. Over and over I reminded myself that I was safe with Reid. It was Carver I needed to fear. Still, being alone with him sent a flurry of apprehension through me. If only we had something to make the time move faster.

Where were Mike's classics when you needed them?

I tapped my nails on the can again, trying not to allow my eyes to wander in Reid's direction. Lucas and Megan had helped him find a soul, so he should remain human for awhile. I didn't know how long that would last, though.

"What?" Reid asked, catching me staring at him.

"Oh, uh—I—nothing," I stuttered, sounding like an idiot.

Reid huffed. "For the love of God, just ask."

I ran my fingers through my hair, brushing it, twirling it around my index finger. "Um, you and Lucas…you, uh, needed a soul, and…."

"You want to know who I killed?"

"Well, not their name, exactly, but…"

"Hospice at the hospital," he answered. "Someone about to die anyway." Reid turned his attention to the window as he said it. "It's better than the alternative."

"A child?" Repeating what Lucas had told me.

"Anyone the demon wants."

I set my Pepsi between my legs, wondering if it was wise to keep the trajectory of this conversation on course. Stupid or not, I kept it going. "Does it hurt?"

Reid twisted in my direction, an eyebrow quirked. "Killing someone?"

My cheeks flushed. "No, no! I...I meant, when you change. When the—"

"—demon takes over?" he finished.

I nodded, nervous. Really, I should stop talking now.

"No. Sometimes I can hold it back for a little while, but the monster always wins. It doesn't let go until it has what it wants. Later, I'm left with the guilt of what I've done."

"Do you remember it? Afterward, I mean?"

Shut up, Carrie!

Reid hesitated before he answered. "Yeah. Even when it's happening, when I'm hurting someone, I know. I even enjoy it. The longer the demon is inside me, the more we become the same entity."

That was hard to absorb. I preferred thinking of Reid as two separate people: one human, one soulless. The realization that the two were merging into one left my mouth dry.

I cleared my throat. "Have you ever—I mean before the other day, here—have you ever put me in a trance?"

His gaze dug into me, making the hair on my arms stand on end. Around me, the air thickened.

Reid couldn't be cycling already, could he?

He blinked, rubbing his face, and all of a sudden I could breathe again. "I held myself back as long as I could that day, but it broke free and overtook me at the football game the night I met you."

"I don't remember it, exactly. Only that something changed and I was scared."

"I've been attempting to fight it off when it rises inside me, and I did that night, before I fully drew you in."

"Thanks for that." I took another sip of Pepsi, trying to determine if his admission made me feel safer or not.

"Most of the time, I lose. You got lucky."

When I looked back up at him, I noticed his hands shaking and sweat gathering at his brow. Again, the atmosphere in the room seemed distorted, and I shuddered. Tension filtered in, slowly expanding throughout the room like a roll of humidity.

Not. I'm going with not *safer.*

"Reid? Are you okay?" I asked, studying him for a hint that I was in danger.

He stood up without answering and walked to the window, his back to me. "I'll never be okay. Not anymore."

A fitting response left me for a moment. I couldn't imagine what it was like to be him, to have something so evil taking over your mind, body, and soul. Would mature-incubus Reid even be Reid?

"I'm really sorry, Reid," I finally said. "Is there a way to stop it? Can you somehow reverse what Carver did to you?"

"No. The more souls I steal, the faster I'll change into a cambion permanently. Forever damned."

Something about his tone tugged at me. Too haunting, maybe? Deep down, I pitied him. His life had been cruelly taken from him, and there was nothing he could do about it. I set down my half-drunk can of Pepsi on the coffee table and inched toward Reid.

I reached out, carefully touching his shoulder. He didn't flinch. "I'm so sorry, Reid," I repeated because there was nothing else I could think of to say.

When he didn't answer, I dropped my hand and scooped up the rest of my Pepsi to dump down the kitchen sink. I watched the brown liquid swirl over the stainless steel and into the drain.

Flipping the can upside down, I put it in the strainer and glanced at the microwave clock.

I had five more hours alone with Reid.

Great.

After squirting a glob of soap on my hands, I lifted the handle on the faucet, letting the warm water spill over my hands longer than necessary. The sound was better than the eerie silence pressing in around me. I shut off the nozzle and hung my head over the sink, closing my eyes. Maybe, if I concentrated hard enough and allowed my soul to open, I'd be able to connect with Lucas. At least see where he was and make sure he was safe.

Lucas, where are you? Can you hear me?

"Carrie?"

I whirled around, startled. "Oh, Reid," I said, sinking back against the counter with my hand over my heart. "I didn't hear you come in."

"I didn't mean to scare you," he murmured, his voice sending chills through me. "What are you doing?"

I froze.

Concentrating on connecting with Lucas, I'd missed the heaviness falling in over me. The evil hue to Reid's tone brought me back to reality, sparking a rush of adrenaline shooting through my veins.

Reid isn't the one who kills you. Reid doesn't kill you.

I repeated the words in my head, reassuring myself. My heart raced, and I struggled to not lift my head.

Don't make eye-contact. It's how they draw you in.

"What's wrong, Carrie? It's just me. *Pitiful*, harmless Reid."

An invisible force compelled me to look up, meet his gaze, but I held my stare on the floor, at his shoes. He took a step forward, and I took two back. The energy in the room had shifted a full one-eighty.

"Um, can I get you something? A Pepsi or maybe a sandwich?" The words rushed out of my mouth, my voice shaking.

He stepped toward me again, and I backed up. I only had a few more feet left before I'd be trapped against the back wall.

"Nah, I'm good. I'm just checking up on you, like Lucas wanted." Slowly, he moved forward, and I reciprocated until my back was against the wall.

"I'm fine," I choked out. I felt my eyes rising up his legs, unable to fight the pull any longer.

Tenderly, Reid trailed his fingers down a strand of my hair, letting go only when he reached the end. Oh, it felt so good! "You don't look fine to me. Are you scared of me, Carrie?"

I tried to slow my breathing, my heart rate. The thought of how I'd lose control if I met his gaze stopped me at his stomach.

Lucas! I need you!

Somehow I knew my thoughts hadn't connected; I was on my own. Defenseless to the power drawing me in, my eyes climbed up to Reid's chest, his neck, his chin, his lips. His delicious, delicious lips. The tip of his tongue ran over them as his hands glided down my arms and locked around my waist. My heart sped up, my body reacting. Wanting him.

"Reid," I breathed, "What are you doing?" Suddenly light-headed, I slammed my palms against the wall behind me to keep my balance.

"Taking what should be mine," he hissed.

"I'm not yours," I whimpered. Reid's head ducked down, his mouth skimming along the nape of my neck. "Lucas, what about Lucas? Your friend, remember?"

Hot breath pulsed against me, while tears formed behind my lids. Oh God! Had Jess's vision been wrong?

"Lucas is weak, always has been. He couldn't stand watching her die, not knowing what was killing her. The little putz took off soon after I got there." Reid licked my skin from my collar bone to my earlobe, and I squeezed my eyelids shut, relishing in his touch. "I guess I can't blame him for that, but he didn't know what I did to her. Ah, she tasted so good."

"What are…what are you talking about?" I panted, fighting to control myself.

"It doesn't matter now. They're both dead." Reid yanked my hips into his. "I think that's enough chit-chat, don't you?"

I dug my nails into the drywall behind me, clutching onto nothing. Reid wedged me up against the wall, and I stifled the cry in my throat.

"Look at me." Reid's commanding voice enthralled me, and I immediately obeyed. Instantly, the fervor of his stare pierced me, cutting through me like millions of tiny slivers of glass invading my bloodstream. His black pupils expanded, eclipsing the caramel color and replacing it with coal.

My heart pounded so fast it vibrated in my ears. But it wasn't out of fear this time. No, I wanted Reid—bad. My body ached for him.

I jumped and wrapped my legs around his waist. Then, I devoured his neck with kisses.

"That's more like it, Carrie," Reid said, moaning into my ear. "Isn't this so much better than fighting me?"

"Oh yes! I need you, please," I begged.

I tugged at his shirt, lifting it off his back and digging my nails into his shoulder blades. All I could think about was how fast I could get his clothes off, and how amazing his body would feel all over mine. I sucked his flesh into my mouth, struggling to get the stupid shirt off him.

"Need some help with that?" The sweet hum of

his voice spilled into the pit of my stomach, making me ache for him even more.

"The bedroom," I gasped. "Over there."

He combed through my hair. "That's a little … traditional." He twirled me around, depositing me on the kitchen counter. "This is a good spot. I'm sure Lucas won't mind."

I locked my thighs on his hips as tightly as I could. "Lucas who?" I asked, running my fingertips over the waistband of his jeans, wishing he'd shut the hell up and get on with it.

Reid laughed. "The guy who lives here."

"Oh," I said as I fumbled with Reid's belt. "Tell him thanks."

"I will definitely have to do that."

Reid's mouth pressed into mine. I couldn't breathe, but I didn't care. He could do whatever he wanted with me. Heck, he could even kill me if he wanted to. Oh God, that would feel so good!

Reid grabbed a hold of the hem of my camisole and lifted it over my head. I giggled when he tossed it behind him.

"About time," I murmured, nipping at his mouth.

Then, suddenly, he threw himself backward, slamming into the counter. He shook his head, washing out the black. Golden irises wandered in jagged motions over me.

"Carrie! Carrie, I'm sorry. I'm…"

The haze lifted, and I sucked in a breath, pulling at my hair. Wide-eyed, I stared at Reid across from me…wait, where was I? I lurched forward, not realizing I was sitting on the counter. On my way to the floor, Reid lunged and caught me mid-air. It took me a moment to realize his hands circled around my bare skin.

"Reid," I whispered, and he set me on my feet and slowly backed away.

I gave myself a onceover. My white cami was nowhere to be seen, revealing my lacy, see-through bra and leaving my stomach exposed. Half-naked in front of an incubus, I flung my arms around myself.

"Did you…Did you do this to me?"

Reid crouched down and bowed his head into his hands. "I'm not safe."

"You're cycling again, aren't you? You put me under." I barely recognized my own voice. "You were going to kill me."

The stolen soul inside of him was dying, and the demon within craved a new one.

A wave of pity washed over me. He was a prisoner in his own body, unable to control the demon within. Keeping one arm over my breasts, I knelt in front of him, grazing his cheek with my fingertips.

He didn't move. "Don't touch me."

My mother always said I was as stubborn as my father. I repeated the gesture. "It's okay, Reid."

Swiftly, he grabbed my wrist and flung it away from him. "No, it's not. I almost killed you, Carrie. Lucas doesn't need another reason to hate me."

I sat down, crossing my legs in front of me. "Lucas doesn't hate you, he just—"

"No, Carrie, he hates me. He doesn't remember why." Reid rose to his feet, leaving me on the floor, and tossed me my shirt from the sink. "I need to go. You're not safe with me anymore."

Without a second glance, he darted to the living room.

According to Megan, he had some time before his next cycle, and maybe the others would be back by then.

I slipped the camisole over my head. "Wait!" I called, slower to stand and follow him. "Reid, don't go."

By the time I stepped into the living room, he already had the front door open. "Whatever you do, stay inside. You'll be fine. "

Before I could respond, he disappeared into the night.

Chapter 17

I fell onto the sofa, frowning at the closed front door, my palm on my forehead.

Did that seriously happen?

Reid walked out, leaving me to fend for myself. With any luck, Lucas, Jess, and Megan would come barging in at any minute. I didn't expect it, though. They'd said midnight, and the clock only read eleven.

Earlier, Megan had talked about taking him to the Moore House, and that had straightened him out. Maybe the demons within had some sort of vendetta against cambions? Whatever it was, I didn't want them to take Reid there. After all, part of him was still human.

And what about Lucas? If he ever found out that Reid had cycled again, put me under his spell while Lucas had left us alone, he'd never forgive himself. Right then, I made the easy decision not to tell—for Lucas's sake as well as for Reid's.

My mind shifted to what Reid had said before he left.

"Lucas couldn't stand watching her die, not knowing what was killing her. Doesn't matter now; they're both dead."

Who were dead?

Then, he'd said, *"Lucas doesn't need another reason to hate me."*

Were the two statements connected, somehow? Both dead. Both. This *her* and someone else.

I threw my head back against a pillow, the thoughts slowly overtaking me. My mind moved from Reid's words to his actions. Like at the football game, somehow he'd controlled the demon enough to stop it from killing me, but not enough to avoid slipping me under its spell.

"The longer the demon is inside me, the more we become the same entity."

A knock on the door popped my heart into my throat. With a hand on my chest, I took a deep breath and glanced at the clock: 11:43 p.m. It was too late for visitors.

"Reid?" I called out.

Whoever was on the other side knocked again.

Okay, don't freak out. Of course, it's him.

"Hang on. I'm coming." I rolled off the sofa, smoothed down my shirt, and jogged over. I unlocked the door and swung it open.

It wasn't Reid.

"I have a delivery for a Carrie Reese?" The dark-haired man held a slip of paper in one hand and a bouquet of white roses in a black vase in the other. "Is that you?"

"Um, it's a little late for making deliveries, isn't it?"

He shrugged, unruffled. "People die at all hours of the day—we deliver twenty-four hours."

"Excuse me?"

"Yeah, mostly to hospitals and stuff."

I eyed him skeptically. The floral design on his polo boasting Flower Express looked legit enough. "Oh, uh, yeah, I'm Carrie."

"Great." He handed me the bouquet. "Sorry for your loss."

"Yeah, thanks," I mumbled as he got in his truck and drove away.

Is this Reid feeling bad for leaving?

I closed the door and locked it again, taking the roses to the table.

Or are they from Lucas? Ooh, with a message?

I sifted through the flowers and found a white envelope with my name on the front. A wave of relief washed over me. I smiled as I ripped it open. Hopefully, this was his "We were successful and safe. Heading home now. Love you" message.

Wait, flowers can't be ordered, prepared, and delivered faster than they could make it back, right?

I pulled out the card and flipped it over. My eyes trailed over the handwritten words. Once they registered, I threw out a hand to keep my balance, and it hit the vase. The flowers crashed to the floor, breaking the glass into a thousand pieces.

I'm coming for you.

—Carver

White roses. Black vase.

Jess's vision and our conversation rushed back to me.

"And a bouquet of white roses in a black vase,

like what you got us over Christmas."

Had Carver been watching us even then?

I fumbled with the card, absently folding it with trembling fingers, and stuffed it in the pocket of my jeans. As panic set in, I ran to the front door to check the bolt. Then I raced around the house, locking every window and pulling the blinds closed. Leaning against a wall in Lucas's bedroom, I finally slid to the floor. This wasn't how it was supposed to be. Tonight, I was supposed to be safe.

I pulled my knees into my chest and rocked back and forth. White roses were Stacy's favorite, and I had specifically asked for a black vase at the store. Whimpering, I scissored my arms and buried my face in the crook of my elbow, trying to catch my breath.

I almost choked on a sob as the realization hit: Carver sent the flowers to Lucas's *house*. He was coming to Lucas's house! I wasn't safe here without Reid to defend me.

I hugged my knees to my chest, hyperventilating now. Jess hadn't seen this, right?

I'm not supposed to die tonight!

Tears formed behind my eyelids, and I didn't wipe them away when they tumbled down my face. Maybe the invisible veil separating my soul from Lucas's had collapsed due to my distress, and he could hear my thoughts now. I had to try.

Carver is coming.

With the back of my hand, I swiped away the tears and stood up. Reid was supposed to be my protector, and he'd left. The only way I was going to survive the night was to find him. Incubus against incubus was a much better match-up than incubus versus human—somehow I'd played the latter game three times and survived. What were the odds that I'd live through another showdown—with Carver, nonetheless?

I grabbed Lucas's car keys from the kitchen drawer and stopped at the front door. What if Carver was already here, waiting on the other side?

I took a deep breath. No, I couldn't think that way. If he was, I was dead regardless. If he wasn't, I still stood a chance.

Reaching for the doorknob, I heard a car drive down the street and jumped.

Settle down, Carrie. You can do this.

Again, I inhaled and blew it out, reaching for the knob. This time I turned it and swung the door open. Cool evening breeze greeted me, swirling and brushing over me. Chilling me to the core.

And that was all. No one stood on the front porch. Empty space surrounded me.

Thank you, Lord.

I didn't waste any more time. I sprinted to Lucas's car and threw myself inside, locking the doors as fast as I could. It probably wouldn't keep Carver out, but it made me feel better.

The moon shone down, and the stars glittered in the night, reminding me of all the times Lucas and I laid outside gazing up at them. In the field behind my grandparents' house, on the hood of his car, on the rooftop… I forced down the lump in my throat. Dying tonight was not an option. For Lucas, somehow, I would outwit fate.

I drove the short distance into town, unsure of

where to start looking for my wayward bodyguard. Heck, if Reid cycled again, he could be halfway to Canada by now. From my experience, supernaturals tended to have mad travel skills, and Reid was part-demonic after all.

Downtown Red Oak at midnight mimicked Villisca during football playoff season: no cars, no people. I drove slowly, scanning the darkened storefronts for any sign of movement. Like in Villisca, the old brick buildings resembled something from old western movies. All different but oddly attached.

I stopped at the south corner, considering whether I wanted to go down the next street or stay on the square when a shadow crossed over the sidewalk. Inching Lucas's car forward, I saw a man duck into an alley halfway down the block. A small light from a nearby store illuminated Reid's bright red hair.

"Gotcha," I whispered.

I turned onto the street and parked against the curb. Hopefully his slower movements meant he was either on the human end of his cycle or he'd already procured a new...

Ugh. I hated thinking of the other possibility that would un-incubus him, but if that had happened, it would ensure my safety with him—for a little while anyway.

Quietly, I eased out of the car. I didn't want him to hear me and bolt. Now that I'd found him, the last thing I wanted was to traipse around town trying hunt him down again. I tossed the keys under the driver's seat and closed the door with as little noise as I could muster. When it clicked, my attention jerked up to the passageway Reid had entered.

"Come on, Reid," I said to myself. "We gotta get out of here."

I hurried along the sidewalk, staying close to the buildings and mimicking Sherlock Holmes in one of Mike's classics. Hopefully, it kept me concealed from unwanted eyes.

As I rounded the corner into the pathway, soft footfalls behind me made me twist and peer down the street. Was it my imagination, or did I hear something? In front of me, empty darkness stared me down, sizing me up.

Since last summer, I had every reason to fear the dark.

I spun back around and started down the alley. At the end, I could see Reid, walking slowly in the opposite direction. I let out a breath, my shoulders falling. Safe at last.

I dug the card Carver had sent with the flowers out of pocket. Picking up my pace, I jogged by the dumpster on my left, dodging a stray cat. My feet sloshed into a puddle, the water splashing up my ankles.

The sound of me running reverberated off the buildings, bouncing back at me like one of the tuning forks we had in music class. Reid was almost at the end of the road.

"Hey, Reid. Wait—"

Cutting me off, someone slammed me up against the cold brick wall. My feet dangled off the ground. Icy fingers laced around my neck, choking me. The card fell from my hand, and whoever it was had my head tilted upward toward the stars.

"Eh… Rei…" I struggled to breathe, my nails clawing at the hand strangling me.

Dark circles blinked into my vision.

My attacker adjusted himself, his mouth teasing my ear. "Well, well. What do we have here?" His hushed voice dripped with evil, and I already guessed who had a hold of me. "Carrie Reese, the pretty little soul I've been waiting for."

I wiggled and tried to kick at him, but it was useless. When his breath slithered across my face, I went limp.

"That's better. Now, where were we? Ah, yes." He loosened his hold enough for me to suck in a lungful of air. "Out by yourself, Carrie?"

"No," I gasped out.

"Hmm, really? I don't see anyone else."

"I'm not alone."

He chuckled in my ear, and I cringed at the flowery scent of his breath. It seemed he'd already devoured a soul for the night. "Surely you can't mean *Reid* is with you." The disgust in his tone when he said the name made me shiver. His voice lowered as his lips clasped onto my earlobe. "Let me tell you a secret, Carrie. Reid. Led you. To me."

"No. He'd never do that. Lucas—"

He gripped my throat harder again, silencing me. "Have you ever asked Reid why Lucas died?"

I shook my head.

"You should ask him. It's such a…*touching* story." He laughed then turned his head away from me. "Hey Reid! You can come out of the shadows now."

What? No!

"Let her go, Carver," Reid said from somewhere down the alley. "It's me you want."

Carver ran his fingers down my cheek, and I took a chance to steal a peek at him. Exactly how Jessica described him to me last summer, Carver's bleached blond hair rose up in spikes on top of his head. Turquoise irises framed by dark lashes stood out in contrast to his tanned skin. A strong jaw clenched below pink lips, curved up in a crafty smile.

"I'm not sure about that, old friend." His nose nestled in my hair. "You smell so good. I bet you taste even better." Low at my collarbone, Carver traced the tip of his tongue up my carotid artery. "Delicious."

I squeezed my eyelids shut, concentrating on how my own heart thumped against my ribs in the beat of a bass drum. Even though I'd known about this impasse since last summer, it didn't stop the panic from engulfing me.

"Put her down, man. She's not a part of this." Reid's voice sounded close, right beside me now, but I couldn't force my eyes open to check. Carver would probably have me in a trance faster than Reid ever did.

"Like hell she isn't!" Carver spat. "*You* and Lucas dragged her into this. She's fair game as far as I'm concerned. Which reminds me, where is our little dead friend?"

"It's just us tonight, Carver."

"That wasn't the deal."

"Deal's off."

Oh, Reid is in cahoots with Carver?

My eyes bugged open in surprise as Carver slid me higher against the brick. The grooves gouged into my shoulders. His other arm shot out, and he circled his fingers around Reid's throat like mine.

"You don't get to call off the deal, Reid," he rasped out.

Stuck in Carver's grasp, Reid didn't move. We locked gazes for a second before he looked away.

"Isn't this a lovely sight?" Carver said snickering. "The snitch comes face-to-face with the prey. Tell me, Carrie, do you still think Reid is your saving grace?"

Yes. No. Maybe. I didn't know what to think, but I didn't dare answer the question.

Carver sighed. "I can only deal with one of you at a time. Let's see." His cunning gaze shifted between Reid and me several times. "Sorry, old friend. I choose the girl."

As soon as he said it, he tossed Reid backwards into the opposite wall. Reid's head smacked against the brick in a deafening crack. I tried to scream, but Carver's hold was too strong. In front of me, Reid slumped over, unmoving.

"That's better. Now, Carrie, where is Lucas?"

Ohmygod! Carver killed him!

Wide-eyed, I took in Reid. Blood oozed from the back of his head, slithering down the pavement in a stream of crimson. Carver slid over, blocking my view. He leaned in, a blond spike tickling my face.

"Where's your boyfriend, Carrie?"

"Gone," I whimpered. "He's … he's gone."

"And where did he go?"

"Um, he…" *What do I say?* "He went with Megan."

"Where, Carrie? WHERE?" He slammed a palm into the brick beside my ear.

I shook my head. "I … I don't know. They didn't tell me."

"Okay." He stepped back without loosening his grip. "We can play the hard way. Evil lingers in all of the dark corners of the world, you know." He grinned, locking his bright turquoise eyes on mine.

"Carrie, you die at the hands of a turquoise-eyed, blond vampire."

No. Crazy-ass cambion with one hell of a grudge.

I knew what came next. Reid had done it to me three times before. Carver's pupils expanded until blackness filled in from corner to corner.

Inwardly, I screamed, "NO!" but my lips formed a seductive smile in response. My fingertips rolled over Carver's full lips. So close. So enticing. So…delectable. When my feet hit the ground, Carver released me, trailing his hands down my arms. Warmth filled me, and I couldn't think of anything except Carver's mouth and how much I wanted to kiss it.

"After tonight, you won't remember Lucas. He's nothing more than leftover dust polluting the earth," Carver murmured, sucking the flesh at my throat.

"Yes," I breathed, and Carver entwined his fingers in my hair, yanking my head to the side. Carver could do whatever he wanted to me.

I wrapped my arms around his neck, pressing my

body against him. Never in my life had I wanted someone this bad. My lips searched for Carver's. Teasing me, he pulled back each time I got close.

"Please," I begged. "I need you. I need you now."

Carver's hands slipped under my shirt, caressing the skin in small, tantalizing movements. He lowered me to the ground and crawled on top of me, his hips pressing into mine. Rocking against me. Beside us, the card from the flower shop floated in a puddle.

"Kiss you?" he asked, teasing me again.

"Yes! Kiss me!"

Carver grinned. "Okay. You asked for it."

I let out a moan as his mouth covered mine, melting me into obedience. My whole body relaxed and tingled with warmth. A consuming fire engulfed me, driving me onward with an overwhelming desire. I laid back, my muscles loosening and my mind given over to utter satisfaction. Silk flowed through my veins, softening and molding me to whatever Carver coveted from me.

I smiled as I let go and fell deeper and deeper into him. Somewhere in my head, my subconscious shouted for me to wake up, but the voice grew fainter until it disappeared completely. Heat extended to the tips of my fingers and toes as Carver's tongue massaged mine.

I'd never felt this wonderful, not when Lucas kissed me nor when I was holding him. This was better. Warmer. Exhilarating. This sensation was what was missing in our relationship, the one Lucas couldn't feel. It was like I'd been standing on top of a mountain for so long, and Carver finally pushed me over the edge, sending me free-falling into unparalleled euphoria.

Then I hit the bottom.

The warmth evaporated into icy cold daggers slicing into me. Shivering on the ground, I could barely make out the man on top of me, rising to his feet.

How did I get down here?

My teeth chattering, I struggled to suck in air. I heard my voice whimpering over and over again, saying something I didn't understand.

The man kicked at my feet. "Humans are weak and pathetic," he growled.

I jerked on the ground in spastic movements, unable to control myself. My vision blurred, and I had to blink several times to make out where I was.

An alley.

Memories crept in, and a single name crowded my mind—Carver.

"Get up, you worthless piece of shit." Carver grabbed Reid by the back of his shirt, lifting him to his feet. Blood flowed down Reid's hair, staining it crimson. "Such a disappointment you are."

Reid groaned. Pale and unstable, he tucked his knees under him and climbed to his feet. Halfway up, he fell back to the ground.

I tried to speak, but no sound came out. Reid's head rose up, and he saw me. Curled into the fetal position, shaking, I peered back through the haze.

"What…what did you do…to her?" Reid rasped out, weakened.

Carver scoffed. "What you couldn't."

On his hands and knees, Reid crawled to me. He put a palm on my forehead as if checking for a fever.

Cold. So cold.

"Carrie," Reid whispered. "I'm sorry. I'm so sorry. I didn't…Please, I didn't mean for this…"

Something told me I should blame him. I should be angry, but I didn't know why.

"What you do with her is up to you," Carver said. "Finish her off or let her die here in the alley with the rats."

"Why? She was—"

"Innocent? Mortals never are, Reid. You of all people know that." Carver bent down beside him. With two bony fingers, Carver lifted Reid's chin until the two were face to face. "Don't you see? I'm giving you a choice, Reid. One which you believe I robbed you of. Think of it as," Carver twirled his other hand in the air, "a gift."

"You're sick."

Carver threw his head back, laughing. "No, Reid. I'm beyond sick." He let go of Reid and stood up, glowering down at me. "Tell Lucas she didn't give much of a fight; it hardly seemed worth the effort."

Evil. Pure evil.

I coughed, blood tinkling down my chin.

"If you're gonna kill her, you'd better make it quick. Ease her suffering. It would be…what's the word? Compassionate." Carver walked backward out of the ally. "Make sure Lucas gets this little message. Maybe it will sink in this time. And you, Reid, we're not finished yet."

d. Nichole King

The last thing I remember was Carver's sadistic laughter echoing through the alley.

Chapter 18

Cold engulfed me, filling my chest. Each gasp for air froze my lungs, making it harder to breathe with each inhale.

The ground dug into my side, and the scent of rotting garbage wafted into my nostrils. Nausea mixed with panting gasps churned my stomach.

Beside me, Reid wiped the blood from his head and smeared it on the pavement. Sure that he was as light-headed as I was, I wondered how he could maneuver himself up. He did, though, swearing at the cat who'd apparently stuck around to watch the show.

"I'm taking you home, Carrie," Reid said, but it sounded like fuzz in my ears.

By "home" I hoped he didn't mean my grandparents'. Then again, I didn't want to be at Lucas's either, and I wasn't sure why I felt that way. Something inside nagged at me, telling me that I should hate him. Hate everyone.

But I don't hate Lucas…do I?

Effortlessly, Reid scooped me up, as if he hadn't

almost bled out. Supernatural power, I guessed.

"Put your arm around me, okay?" With Reid's help, I lobbed an arm behind his neck. "Let's go."

He staggered down the alley, leaving in the same direction I'd come in. It had to be well after midnight by now. Quiet, the night kept its secrets, and all I heard were the sounds of Reid's shoes hitting the cement.

When he opened the door to Lucas's Jeep Compass, it hit me that he knew I'd driven here and where I'd parked. I'd been following *him*.

I narrowed my eyes as he carefully laid me into the backseat. When my head hit the leather, I winced.

"Sorry," he mumbled.

I curled my legs up on the seat, my arms wrapped around me, attempting to calm the icy trembles rocking my body.

Reid slammed the back door and slipped behind the wheel then he bent over to retrieve the keys from where I'd hidden them.

How did he know that?

"*Reid led you directly to me,*" Carver had murmured in my ear. I could still feel his breath sticking to my neck.

Was Carver right? And if so, why? Had Reid tricked me?

I coughed again. This time, I managed to cover my mouth. I hacked until I was sure my esophagus would come up next. Liquid spewed out, rolling down my chin. Gasping for air, I held my hand out and gaped at the blood dripping through my fingers. It poured down my arm and fell onto the seat.

"Oh shit," Reid muttered, staring at the blood. "We gotta go."

He flung the Jeep into gear and spun backward out of the parking space like an Indie 500 driver. The tires squealed as he floored it down the street. I'm not sure how fast he was driving, but it took no time at all before he stopped in Lucas's driveway.

Two seconds later, he had the door open and eased me out of the backseat. Trembling, I wrapped my arm around his neck again, mixing my blood with his on the shoulder of his t-shirt.

He kicked the front door open, breaking it at the jamb, and didn't bother with the lights. My eyelids dropped, and I could barely make out Lucas's bedroom. The empty white walls seemed dull. The evil presence in my head pushed in on me. Even the room smelled like Lucas, and the scent that once filled me with longing now nauseated me.

The realization that my mind wasn't right tugged at me. Rolling thoughts of needing Lucas here to hold me contradicted the loathing I also felt. It was like I was losing myself.

Gingerly, Reid deposited me on top of Lucas's white comforter. "Hang on."

I collapsed immediately, too weak to hold myself up. The feather-filled duvet caressed my face, and despite the stench of Lucas pouring off it, I wanted to sink into the softness and stop breathing. Pain radiated through me, starting at my heart and slowly spreading outward.

Ripping back the comforter, Reid gently dragged me across the bed. Blood stains now tainted the beautiful white, ruining its innocence. Reid tucked my shivering body under it, and I couldn't help but think of the symbolism.

"Okay, um…" Reid breathed out, scanning the room.

He rushed over to Lucas's closet, slinging open the doors and rummaging through the clothes. When he didn't find what he was searching for, he shot me a pained glance and left.

Don't come back, a voice hissed in my head.

Had I thought that? No, I couldn't have.

I tried to grab hold of the warmth the blankets were supposed to offer, but it was useless. As a matter of fact, I wanted to die. Let go and be free.

Something inside me fought, though. Like it was controlling me, my thoughts, and my will obeyed it when it called, and I was powerless against the master.

Lucas, I need you. Please!

And then it shifted. Inside me, the monster broke free. Taking over.

Lucas did this to me. It's his fault, and he needs to pay.

Reid ducked back into the room. "I only found one," he said, draping a thermal over me. "I…I don't know what else to do."

Fumbling, I gathered the top of the new blanket into my fists, holding it to my chest. The sight of it triggered a memory from last summer. Lucas and I lying on this blanket, in the middle of nowhere, gazing up at the stars.

The sting of tears burned my eyes.

My earlier conversation with Reid beckoned to me from the back of my mind. He'd said that the longer the demon was inside him, the more they became one and the same, and I wondered if that was what was happening to me. Normally, incubi couldn't create more of their own kind—with the exception of Carver and his experiment, which I didn't think he performed on me—so I was going to die. And from the sounds in my head, I'd die evil.

"Kill me," I rasped out. "Lucas can't see me like—"

Reid shook his head. "They'll be back soon. They can heal you—I think."

He didn't sound sure, and I didn't know if I wanted to wait that long. I needed to silence this voice before it consumed me.

"What," I swallowed back the blood rising in my throat, "is happening to me?"

Reid clutched my hand in his. "Carver stole your soul. Well, most of it anyway, and he poisoned the rest. You're dying, Carrie."

This slow, agonizing death isn't what Jessica saw, though.

"I'm sorry," Reid said. "This is my fault, and I'm so sorry." He laid his head on my shoulder, sighing.

I tried to fight back the thought, but the voice broke through.

No. It's Lucas's fault. I hate him!

"CARRIE!"

I didn't hear the door open, but at the sound of Lucas's voice, a burst of joy exploded inside me. For half a second, I felt normal.

Lucas!

As soon as I thought it, hate filled me, and I closed my eyes so I didn't have to look at the bastard. He left me! So many nights he'd been gone, chasing some half-demon who was more important than me. More important than protecting me!

He spent far too much time with Megan, sharing everything with her, and keeping secrets from me. Like why he was so tired before and whatever the contents of the Incenamus book said. Sure, he'd told me that he hadn't translated all if it, but some of it he had. The two of them knew it all.

I took a deep breath and waited until the thoughts faded away. When I opened my eyes, I saw Lucas standing in the doorway, pale and flickering in and out of transparency. His expression changed from shock to grief to murderous rage. He set his gaze on Reid.

Come to me, baby. I need you.

"What the hell is this, Reid?" Lucas growled.

"I'm so sorry, man. Carver—"

Suddenly, Lucas lunged at him. Wrapping his fingers around the incubus's throat, he squeezed. His face contorted in fury.

Reid didn't move a muscle, allowing Lucas's anger to destroy him.

Yes, kill him!

Lucas's head snapped in my direction, his mouth in a surprised O at my thought. He loosened his grip, light green irises boring into me.

"LUCAS!" Megan screamed, running to them and peeling Lucas away from Reid. Still stunned by my reaction, Lucas didn't fight her. "Let him go!"

She shoved Reid into a corner and said something to him. Slumping back against the wall, he nodded his agreement.

Jessica rushed over to me and pressed the pads of two fingers against my neck, checking for a heartbeat. "How are you still alive?" She ran her brown irises over me in bewilderment. "My vision never changed regarding this."

You and your useless visions. How dare you touch me?

Lucas sat down on the bed on the other side of me, taking me in.

"Incenamus." Megan pursed her lips as it dawned on her, answering Jessica's question. "Her soul is dying, but since it's connected to yours, Lucas, you must be keeping her alive."

"Yeah, but for how long?" Lucas's voice trembled, the sound sliding into my heart and making me ache for him. Losing me was his greatest fear.

"I don't know."

"How do I save her?"

The silence thickened around us, drowning out the strum of my quickening pulse.

"I think you know, Lucas," Megan whispered.

What does Lucas know about saving me? Is this another secret he's been hiding?

The monster in me began to rise again, and I could feel my own thoughts converging with it.

Lucas drew my hand to his lips. "This wasn't supposed to happen now, damn it! How did he get to her?"

"Carver did this?" Megan asked, and from the corner Reid nodded. "Then…"

Jessica's gaze wandered over me, her mouth taut

and her brows furrowed in dismay. "This isn't what I saw. It isn't…"

"I can explain," Reid said, taking a step toward us.

"It'd better be good," Lucas mumbled.

Megan hesitated. "Maybe you should explain from there."

"No," Reid answered quickly. "Whatever Lucas wants to do to me is well deserved."

He walked to the end of the bed where all of us could see him. His shoulders rose and fell and he brushed both hands from the back of his head forward.

"I came here for two reasons. As a human, I needed to find Lucas and warn him. As an incubus…I came to hurt him. Carver sent me to target Carrie."

"WHAT?" Lucas would have shot off the bed if his secret-keeper Megan hadn't grabbed his arm. "You came here to kill Carrie?"

You make me sick. Get out of here.

Dejected, Reid bowed his head. "I'm so sorry, Luke. Carver said—"

"I don't give a shit what Carver said to convince you!"

"It changed, man. Tonight, I was going to cut him off before he arrived to tell him the deal was off. I'm not working for him anymore."

Lucas ran his fingers through his hair, a gesture I remember I used to love, but right now, it annoyed me. "Tonight? Well, gee, Reid, doesn't that make it all better?"

"Why?" Megan prodded. "What made you

change your mind?"

Reid hesitated. "That's not important."

"Oh, I think it is," Lucas said.

Reid's eyes cut to Lucas. "Our history. What I did to Carrie. I owe you."

"I'm not sure I buy that," Lucas replied.

"It's all I've got, man. Take it or leave it, but I'm helping you kill Carver regardless. He's stolen lives away from me too."

"That's what changed," Jessica mused out loud. "When you picked a side, Reid, it altered the course of the future. It made the vamp, Julianna, and Mike necessary to end this thing."

"So instead of the four of us at risk, Reid decided to make it six," Lucas said.

Megan whipped her hands in front of her. "Wait, back up. What does Carver want with Carrie?"

"Nothing, really," Reid said. "He wanted to use her to get back at Lucas."

"For searching for him?" Megan's brows knit together, confused.

"Not exactly, though that pissed him off even more."

"Me? What did I ever do to him?" Lucas asked.

"It's a long story," Reid muttered.

"I'll bet it is." Jessica trained a cold stare at him. *Get out of the room. All of you. Just GET OUT!*

Lucas squeezed my hand and kissed the back of it, leaving his lips pressed against the skin. The gesture and the way his shoulders fell should have made me want to hold him close, do anything to take away the hurt my thoughts caused him. Instead, it made me angrier.

"Okay, um, let's take a break, shall we? I'd like to have some time with Carrie—alone."

No. You most of all. Get the hell out!

Swiveling his head to me, he opened his mouth to speak then shut it.

"Whatever you need, Lucas," Jess said, standing. She bent over and kissed my forehead. "It'll be okay, Carrie."

What do you know? Worthless witch.

I sneered at her back as she walked away, led out by Reid. At the door, Lucas caught Megan's elbow.

"Her thoughts, they're…"

"Lucas, her soul is dying because Carver ripped it apart and took the biggest slice. It's," she paused, "it's like Reid's cycles. Her being is at war with itself; each piece is pulling her in a different direction. What's left of her soul has been poisoned, and her spirit is struggling to balance it out. Lucas, if you don't do something soon, her body will win and she'll die."

Yes, let me die, please, the real me begged.

Lucas glanced over his shoulder at me, frowning. He sucked his lower lip into his mouth, furrowing his brow. I hated that pained expression. It was part of the reason I didn't want Reid to bring me here.

Lucas faced Megan again. "Do you have the book?"

"Not here."

"I'll do it. Get it for me."

"Are you absolutely sure, Lucas? You do this, and there's no going back."

"It's not even a choice, Megan."

"Okay, I'll leave right now. Be back soon."

Megan closed the door behind her and Lucas drifted back to me. His darkened green irises swept over the blood smudged on the blankets.

"Care, I should never have left you. I should have come back. I should have—"

On top of the mattress, he pulled me into his arms. Combing through my hair, he moved the locks aside and kissed the base of my neck.

My vision blurred, and I moaned through the ache in my stomach. In this very second, I was me, and I didn't know how long I'd stay this way. A bubble I couldn't hold back rose in my throat. I coughed, blood sputtering everywhere. I was a dying mess.

Don't leave me.

Lucas sat up and yanked his shirt over his head. "I'm right here. Forever." He dabbed the material over my mouth, wiping away the blood. "I'll save you, Carrie. I'm going to fix this."

How?

"The Incenamus book. It can restore you."

Through the shivers, I nodded, but the voice in my head returned.

He lied to me. He said he couldn't translate the book because it was in Cumbric.

Lies. Lies. More lies.

Now drowning in anger, I couldn't think. My mind screamed in a voice I didn't recognize. He needed to pay for lying to me.

"Fight it, Carrie, fight it," he begged.

Tears swelled in the corners of my eyes as I struggled to do what he asked. Slowly, with a shaking hand, I reached for him and glided my

fingers over his cheek.
    "Save me."

Chapter 19

With Lucas beside me, I fought against the darkness when it overtook me. I squeezed my eyes shut as the voice—my voice—screamed in my head.

"I'm not letting go of you, Carrie," Lucas murmured in my ear, holding me closer.

Stay away from me. Don't touch me!

"Fight it."

I hate you.

"I love you. I'll always love you."

The walls closed in around me. My whole body tensed as if the pressure inside would make me explode. When the screaming in my head forced its way out my mouth, I thrashed on the bed like a caged animal, no longer weak. A small piece of me wanted to stop myself, but I was paper in its hand, and it was crushing me.

Lucas held me down as I snarled and snipped at him. "Let me go, you son of a bitch!"

He didn't answer me, his eyes flickering to the door.

"It's the poison," I heard Jessica remind him. "It's not her."

Lucas nuzzled his face in my hair, his fingers tightened around my wrists, pinning me to the mattress. I hated how calm he was. I hated his cool touch. I hated every word that came out of his stupid mouth. Lucas was my enemy.

I twisted violently under him, kicking at whatever part of him I could hit. My teeth snapped down on his arm, but he never flinched. Of course he wouldn't; he couldn't *feel* me.

The thought bit at me. Memories of touches, kisses. Every caress he never felt saturated me with bitterness. In his kitchen, on the roof that night, each time he stayed the night was tainted with insincere love for me. I'd given him everything I had, and what had he reciprocated?

Lies. Rejection. Fake embraces.

Then, as fast as the cycle began, it stopped. The fires within me burned out, and I shook uncontrollably. Weakness settled back into my bones. Pain cut at my core like my insides were transforming into stone. I whimpered, nestling into Lucas's body.

"Save…me," I murmured. A tear trailed down my cheek and landed on Lucas's chest. The fight alone was killing me.

His lips pressed against my forehead as he held me closer. "I will. Megan will be back soon, baby. Hang on a little longer."

"The…book," I sputtered out. "Incenamus book?"

"Yes."

"Why?"

Lucas's brows furrowed. "No, don't talk. You need your energy."

I shook my head. I had to know why he needed a book that he hadn't translated. "Tell...me."

Lucas smoothed my hair, avoiding my gaze. "Just rest. We can talk later."

"No. Now."

Again there was something he wasn't telling me. The book contained powerful information, including how our soul-link could bring the dead back to life. Still, Lucas had wanted nothing to do with it...until now.

Please. You're scaring me, I thought too tired to speak. He'd hear me.

Pain emanated from his beautiful irises when he looked at me. I hadn't meant to hurt him, but I wanted to know before the beast took me over again with all its anger and twisted words.

"It has the answers we need, Care. There's information in the book that can keep you alive."

I tried to absorb it, but through the shivers, I had a hard time sorting out my thoughts and connecting the pieces.

But you only know the parts in Latin. You said without knowing the sections in Cumbric, it wasn't safe to use.

Lucas rolled his fingertips on his chin. "It wasn't safe," he finally said, not elaborating.

Is it now?

The muscles in his jaw clenched, and he raked his hand through his hair, dark locks falling over the back of his hand.

"As safe as it will ever be," he sighed.

I studied him, waiting for him to flinch or look away so I'd know something was wrong. But his gaze locked on me and held, staring at me as if he wanted me to read his thoughts because he didn't want to say them out loud. Trembling all over, I couldn't concentrate on him long enough to even try.

Silence hung in the air, and I finally put it all together. The monster had been right.

You lied to me.

"I protected you."

How long have you had it all translated?

He slid his palm down his face. No, of course he didn't want to tell me.

"Since before Christmas."

Since before Christmas? What the hell? All this time passed and he never once tried to get his life back, attain a body. How badly did he really want to be with me? I fought to hold back the tears. How many more secrets was he hiding?

I sobbed as heat began to flicker around my heart again. Moaning, I tossed and turned on top of the mattress. The poisoned spirit within me was taking over; my master had returned.

My other voice, the one I hated, rang out loud and clear in my head.

Lies. All lies. He doesn't remember his life or who he is. How can I really know him?

Even the small part of me that remained me couldn't retort. It fell silent, and I entered the shadows of hate consuming me. Losing myself in its demands.

The poison Carver left in my soul burned in my veins, and I screamed until I ran out of breath.

I felt Lucas's arms wrap around me, pulling me into him. He whispered some sort of bullshit in my ear about fighting and loving me. For all I cared, he could go to Hell and stay there. The liar meant nothing to me.

Go away! I hate you!

"Don't let it control you," Lucas said, cupping my face and peering into my eyes.

I spit on him. "I don't want you. Get away from me!"

He shook his head. "I'm not leaving you."

I struggled against him, clawing at him and ripping at his shirt. All I wanted was to tear him apart.

Finally, my spirit stopped fighting, releasing the white flag of surrender. The fire inside me burned hotter, and I cried out in anger and pain. Faintly, I registered how I sounded like the screaming souls I'd heard in the attic of the Moore house last summer. Yes, Hell was now invading my mind and body, and nothing stood in its way.

I coughed, blood splattering over the comforter. My head thrashed from side to side as the voices squeezed in. I knew I couldn't take it any longer, but I didn't know how to make it stop.

The bedroom door flew open, and Megan rushed inside.

"I got it, Lucas." She shoved an old leather book into his hands, and he whipped through the pages like he knew exactly where to go.

"Here," Lucas said, sliding a finger over a page.

"It's right here."

He passed the book off to Megan and stood over me. Megan skimmed the words as Lucas closed his eyes and placed one hand on my heart and his other on my forehead.

Still wailing, I tried to shake him away, but he pushed down on me harder with strength I didn't know he had. At least, not with me.

"Call Jessica in," he instructed. "We'd better hurry."

Megan laid the open book on the bed and went after Jess.

"I'm gonna make this right, Care," he murmured. "I need you to fight this a little bit longer."

Jessica, Megan, and Reid bolted through the door.

"Jessica, hold onto Carrie's arms," Megan commanded, picking up the book again and scanning the words.

Lucas took a deep breath, concentrating. "I call on the power of Incenamus—"

"Wait, Lucas!" Megan cried out, grabbing a hold of his wrist. "What are you doing?"

"Starting the spell," he replied, pushing her away. Megan stumbled backward at the force. Lucas closed his eyes again. "I call on the—"

"Lucas, STOP!" Megan urged. "You can't."

She grabbed the book and thrust it in front of his face. "You'll waste it if you do it now. Lucas, she has to die first."

Chapter 20

I sunk into the mattress, dizzy. The room spun around me, and with it, the blur of faces in a never-ending slur of motion.

Lucas sat beside me, serene and silent. I felt him inside my head, soothing me. The fire hadn't returned in a while, and I dreaded when it would. Maybe, though, I'd be dead first. Tired of fighting, I was ready to let go.

"Carrie," Lucas began.

Megan touched his shoulder as he bowed his head. "It's the way has to be."

"What if I can't do it? What if I can't bring her back?"

Not answering, Megan's eyes drifted over me. "I'll wait in the living room, Lucas. Let me know when you're ready to begin."

When I'm dead.

The door closed behind her, leaving Lucas, Jessica, and me to wait it out. Death was coming for me and soon, that much I knew. The other stuff, however, I hadn't figured out yet. The monster within weakened me, making it impossible to think.

I moaned as pain shot into my stomach, twisting and churning as if my organs were rotting out. When my great-aunt died in hospice a few years ago, she had a constant morphine drip. When I asked why, the nurse told me that dying hurts, and the meds help control the pain so she'd pass peacefully. I wonder if morphine would work for a dying soul like it did for a dying body.

This wasn't how I thought it would end.

"We won't be long, Jess," I heard Lucas say as his arms folded around me.

"Fine," Jess replied, her voice softer than usual. "I'll see if Megan and I can mix up a potion to help soothe her. There has to be something."

"Yeah." Lucas's voice broke.

He scooped me up, blankets and all, and hugged me against his chest. "Hold onto me, Care."

I tried to lift my arms around his neck, but I couldn't. There was no strength left in me.

I can't.

His disappointment radiated through me, chilling me. "It's okay, baby. I've got you, and I won't let go."

I nodded into him, shivering in his cool arms. Closing my eyes, I rested my head into his shoulder, and air squeezed in on me as we disappeared.

The next breath I drew was outside. The breeze picked up my hair and twirled it behind me. Usually, when this happened, it annoyed me, but not this time. This time it felt good.

The moon shone brightly, unobstructed by the lingering clouds. A few stars twinkled overhead as if they were waving at me, beckoning me to come and play. Yes, I'd rather live, but if whatever Lucas attempted didn't work, I embraced the comforting thought that I'd be among the stars that Lucas loved so much.

Sitting on his roof, me secure between his legs, Lucas's hands glided down my arms. I leaned back against him, needing to feel him close. Neither of us knew what the morning would bring.

"I…love…you," I rasped out.

Lucas dipped his head low and sucked on my neck, his lips still against me as he spoke. "This isn't goodbye."

You don't know that.

"I won't lose you like this."

I rotated my head slightly to accept his lips on my own. For an instant, sheer joy made my heart flutter, reminding me of the miracle that was the two of us. How being with him filled me with the comfort that I only found in his embrace. The satisfaction of knowing he was mine.

The burning in my stomach made me grimace, but no matter what anyone said, saying goodbye hurt worse than dying.

He picked me up just as I began to convulse.

"Let's get you back inside. Hopefully Megan has something for the pain." Lucas picked me up, and instantly, we were back inside his bedroom.

"Megan!" he yelled, holding me down. "Megan, help me!"

Jess and Megan burst through the door and pulled Lucas off me.

"Stop, Lucas. It's not the poison; it's

happening," Jess explained. "Hold on, Carrie. Be brave."

"Lucas," I wheezed out.

Then everything stopped.

***

They say the last thing to go is your hearing.

Lost inside myself, I heard everyone around me.

Most of the time, the three of them were quiet, patiently waiting for my heart to stop. Once, Reid tried to come in, but Lucas went berserk.

"Get the hell out of here!" he screamed, and the door slammed shut. Through it, I heard a muffled voice repeating "I'm sorry. I'm so sorry."

Megan sighed but didn't respond.

"How do we know when…?" Lucas trailed off, and I hurt for him.

If he held me, I couldn't feel it. It was like pure torture, and I realized how he must have felt every day with me.

"I think you'll notice, Lucas," Megan said. "Incenamus will tell you."

The tap of his fingers on the nightstand reverberated in my ears, and I imagined him sweeping a hand through his dark hair.

Delving lower into the darkness, I let myself sink further and further away. I no longer felt the softness of the blankets or smelled Lucas on the pillows.

Deeper and deeper.

Soon, the sounds of Lucas's sighs and his fingers rapping on the nightstand evaporated. I couldn't even hear the air escaping my own lungs.

My soul was like a candle as the wax gradually melted. The wick burned too low, dancing in a puddle beneath it. Not wanting to be blown out, the flame flickered, waiting to fade away.

The time for goodbyes was over, and those people I cared most about ran circles in my head, their faces clear as the last time I saw them. Stacy. Jessica. Megan. Mike. Grandma and Grandpa. Mom. Even Dad.

And Lucas. Always Lucas.

Swirling in my memory, the faces began to dull, the colors losing their luster. Everyone slowly seeped into the dark, blending into it until they vanished.

I took one last breath and let go.

Chapter 21

Blackness surrounded me when my eyes fluttered open. I blinked, attempting to wash away the blur. Haze filtered into the corners of my vision, but I could still make out Lucas's bedroom.

To my left, the large window with black curtains drawn slightly back allowed a sliver of moonlight to spill in. Further down the wall, Lucas's closet doors were open, one of them grazing the empty armchair. The white walls seemed brighter to me, even in the dark.

Is this how Lucas felt when he died?

No, I answered myself. If I woke up as a ghost, I wouldn't remember my life, or Lucas.

I shifted on the bed, my head dropping to the side like my muscles hadn't woken up yet. Letting out a moan, I reached for the glass of water on the nightstand. My stomach did a somersault at the motion, and the urge to throw up became eminent.

Nope, definitely not dead.

I felt strange, though. My heart beat in a continuous rhythm, but with a dull ache inside it—

inside my whole body. Like…like my organs were coming to life?

I swallowed back the vomit with a gulp of water and set the glass down.

As my sight adjusted, I focused on a dining room chair beside the bed. Empty, but…not. The knowledge of his presence rushed through me from the inside out, stronger than ever before. I squinted, waiting for Lucas to materialize.

For what seemed like hours, I heard his voice in my head. Felt his presence flood me with warmth. His spirit flowed through me like blood in my veins.

I thought he'd be here if I woke up. *When* I woke up.

I rolled back onto the pillow and stared at the ceiling. "I can feel you, Lucas. Where are you?"

A sense of doubt crept in as I remembered the hateful words I'd spit at him. Evil thoughts that he'd heard. Things I didn't mean. Things I couldn't control.

Suddenly, a slash of pain sliced through my head and I cried out, covering my temples. I flung a pillow over my face to drown out the sound of my howls reverberating in my ears.

Oh, God. Am I dying again?

The edge of a knife skimmed down my neck and stabbed into my chest. At the sensation, my body curled in on its own, my knees pulling into my chest.

Make it stop!

The bedroom door jolted open, and Jessica and Megan raced inside.

"Carrie!" Jessica threw herself down on the bed,

shaking me by the shoulders. "Carrie, what's wrong?"

In the middle of the room, Megan turned in a circle, scanning the air. "Lucas?"

"It hurts," I sobbed.

"What hurts?" Jess asked, smoothing my hair.

"Um, everything. Everywhere. My heart."

Jessica's attention snapped to Megan. "Is she having a heart attack or something?"

"Lucas!" Megan called, her eyes searching the room.

I buried my face in the pillow again. "He's gone, and it's my fault."

"No, he's here, Carrie. Trust me," Megan assured me. "He's just—"

Jessica shook her head, cutting Megan off. Eyes-wide in warning, Jessica stared at Megan for a moment before Megan broke the connection.

"He's whaa—" I wailed out as a wave of pain crashed into my gut.

"Lucas, you have to stop," Megan snapped. "Lucas."

Jessica wrapped her arms around me, soothing me with the hushed coo my mother used when I was a child.

"Control it, Lucas. You have to control it," Megan said into the air.

Like smoke being sucked out of a window, the sting slowly dissipated. Little by little, it freed me until I sunk into the mattress, panting. Along with the pain, the sense of Lucas had permeated me before it too, dissipated, and I was left alone inside myself.

"That's it," Megan murmured. "It's okay, Lucas."

Lucas did this to me?

Jessica rested a hand over her heart in relief. She nodded at Megan, both of them relaxing a bit.

"Jess?" I whispered. "What's going on?"

Megan crossed her legs at the foot of the bed. "Lucas is okay, Carrie," she answered. "When you died, he used the power of Incenamus to bring you back."

Panic gradually replaced the concern as Lucas's warnings repeated in my mind.

"It can't be that easy. We shouldn't mess with fate."

"We don't get something for nothing."

At the realization, I choked back a gasp. He'd used it. He used the book and Incenamus to bring the dead—me—back to life. But…

So, if Lucas brought me back, what did he have to give up?

Using Jess's arm for support, I lifted myself up into a sitting position. Jessica stuffed a pillow between my back and the headboard to keep me comfortable. My death must have activated her motherly side.

"Megan, where is he?" I rasped out, catching my breath.

Megan bowed her head before peering up at the empty chair beside the bed. Her stare bored into it as if she was willing it to move with her mind. As far as I knew, her powers weren't that strong.

I looked over, and for a fraction of a second, Lucas shimmered into existence and then blinked out.

"No. Come back!" Tossing the blankets off me, I scrambled toward him.

"Carrie." Jessica crawled after me, hooking an arm around my waist to keep me from losing my balance and tumbling off the edge. I hadn't noticed how wobbly I was.

I waved my hand over the chair, feeling nothing except cold air.

"I don't understand." I slouched, scooting my knees up into my chest. "Why can't I feel him now? Was Incenamus used up?"

"No, Carrie, it doesn't work that way," Megan said. "It wore him out, is all. I'll let him explain when he regains his strength."

The way her voice lowered told me she was lying. Whatever he'd done to save me did more than just wear him out.

I frowned. "I don't think so. Lucas told me that you don't get something for nothing. What was his something?"

Megan hesitated, glancing at my invisible boyfriend, as if asking his permission before answering me. My guess was that it had to do with the book and whatever information Lucas hid from me.

Why he hadn't used its power to procure a body and come alive himself.

"You know that a living being needs three things to live: a spirit, a body, and a soul. When one dies, you die. Because the two of you have connected souls, it's like you are one living being. Incenamus offers a way for one of you to give a piece of the missing part to make the other person whole." Megan cleared her throat, again stealing a quick peek at Lucas.

She continued, "In your case, Carver poisoned your soul. Your soul died, Carrie, and Lucas used Incenamus to give you part of his."

He did what? "Okay, now what? His body died, right? That means I can just use Incenamus to give him part of mine...somehow. Easy peasy. Fixed." Even as I said it, I knew it wouldn't work. If it were that simple, Lucas would be alive right now, holding me in real, solid arms.

"I'm sorry, Carrie. It's a one-time thing, one way. He gave his soul to save you."

One time. One way.

The power to bring him back was gone. Sacrificed for me.

"He gave me part of his soul," I whispered, "so, is he...fading away?" My lips moved at the last words; I doubted if any sound came out.

"No, it drained him, though. He needs time to recuperate."

"What happened earlier then? When you told him to control something."

"His spirit is adjusting to the partial soul, and since you two now share the same soul, the pain resonated in you too."

I clasped my hands on my lap, considering what Megan had explained. It seemed too easy with all the stuff Lucas had warned me about. Incenamus gave me my life back at the expense of part of Lucas's soul, so what did that mean? How did only having part of a soul affect him? Surely, not just that his strength would be depleted for a short time. There had to be more to it than that.

Both Megan and Jessica stared at me, probably waiting for me to explode, flip out, or something. Instead, I focused my attention on the empty chair, trying to understand.

Again, the outline of Lucas flashed and disappeared.

You don't get something for nothing. So what? Lucas gave me part of his soul, what was the big deal?

His soul. His soul. I repeated over and over in my head.

Susan Taylor's words filtered in, and the missing piece materialized. Without his soul—his entire soul—Lucas would fade away, cease to exist. She'd told us that when he stayed in corporeal form, he wouldn't feel his soul pulling him to it. And how much time he had left to find it varied for all ghosts. Some have a hundred years, others mere days.

"Ohmygod," I muttered to myself. "His soul. He gave up a part of his soul…and how much time he has to find the rest of it."

Last summer, when the town necromancer Susan Taylor had explained why Lucas was trapped between the living and dead, she said sometime before he died, his soul was ripped from his spirit. But even though the two entities were separated, they were still a part of his being, unlike the soulless, whose souls were dead—like mine now.

Silence hung heavy the air. Jessica and Megan's eyes fixed on me.

"That's it, isn't it?" I asked. "Isn't it?"

"Yeah," Megan confirmed. "He may never feel the rest of it calling him again."

"How much time?"

Megan heaved a sigh. "A fraction of whatever he had left."

***

I was supposed to be sleeping, gathering my strength, but thinking about what Lucas had done crushed me.

Now I understood why he'd been so hesitant to use the power of Incenamus before. To bring someone back to life took life away from the other person.

I stared at the empty chair beside the bed.

For all I knew, Lucas was still sitting in it. It was morning, and I still hadn't felt him in my head.

"Hey Carrie," Jess said, carrying a tray of breakfast food. Seeing the scrambled eggs, perfectly fluffy pancakes, and crispy bacon shot a sting through me. I'd much rather have Lucas's version.

I smiled, though. "Thanks."

I sat up, and like before, Jessica wedged a pillow between my back and the headboard. When I was settled, she placed the tray of food on my lap.

Jessica climbed in bed beside me. She lay on her stomach, her chin propped up on two fists. "How're you feeling?"

I shrugged. "Tired."

"Dying and coming back to life is exhausting," she said, and I giggled.

"Who knew, right?" I picked up my fork and

moved the scrambled eggs over my plate, suddenly realizing: "Hey Jess?"

"Yeah?"

"No one is supposed to know you're here, so what did you tell your parents?"

"My parents, believe it or not, were easy. I told them you and some friends of yours were going to Aspen—with parental supervision, of course—and had invited me along. They think I'm whizzing down the bunny slope for the week." She whistled as her hand plunged into a pillow.

"That had nothing to do with the Colorado line we fed Stacy, was it? Speaking of Stacy…" I scrunched up my nose and narrowed a brow. "What did you tell her?"

"Um, yeah, about that." Jess blushed. "I sort of compelled her to go with her parents to Costa Rica for spring break. She doesn't know where I am."

"Whoa, wait? You charmed Stacy?"

Since Megan had charmed my grandparents, I hadn't even considered calling them, and according to Jessica, I was supposed to be in Aspen anyway. Probably a good thing I hadn't contacted them, or I'd have a lot of explaining to do.

Jess covered her mouth to hide her grin. "It was for her own good. Seriously, the girl is living it up in a decked-out cabana, catching the gorgeous Pacific rays, and ogling half-naked guys with six-packs that are undoubtedly all over her. I did her a favor."

I shook my head with my lips tucked between my teeth. "I'm not so sure she'll see it that way, but yeah, she doesn't need to be involved in this crazy mess."

"Speaking of people involved in this crazy mess, I hate to say it, but if you're feeling up to it, I think you need to talk to Mike today." She said it slowly, carefully gauging my reaction. I dropped my fork onto the plate.

Suddenly, what little appetite I had disappeared completely. "The vision hasn't changed, has it?"

"No, Mike needs to be there. And it may come sooner than we thought."

"How soon?"

Jess heaved a sigh. "Soon. The visions are coming hourly now."

"What do I tell him?"

"Everything."

She must be joking. He'd never believe me.

"Everything? Like, every. *Thing*?"

"It's safer for him if we don't keep him in the dark. Besides, I think I know why we need him, and absolute honesty is a necessity."

***

By mid-afternoon, I felt more like myself. Weak still, but my head had cleared, and I could at least stand up on my own without losing my balance.

Seated in his usual spot on the armchair in the living room, Reid looked up at me as Jessica led me to the sofa. I avoided making eye contact; I didn't have the energy for a confrontation with the traitor.

"I'll get you a glass of water," Jess said, patting me on the shoulder.

"Um, Pepsi?"

She laughed. "Of course. Be right back."

I fiddled with a sofa pillow in my lap, wondering when Lucas would appear and trying to watch television to distract myself. For a second, I was transported to my grandparents' living room; The Weather Channel glowed back at me with Local on the 8s.

"High of seventy-eight with lows stretching down into the mid-fifties. Tomorrow, expect cloudy skies with a high of only sixty-one. Thunderstorms roll in late evening, bringing heavy rainfall and even hail in some areas. These storms are likely to produce possible rotation overnight."

Jess settled in beside me, handing me a can of my favorite beverage. I gulped down half of it before asking, "Where's Megan?"

"Outside, talking to Julianna on the phone."

"The vampire from the Cambion Council?"

Jessica nodded. "I told you Carver's returning soon, and we need to be prepared."

I blew out a groan, a wisp of hair hanging over my forehead flying to the side. "I didn't think you meant *that* soon."

"Ready to call Mike?"

"Give me a minute. I need to figure out what to say."

I leaned back on the armrest, dreading making the call. Forcing Mike into this craziness was so not fair and extremely dangerous. Not exactly horseback riding on Sunday afternoons.

I almost smiled to myself at the memory of how freaked out I was during my first lesson. I'd come a long way since then.

"Julianna's coming." Megan jetted through the front door, a relieved smile on her face. "She agreed."

Jess grinned smugly. "I knew she would."

"You're up?" Megan said, noticing me. "Good. And Lucas?"

"Nothing yet," I murmured.

"Don't worry. I'm sure he'll—Jessica?"

Jess fell back into the cushions, her irises clouding over, her face tilted up to the ceiling. Other than her hands shaking slightly at her sides, she'd gone rigid.

Megan rounded the sofa and crouched on the floor next to Jessica.

The three of us stared at her and waited for her to come to. Her nostrils flared and moisture gathered at the corners of her eyes. Ever since we were little, her nostrils pulsed whenever she was frightened.

"Jess?" I whispered. "Jess?"

Her chest rose, oxygen expanding her lungs. She blinked, taking a moment to catch her breath before she sat up.

"Hey, you okay?"

"Yeah, yeah. I'm fine," she answered, and if I hadn't known her all my life, I would have believed her.

"What did you see? Anything different?" Megan offered Jessica a hand.

Jess grabbed it, and Megan pulled her to her feet. It seemed my precog bestie was getting used to these visions.

Focused now, Jessica straightened her peasant top. "Again, it's only glimpses, nothing solid. Um, silverware. The same thing I've been seeing for months. A drawer full of it falling to the floor."

"Details," Megan said. "For instance, does the silverware have any patterns on it?"

"Uh, no, they're plain Jane. The drawer is white with peeling paint, and the floor is wood. Old wood."

"Okay. What else? You said earlier something about a cemetery with a large oak tree and the numbers 314."

"No cemetery or numbers this time. There's a broken window, though. Wooden chairs. I still see someone being thrown onto a table, and the table collapses."

"Who?" Reid asked, stepping forward from his perch in the corner.

Jessica studied her hands as if she was concentrating on them. Her eyes narrowed, and she hesitated. "I don't know. I can't see."

"Anything new?" Megan asked.

"Rain," Jess answered quickly. "Lightning. Thunder."

"Oh no," I moaned, staring at the television. "Tomorrow night."

Three sets of eyes cut to me.

"Whatever's going to happen is going to happen tomorrow night. The weather's supposed to be stormy." I set my empty Pepsi can on the coffee table. "You said soon."

"I don't know," Jess sighed. "These visions of stuff may not even be connected. A glimpse from one event here and another from there. Heck, I interpreted Carrie's death all wrong."

"Yeah, but it's the best prediction we have right now," Megan said, sounding calm and collected. "It's cliché, I know, but I suggest we hope for the best and plan for the worst. Regardless of when, Carver's coming for us, and we need to be ready."

Chapter 22

I wasn't sure what was worse: waiting for the impending battle or the actual confrontation. At the moment, I'd choose the waiting.

Tension grew throughout the rest of the day. Lucas had yet to make an appearance, and it made me apprehensive. I paced the floor, gripping the phone like I was strangling it.

Take that, new iPhone!

Minutes ago, Jessica filled me in on what little plan they had, and when she mentioned the proposed battleground, I stopped breathing for moment. However, being non-strategists, and with a large group with varying strengths and predispositions to evil, neither Jessica nor Megan felt qualified to head up the attack. We needed a leader, and it sure as hell wasn't me.

"Carrie." Megan placed a hand on my shoulder. "It's now or never, girl. We can't do this without him."

I ran a hand through my hair and nodded. "Okay, I'll call."

I padded into Lucas's kitchen and leaned my back against the far wall, the same place Reid had cornered me before he darted out of the house.

Earlier, I'd decided that telling Mike over the phone would be something only a jerk-friend would do. Like breaking up with someone in a text instead of in person. Mike deserved better. So, my plan was to wait until after baseball practice, call him, and have him come over to Lucas's house where I'd tell him in person that Lucas was dead, Megan and Jessica were witches, Reid was an incubus, and that we needed his help to kill another incubus who had it in for Reid, Lucas, and me. Breathe in.

After three rings, I considered hanging up and trying again later, but on the fourth, Mike picked up.

Crap.

"Hey, you. I haven't heard from you in a while."

"Yeah, I know. Sorry about that. I've…been busy," I said, twirling a lock of hair around my index finger. "Um, hey, I was kinda wondering if you had any plans for the night?"

"Well, I was going to watch some mermaid show with Mandy, but if you have a better offer…"

My heart literally took a nose dive into my stomach at the mention of Mandy. She was half my reason for not wanting Mike to do this. "Oh, well, I don't want to ruin sister time."

"Carrie, I was joking. What's up?"

I sighed into the receiver, knowing full well that Mandy probably *had* planned on them watching mermaids.

I'm sorry, squirt.

"I'm at Lucas's, and I was wondering if you would come over?"

"You're kidding, right? You want me to come to Lucas's house? He not enough entertainment for you?" His voice dripped with disappointment, and I flashbacked to when he'd showed up at Renae's Antiques.

"No...I—"

Mike interrupted my mumbling. "Is everything okay, Carrie? You don't sound so good."

"I'm fine, I just...please? We need to talk."

He blew into the phone as he relented. "Okay. Text me the address and give me an hour."

"Thanks. Oh, and can you not tell anyone that you're coming here?"

"This is getting weird, Carrie."

I made a face into the air. "You have no idea." I switched the phone to the other ear to give myself a moment. "I promise, I'll explain everything when you get here."

"Yeah, well, I'm looking forward to it," he droned out.

"See you soon."

Memories of Susan Taylor's funeral whipped through my mind, reminding me why she'd died. The demons had targeted her for helping us, and she'd paid for it with her life. Wasn't I doing the same thing with Mike?

I hit end and slid down the wall, knocking my head back against it. "Stupid, stupid, stupid."

Closing my eyes, I let out a long sigh.

"Jess?" I called out.

"Yeah?" She stepped into the kitchen as if she'd

been listening in right around the corner.

"He's on his way. Let me talk to him first, though."

"Sure thing." She smiled sympathetically and walked over to me, sliding down the wall with me. "I know how hard this is for you, and if it's any consolation, if we defeat Carver, Mike will walk out alive. I swear it."

"And unharmed?"

Jessica swallowed, and I took that as a "no." "I don't think any of us will get that lucky."

"And if we don't defeat Carver?"

Jessica averted her gaze.

"Come on, Jess. Be straight with me here."

She looked up, her eyes locking on mine. "None of us survive."

"We *will* kill Carver. I won't let him live after what he did to you." Lucas appeared in the doorway, and the sight of him sent a jolt of relief through me. To me, he'd never looked more amazing than he did at that moment.

I scrambled to my feet and ran to him, jumping into his arms and wrapping my legs around his waist. "You're okay!" I showered his neck with kisses, slowly moving to his mouth. He kissed me firmly, separating his lips so I could drink him in. Right then, the stars were perfectly aligned.

"I'm so sorry for acting like I did when…" I murmured against his mouth.

He swept the back of his hand down my cheek. "No, baby. You weren't yourself. The poison killing your soul controlled you."

From somewhere next to me, I heard Jess clear

her throat and I swore she was smiling when she did. "I'll leave you two alone for a minute."

Lucas crushed me against him as if…well, as if I'd died and had been brought back to life again. His head lowered and cool lips pressed into my neck.

"I'm perfect, Care; I have you."

A tear slipped from my eye, and I buried my face in his shoulder, breathing him in. His perfect scent washed through me. Consuming me.

Then, suddenly, I could feel Lucas in my head and all over me. His presence filled me up, making me whole. Sure, in the past I'd felt this before, but this time it was stronger. Much stronger.

I sucked in a breath at the sensation, allowing it to engulf me. When it passed, I smiled at the wonderful flutters beating in my stomach.

Legs still hugging him, I leaned back a little in his arms to meet his gaze. "Incenamus?" I asked, sensing that whatever just overwhelmed me had overwhelmed him as well.

He nodded. "Yeah."

"How'd you do it? How am I…?"

"Alive?" he finished for me, pressing his lips on mine again. "I placed one hand on your forehead, the other over your heart, and said the words in the book. Incenamus did the rest."

I studied him for a moment. Dark, disheveled hair that looked as though he'd run a hand through it a dozen times, emerald eyes, and a smile that entranced me enveloped my senses.

Lucas was amazing. Better than amazing.

"You gave up—"

"Nothing," he finished, a thumb gliding over my lips. "I gave up nothing, nothing that I couldn't live without."

"But Megan said your soul will no longer draw you to the rest of it. How will you be able—"

Stopping me, Lucas placed a palm over my heart. "It doesn't matter. My soul lives in here now. Where it belongs."

His words sounded so sweet, but still. "If part of it is in me, does that mean…Will you cross over?"

"When I read the words out of the book, the power drew from my spirit, connected to my lost soul, and brought back half for you. The other half is still out there somewhere, waiting for me to find it and leave this world."

A sliver of hope made my heart beat faster. "Can we use the book then, to find the other half?"

Lucas shook his head. "No. That's not what the book is about. It's only about the secrets of our connection, nothing more. I think," he paused, running his fingers through my hair, "I think that's the point. There's no magic that will help me find my soul. Like searching for it is part of the journey to leaving this world and moving on to the next."

I frowned. "So, we're back to square one. And now we have even less time to find it—or be together before you fade away."

"Giving part of my soul to you wasn't even a question, and I'd do it again in an instant." Lucas cupped my chin between his fingers. "I love you, Care."

***

Laughter and applause broke our reunion, and we meandered into the living room.

I nudged Lucas in the ribs. "What's this?"

Megan stood in front of the television in the corner with a bowl of grapes. Reid sat in the armchair, and Jess was perched on the far end of the sofa.

"Ready, Reid?" Megan asked.

"Let it fly, baby."

It seemed to defeat Carver, we needed Reid, so for now, he'd been forgiven. At least on the outside. I, on the other hand, still had my doubts about the guy.

Megan aimed a grape and tossed it at him. It fell short and Reid lunged for it. The grape bounced off his chin and landed in Jess's lap.

Megan laughed, and Jessica handed the grape over to Reid, who popped it up himself and caught it in his mouth.

"That, my love, is fun," Lucas said, answering my question. "Come on. We could use some time to let go for awhile." He tugged me behind him to the sofa.

I guess without Mike in the know yet, there was no need to talk strategy until he arrived. So, of course, everyone jumped face-first into play mode.

"Heads up, Lucas." Megan lobbed a grape into the air as we rounded the corner.

Lucas threw his head back, opened his mouth, and the grape fell inside. Nothin' but net.

"That's how it's done, Reid," Megan teased.

Her lightheartedness with the incubus made me a little uneasy.

"My turn! My turn!" Jessica scooted to the edge of the sofa. Whatever—besides my death—prompted her somberness since coming to Iowa seemed to have been pushed aside for now. Now she was her fun-loving self. Much better.

"Okay, here it comes." Megan launched the grape in the air.

Jessica muttered a word in Latin, and the grape stopped and hovered in mid-air. She offered a sly grin in Megan's direction, stood up, and plucked the grape out of the air. Sticking it in her mouth, she took a bow.

"Cheater," Megan muttered and shot Jess a wink. "How about you, Carrie? Ready for this?"

I groaned. Even before I died, I'd never been good at catching flying objects in my mouth. I opened up anyway and watched as Megan let the grape fly at my face. She tried to be gentle, but it soared through the air and smacked me square in the forehead. Not to let Jessica out do me, I picked it off the cushion, stood up, ate it—and took a bow.

"And that's how it's done," I repeated Megan's tease to Reid.

Applause erupted, and I stayed on my feet for an encore, which I caught with Jessica's freaking awesome cheater trick.

Megan went around the room again, launching grapes into the air for Lucas, Jessica, and Reid. It was a much-needed break, the calm before the storm. The tension was still there, but we camouflaged it well.

As soon as Mike knocked on the front door, though, reality struck, and the game was over. Time to get back to business.

In the silence, all eyes flashed to me. I scooted off the sofa and sighed. "Let me talk with him outside first."

Hesitant, Lucas let my hand slip from his. I was sure he didn't want me out of his sight as much I didn't want him out of mine. This was only Mike, though, and I wanted to get this over with.

I opened the door, and Mike stood there, pointing toward the sky. "Looks like a storm is brewing."

"You could say that."

He stuffed his hands in his pockets. "You called me over; are you going to invite me in?"

I stepped onto Lucas's tiny porch, closing the door behind me. "Let's talk out here." I sat down on the step, and Mike did the same. He ruffled his still-wet blond hair and leaned forward on his knees, cocking his head to me.

"So, what's up?"

I took a deep breath and let it out slowly as I stared at the sidewalk. "You said once that you believe in ghosts."

"Yeah…"

"How about other creatures? Like, witches and vampires and stuff?"

Once it was out of my mouth, I realized how stupid I sounded.

"Uh," he hesitated. "No, I guess."

I peered up into the sky, holding my breath. Gray clouds rolled in, fully blocking the sun. For two in the afternoon, it sure looked more like late evening. The dreariness reminded me that I didn't have time for small talk. Carver was coming tonight.

"What if I told you that I believe in all of it? Ghosts, witches, vampires, demons, incubi? That there's a whole other world living around us. With us."

Mike studied me for a minute, probably waiting for me to burst into laughter and tell him I was only kidding.

He smoothed a finger over his chin. "If it weren't you, I'd say you were crazy."

Yeah, me too.

"But I am me."

He nodded, pursing his lips. "Then I'd say okay."

"'Okay' as in what? You're going to take my word for it and trust me, or you're cool with having whack-job friend?"

Mike chuckled, his hazel irises morphing into a beautiful gold color in his amusement. "I have more whack-job friends than you. Have you met Logan?"

I giggled, thinking of Mike's unreliable co-captain who'd asked me to place bets on their losing the game.

His face turned serious. "I mean okay, as in I trust you. Friends do that—trust each other."

I chewed on the inside of my cheek. Unfortunately, I knew from experience that trust only went so far with some people, i.e., my father. "This isn't me giving you answers for a review sheet, Mike."

With gentle strokes, he pushed wind-blown strands of hair away from my face. "Yeah, I know that." His tongue rolled over his lips as his gaze dropped to mine for a second. "I'm on your side, Carrie. For whatever."

I glanced away at his words, knots tightening in my stomach. "You might as well come inside then. We need your help."

Honestly, I wasn't sure what I wanted him say. Part of me, though, hoped he'd tell me I was crazy and walk away from this mess.

I pushed up off the step, and Mike followed me into Lucas's house. I shivered from nerves. What would he think when he found out the truth about Lucas?

Mike sauntered in like he owned the place, seemingly unfazed by the others in the room staring at him. And here I'd thought his cockiness, as Lucas put it, was a façade.

"Um, you might want to sit down," I said, and Reid actually offered the armchair to Mike. Impressive.

Mike nodded to the girls before he settled in as if he were here for movie night. Relaxed, he leaned back, arms propped up on the side cushions.

"Hey Luke," he said. "Nice place—a little drafty, but nice. Got anything to drink?"

Lucas's brows rose, and I snickered to myself.

"Thanks. There's some soda in the fridge. Go ahead—help yourself, man," Lucas answered, mimicking Mike by leaning back and making himself comfortable.

Mike snorted a quiet laugh, a smug grin on his face. "Maybe later. So, Carrie says you need *my* help."

Lucas massaged his chin, and before they could

continue their pissing contest, I positioned myself in front of the television, ready to do the talking.

"Since there's no best place to start..." I cracked my knuckles, and on my way around the room, I pointed to each person as I said their name. "Megan's a witch, Jessica's a witch, over there is Reid, he's an almost-incubus, and Lucas is dead." I held my breath, waiting for Mike to react.

When he didn't even flinch, I continued. I caught him up on the events of last summer, spending more time than needed on how Incenamus linked Lucas and me together. I expected something out of him—an eye roll, perked brows, a grimace—but he listened with the best poker face I'd ever seen. Dude had skills.

"Got it," he said after I'd finished. Then he nodded toward Reid. "So, where does he come in?"

Megan must have noticed the bad-ass glare I shot at the incubus, because she jumped up and filled Mike in, leaving out where I died. The knowledge of Reid's back and forth with Carver seemed to be too much to add to the pile right now.

"We've been searching for the person who saw Lucas after he died, thinking he may hold some clues to the whereabouts of Lucas's soul. In our attempts, we came across a name: Carver. My sources say if anyone knows, it's him."

"Only Carver isn't what we expected," Lucas interjected. "A half-demon, yes, but one more brutal and cunning than most, even of *his* kind."

"This Carver, he's half-demon, half-what?" Mike asked, tapping his fingers on the armrest.

"Human," Megan answered.

Mike's brows shot up. "A human…did *stuff*…with a demon?"

His gaze wandered to Reid as I muttered, "Don't ask."

"And you… ?" Mike breathed out, not bothering to finish his thought.

"I'm an experiment—made, not born," Reid huffed, probably tired of answering the same questions the rest of us had asked.

"Huh," Mike tsked. "Okay, go on."

"Instead of killing solely to survive, as most incubi do, Carver is a psychopath, murdering innocents by stealing their souls for fun," Megan continued. "Somehow, he figured out how to create other incubi out of mortals, and Reid is his first."

"First successful one anyway." Reid leaned up against the wall, crossing his arms.

"Okay, let me guess the rest. Reid is who you actually wanted, right? But instead, somehow you pissed off Carver, and now he's coming here to bury you all," Mike said, flicking a look at Lucas and crowning himself King of the Hill. "Am I close?"

"Pretty much." I nodded.

Mike's finger tick-tocked from me to Lucas and back. "What does he want with you two?"

"He has some grudge against me from a long time ago, and since he can't kill me, he plans to hurt me by hurting Carrie, we think," Lucas answered.

"Well, shit. Nice work there, Lucas. You have successfully brought a madman—"

"Mike," I pleaded, "it's not his fault."

"Yeah, it is," Lucas murmured. "And I take full

responsibility."

My eyes flitted to him. In a tiny motion, I shook my head.

"This is Carver's fault," Reid piped up. "Beginning to end, let's agree on that. The details aren't important right now."

"Reid's right," Megan agreed. "Carver is the enemy here."

Mike hunched forward. "So, what do you need me for? Am I the peace offering or the bait?"

"Actually, I'm the bait," I said quietly, repeating what Jess, Megan, and I concluded from our earlier conversation.

That didn't go over well.

"What the hell, Lucas?" Mike stood up. "Are you out of your damn mind?"

"I haven't agreed to this, man, so back off."

Jessica stepped between them, throwing her arms out. "Stop it, you two. We can't defeat Carver by being at each others' throats. We need everyone here if we're going back inside the Moore House."

Chapter 23

I bowed my head. It had been Jessica and Megan's plan all along. Ironic that our only escape was to go back to the demon house that tried to kill us last summer, but with the rift to Hell inside, it was our best shot.

Jess lowered her arms, frowning. "Speaking of everyone, where's Julianna?"

"The Moore House? And who's Julianna?" Mike asked. To him, the only new face in the room was Reid.

"The last member of this 'team,'" I said, using air quotes. "She's a vampire."

Mike closed his eyes, pinching the bridge of his nose. "Can we talk outside again?"

I gave Lucas an apologetic glance. "Yeah, sure."

Mike opened the front door and waved a hand in front of him.

"This is crazy, you know that, right?" Mike said as soon as we were both outside. "I can't decide if I'm in a dream or some crazy-ass nightmare."

"Both?" I suggested, grimacing. "You said you

trusted me—"

"Oh, I trust you all right, but that doesn't make this any less insane. Your boyfriend is dead, Carrie. DEAD!" Mike tilted his face to the sky. "This shit is messed up."

"You can walk away," I said. "We won't blame you—I won't blame you. It would safer."

"Safer for who? Me? Then what about you?"

"I'll be fine. Lucas will take care of me, as always."

"Lucas?" Mike dropped his head, gaze still trained on me. "He's done a bang-up job so far. You're in the same room as an incubus, and why the hell is a vampire on its way? God, Carrie." He paused, and I could see the wheels in his head turning. "I believe you. I've seen it, but Carrie, this isn't a game. This is dangerous shit."

I closed the gap between us, anger flushing my cheeks. "You don't think I realize that? Who do you think you are? Since the moment I stepped foot in Villisca, I've been a part of this. I know more about what we're up against than you ever will, so don't you dare insinuate that I—"

Mike braced me with both hands. "—I don't want to lose you, and I'm not walking away."

"Lucas can hear you, you know," I whispered, mentally attempting to break away from how Mike's words struck me.

"Good. He needs to know that he's not the only one who cares about you."

I took a step backwards, Mike's hands falling from my face. "Trust me, you've made that loud and clear."

Above us, storm clouds rolled in, and a rumble of thunder sounded in the distance, bringing back memories of last summer.

"If you're staying then come on," I said. "We don't want to be caught out here alone when Julianna arrives."

Inside, Lucas shot Mike a glare and pulled me close—yeah, he'd heard every word. Mike went back to the armchair, avoiding Lucas. He leaned forward on his knees and picked up where he left off.

"Assuming Julianna will be here soon, what's the plan and where do I come in?"

"That's just it, Captain," Jess told him. "You're running the show. Your plan."

"It's where you excel, right? Leading the team," I said.

Mike scanned the room, stopping momentarily on each person. "You're telling me Carver is on his way *tonight*, and you don't have a plan?"

"Oh, no. We have a plan. *You're* the plan. We gathered the players from my vision, and the only way we can win is if you lead us," Jess explained, arching a brow. "Please."

"That's the future you saw?"

"If we want to survive, yes."

Mike's eyes landed on me, his expression reminding me of how crazy this was. He wasn't wrong; we had to be crazy if this was going to work.

"You're all out of your freaking minds, you know that, right?" Mike rolled his eyes, reaching for the coffee table and scooting it to him. "I need a notebook, a pen, and a list of the special powers Carver has. I need to know everything about our opponent and everything each of you are capable of. We only have a few hours, so let's get to work."

***

Mike ran his fingers through his hair. "Okay, Megan first: can you explain that again in English? If Carver is a…"

"Cambion. They're half demons," Jessica finished.

"Right. If Carver's half-demonic, why are we going to the Moore House, and how will the full demons destroy him?" Mike asked, weaving together what was happening now with what I'd explained from last summer's events.

"Cambions are also *half* human, Mike. Demons are the spawn of Hell, and incubi, unlike other cambions, are the spawn of demons. They're tainted with human life. I can't pretend to know how a demon thinks, but it's like cambions are competition for evil doings, so they need to be wiped out," Megan explained.

Mike tapped the end of his pencil on the notebook. "So we don't really have good versus evil here?"

"More like good versus evil versus evil-er."

"In a language I can understand, offense/defense-wise, where does that leave us?"

Megan twisted to look at Reid, who dropped his crossed arms and stepped forward. "Essentially, it's us against Carver. However, with me and Julianna in the mix—especially Julianna, whose soul died years ago—you need to be careful. Julianna's unpredictable at best, but don't ever think she's out for anything other than her own personal gain. She's on no one's side except her own. As for me, I'll control this monster inside me the best I can, but make damn sure to have a back-up plan just in case."

"Even with Julianna, two witches, Lucas, and you, the Moore House with the demons inside is our only option?" Mike asked.

"It's our best option," Megan clarified. "Less room for error."

"Seems to me that leaves a lot of room for error."

Megan snickered, nodding in agreement. "There always is when you're dealing with evil."

***

The air in the living room had begun to thicken again, and my eyes wandered to Reid. Jessica sensed it too and called me into the kitchen for a pow-wow.

Standing at the doorway, she muttered a phrase under her breath, but as far as I could tell, the spell did nothing.

"Sound barrier," she explained.

"Because of Lucas?" I asked, though I didn't know why he needed to be kept in the dark about our conversation.

"And Reid and Julianna, if she shows up. Especially Julianna."

The sound proofing worked only for noise, so I

could still see everyone gathered around the coffee table. Reid's hands clenched and unclenched at his sides as he worked to keep the monster at bay for a little while longer.

"You think he'll cycle when we need him to?" I asked, watching his knee bounce in agitation.

"He'd better. Our lives could depend on it. He said that willing the demon to come out is fairly easy, unlike keeping it caged inside," Jessica said.

I twisted around and leaned back against the counter. "So, what did you want to talk about?"

"This," she said, slipping her crossbody purse over her head. She set it beside me and unzipped it. From inside, she pulled out a small red-tinted glass bottle, pointed at the end—the same bottle that Megan had given her before they left for Corvin Castle and the Cambion Council.

"What is it?" I asked.

"Liquid Fire," Jess answered. "To kill a cambion—specifically, a vampire."

"A vampire? You mean Julianna?"

"She's helping us, sure, but that doesn't mean she can be trusted. You heard Reid. This is our back-up plan." Jess handed me the vial, and I turned it over in my palm. "The potion is almost impossible to make."

"Wait, you said cambion in general. Why can't we just use it on Carver?"

"At one point in my visions, it was a possibility, but something always went wrong. When the images cleared, the Moore House and the demons became the best answer. This potion works a little differently with incubi, but if it comes to it, we can use it on him—or Reid, if necessary. I doubt it will come to that, though. It's not what I've seen. Keep it safe, Carrie."

My head snapped up in surprise. "What? Me?"

"It has to be you."

"Why? Where will you be?" I shook my head. "No, I can't. Here." I held it out to her.

Jessica took a step back, away from my outstretched hand. "In case you need it."

The small crack in her voice made me uneasy, and I backed down. "Will I need it?" I swallowed, afraid of the answer.

She avoided the question, blinking and shifting her eyes to the potion. "To use it, twist the cap and pour the contents directly on skin. The closer you get to a vital organ or artery, the quicker it will work. As soon as you do it, though, get out fast. Understand?"

"Yeah, I understand," I said, taking a cue from Stacy and sticking the bottle between my breasts like she did with her lip gloss.

"Good."

***

"That's not going to work, Mike," Megan said as if she'd been repeating it for hours.

"If I say it's going to work, it's going to work."

Reid's cycle had diminished for now, and Jessica and I rejoined the others.

Pieces of paper coated the top of the coffee table. A diagram of the Moore House block mixed with Mike's game strategy X's, O's, and arrows dotted the pages.

"No, it's not," Megan insisted. "You have to use Carrie to draw in Carver. There's no other option."

Lucas sat on the sofa, arms crossed. "Me. Use me."

"Do you know how ridiculous that sounds?" Megan groaned.

"Reid said Carver wanted to make sure I received some message by him killing Carrie, and I need to know what the hell he's talking about. If you use me, he can deliver it directly."

"Carver can't hurt you, Lucas, you're already dead. He's not going to risk his life by entering the Moore House for you, when he can't do anything to you. That's why he's after Carrie."

Lucas raked a hand through his hair, frustrated.

"Guys, it's Reid and Carrie that will draw him, not the two of you." Megan's voice lowered as she shifted her gaze between the Lucas and Mike.

Mike rubbed his face with his palm, his hand settling on his chin. "What other options do we have?"

"None."

"And what if Reid cycles early, huh?" Lucas asked. "Who's going to save Carrie then?"

From the corner of the room, Reid stepped forward. "I won't let it happen. I want Carver dead as much as you do, Luke, and I will fight the urge with everything I have. I'll control this thing, and I'll protect her, I swear."

Lucas stood up to face him. "Like last time?"

"You don't trust the demon within me, I get that. But trust *me*, Lucas."

"Why should I? From the second you stepped foot in this town, you've done nothing but lie and deceive, and I can't figure why you're still here. So, if you're going to tell me something, at least tell me something real."

"Okay," Reid agreed. "The night Carver kidnapped me, he was actually targeting my best friend. You, dude. He wanted you, and I saved your sorry ass. You came out of that attack with a concussion and eight stitches, and I was turned into a monster. How's that for real?"

The room went quiet.

"Why did he want me?" Lucas's low voice rumbled in my chest, making me ache for him.

"You got in his way, man."

"How?"

Reid stared at the floor before locking his eyes on Lucas. "Your sister, Rachel. You saved her from him, and he never forgot."

Slowly, Lucas lowered himself onto the sofa, fading into transparency. My hand fell through him onto the cushion.

Lucas had a sister. And suddenly, Lucas's words from the hospital rang out in my head. *"Then I saw Mandy and how she ran up and hugged you, wondering if her brother might die. Do I have a sister? Does she still think about me?"*

"Lucas?" I whispered, reaching out to touch the air that was his cheek.

"I have a sister," he murmured to himself. "Rachel."

After a few moments, Lucas re-materialized beside me, his glowing irises dimmer. He faced

Reid again, clenching his jaw.

"When you said I saved her from Carver, what did you mean?"

"I think you know, dude. It's what we incubi do."

Lucas's nostrils flared. "Kill her?"

Reid circled the sofa to stand in front of Lucas. "He'd have his fun first, but you rescued her, took him by surprise and beat him up. It pissed him off. We got her out of there—"

"We?"

"Yeah. I was your wingman. Rachel was…" Reid trailed off, his shoulders falling. "Rachel needed us that night, and we were there for her. Tonight, I won't let you down, man. I want to kill this son of a bitch as much you do."

Lucas rose to his feet, almost nose to nose with Reid. Reid didn't budge, and I worried from the glint in Lucas's eye if Reid should back away.

Lucas thrust out a hand. "If you're telling the truth and we beat him before, let's beat him again, but you sure as hell better be telling the truth."

"I bet my life on it, man."

They shook hands, and Lucas nodded at Mike. "Reid can handle this."

Mike's gaze flashed to me, and he sighed. "Everyone good on the play then?"

Hushed yeses hissed out. Outside, a crack of lightning ripped through the sky, brightening Lucas's living room for a second. I slumped into the sofa; time was running out.

A knock on the door startled me. As if sensing who was on the other side, Lucas instantly slid me closer to him.

"I hope that's our last teammate," Mike mumbled, and Megan rushed to the door.

"Julianna," Megan greeted. "Thanks for coming. Please, come—" The vampire stepped inside. "—in."

The girl in front of me had long black hair flowing down her back, shining with unnatural brilliance under the canister lights. Black eyes scoured the room of people, settling too long on Mike and me, the only humans. Dark lips reddened even more when she licked them, zeroing in on Mike like she wanted to taste him.

"This is Julianna," Megan introduced her unnecessarily.

Standing less than five feet tall, the thirteen year-old Cambion Council member strutted over to Mike, the heels of her black boots clicking on the wood floor. She stopped in front of him, slowly bending over until their noses touched.

I jerked forward, but Lucas held me back. "She won't try that here," he whispered into my ear. I glanced at Megan, who had a hand poised ready and a spell on the tip of her tongue.

"What's up?" Mike said casually to Julianna, not even flinching.

Beside me, Lucas suppressed a chuckle, for the first time amused by Mike's cocky attitude.

"Aren't you going to offer me your seat, *Mortal*?" In her thick Spanish accent, Julianna said 'Mortal' as if it were a dirty word.

"Nah, I'm good." Mike leaned forward, pushing Julianna back as he did. "Since you finally decided to show up, there're some things we need to go over: a.k.a., the plan of attack."

Oh, Mike. Let's not piss off a vampire, 'kay?

Julianna's brow furrowed. Since she died, no one had probably spoken to her like that, especially not a *mortal*.

"As you can see here," Mike continued, ignoring her lethal expression, "I've tracked your movements with the X sub j. Now, I understand the Moore House is as deadly for you as it is for Carver, and that's where Jessica comes in."

Apparently it took a few seconds for her surprise to wear off, because Julianna suddenly leaped toward Mike, her arms outstretched. Megan dove forward and Jess bolted to her feet, their palms up, and Julianna stopped in mid-air like Jessica's grape.

Untouched and seemingly unfazed, Mike peered up at her. "See? Jessica's pretty good," Mike said.

"If you want my protection, I suggest you keep your hands and mouth off my friends," Jessica warned.

"I will not be treated like a house pet," Julianna hissed. "Especially not by a *mortal*."

Again with the mortal stuff? Geez.

"Yes, well, that mortal is leading this attack, and if you want to live through it, I suggest you listen to him."

"Or I can see myself out."

"Absolutely, there's the door. But let me warn you first, you leave here tonight and let Carver survive, your seat on the Council will be *very* short-lived." With her free hand, Jessica pointed to her eye, reminding Julianna what she'd fake-seen.

"If you help us, I'll make sure the Sisters of the Seven Stars hear of your valiant efforts in this matter," Megan added. "They protect the other council member, Sorin, do they not? Prove you're worthy, and they may do the same for you."

Julianna sneered. "Put me down, *bruja*."

"As you wish," Jess said, both she and Megan lowering their hands and giving the vampire the dignity of landing on her feet.

Julianna made a show of dusting off her skin-tight pants and tank top. She narrowed her eyes at Mike. "Fine, *Mortal*. What do you want from me?"

Chapter 24

I didn't like the way Julianna watched Mike, and I was beginning to question why we needed her in the first place. She sent off a serious *I can't wait to get you alone so I can suck you dry* vibe. Apparently, Jess caught me boring holes into the barely-teenaged vampire, because she nudged me in the ribs.

"This won't work without her," Jess said. "Trust me. If there was another way…" she combed through her hair with her fingers, pausing for a second. "I'd gladly take it."

Outside, the thunder rolled, and gusts of wind rattled the windows. That was our cue.

"You ready?" Mike said, addressing all of us but only looking at me. I kind of wished he wouldn't.

I nodded, and Lucas squeezed my hand. With his other hand, he brushed some of the fallen strands of hair out of my face. "Listen to Reid, okay? I won't be far away, and if I have to sweep into that damn house and—"

"You can't," I cut him off. "Not until Carver is

dead, and the demons are gone. Besides, the two of us can't be in there at the same time. Ever."

Or we'll have a repeat of last summer.

"I don't care. I won't lose you, Carrie."

"If you lose me, we lose everyone. It's all or nothing tonight," I repeated what Jessica had told me earlier.

Lucas pressed a palm against my chest, my heart pounding in response. "Take care of my soul, baby."

"Always."

As if no one was around, Lucas leaned in and kissed me. A pang of fear dipped into my chest, but it didn't belong to me. It was Lucas's, and the force of it made me wince; my body was having problems adjusting to its strength.

I broke away from him, still trembling from the overpowering sensation lingering inside me. Lucas cupped my face, the intensity of his stare drilling into me.

"Be safe," he murmured.

In the corner of my vision, I saw Reid's shadow stir until he stood next to me. "Time to go."

Reluctantly, Lucas let go of me and I took a final scan of the people in the room, avoiding Julianna, who oozed more evil than Reid in incubus form.

Megan sat with Mike on the floor, taking a final inspection of the diagram he'd created. "See you on the other side," she told me.

Mike said nothing, his gaze holding mine until I looked away.

Jessica tapped her chest twice and nodded. As she did it, the vial of Liquid Fire in my bra shifted, reminding me of its presence. "You know what to do," she mouthed.

"Come on, Carrie," Reid said, opening the door for me.

I crossed the room as a shock of thunder rocked Lucas's house. Earlier, I'd been fine with our arrangement of me as the bait, but now that the time had come, I wasn't so sure. From what Jessica had said, she could only see the outcome of the plan and tiny glimpses of the in-between, which meant we were mostly in the dark about how this would play out.

I took a final glance over my shoulder at Lucas.

His green irises glowed as they settled on me, holding me in place.

I'll be okay. I love you.

Lucas bobbed his head once, letting me know he'd heard me before I followed Reid out the door.

***

Reid and I took my car and parked it a block away from the Moore House so as to not attract unwanted attention. To this day, I couldn't drive by it and not shudder, and tonight, I'd be back inside its walls. Ironic that *this* was the one place that held the power to save my life.

"You good?" Reid asked as soon as we stepped over the property line of Lot 310.

"Yeah, I think so."

"Listen, Carrie, all you need to do is stick to the plan. Don't make eye contact with him. Or me, for that matter. I'll get you out as soon as I can."

"Right." I tilted my face to the sky, watching the clouds continue to roll in. Since last summer, I'd come to dread the rain.

"Okay then let's get you settled inside, and I'll go find Carver."

I let out a breath. "Fantastic."

***

This plan totally sucks.

Even though we'd talked about it and decided it was the best way to go, I still hated that I was now tied up to a chair in the middle of the Moore House kitchen, in the dark no less. At the moment, I loathed the fact Reid was playing double agent again and I couldn't help doubting that he'd ever stopped.

Lucas trusts him.

What if Lucas was wrong, though? With Reid, only little bits of truth seemed to come out of him at a time, and I'd bet my left kidney that we hadn't seen it all yet.

But it was too late to turn back now. The knots Reid tied in this rope were impossible to break. Before he left, he had me struggle against them to make sure they were secure enough. My only hope hung on Reid's ability to convince Carver the two of them were still a team and lead him to this ambush—inside the Moore House. Reid better be a smooth talker.

In my experience with Reid's mouth, so far so good.

Raindrops landed on the window across from

me, and to pass the time I listed off Jessica's vision points in my mind, leaving out the ones that obviously came to pass when Carver killed me.

Okay, one: *It was raining this time.* Check.

Two: *A kitchen.* I rolled my eyes—obviously check.

Three: *People—I can't make out who—are fighting.* Soon-to-be check.

Four: *A window breaking.*

Five: *I hear screaming, and I see blood. Someone is cut, I think.*

Six: *A wooden chair shattered into pieces on the floor.* I was sitting on a wooden chair, but as of now, it remained in one piece. If this was the one then half-check, I guess.

Seven: *Numbers—314.* I had no clue what that meant. The Moore House sat on Lot 310, and the house numbers were not 314. We're either missing something, or this glimpse was from a different situation still to come.

Eight: *Nails scrape over an arm.*

Nine: *A table, split down the middle.* Under the window being pelted with raindrops stood an old wooden table. That must be the one.

Ten: *A body is thrown through the air. The person, they're not moving. I think they're dead.* I squeezed my eyelids closed. *Please be Carver.*

Eleven: *A cemetery with a large oak tree.* I had no clue where this fit in either.

Twelve: *Silverware falling from a drawer.* Probably from the upcoming fight.

After twelve small glimpses from the future, Carver would be dead. We could do this.

The sound of footsteps on the back porch jolted my heart into my throat, and I froze.

I guess it's showtime.

***

I didn't look up when they walked in. Instead, I focused on a stain at the foot of the wrought-iron stove.

"You should be dead." The sound of Carver's voice made my skin crawl, and I held back a shiver. He came closer, circling behind me. From my peripheral vision, I saw Reid hanging out at the door.

Carver grabbed a handful of my hair and yanked my head back. I cried out, not expecting the force.

"Nice job, Reid," Carver said, tugging at the ropes securing me to the chair.

His mouth slid in next to my ear, and goose bumps pricked over my skin. "Gave. You. His. Soul. How touching." Slowly, he ran his fingers over my neck, and I gulped. "Lucas, Lucas, Lucas," he murmured. "Always ruining my fun, but not this time. Oh, no. Not this time."

"Fun is a fairly subjective term," I sassed.

Suddenly, Carver was in front of me, straddling my lap and still holding my hair behind me. God, I hated how attractive this incubus was—or was making me think he was. Just like when Reid cycled, the air around me thickened, and my body responded to the seductive presence Carver radiated.

Then he backhanded me across the face.

"You speak when I tell you to speak, otherwise keep your damn mouth shut."

Already, I could feel my cheek welting up.

Carver sighed, his breath spilling over the burn on my face. "I thought taking *your* soul tasted sweet, but now I get Lucas's? This couldn't have worked out any better." Carver's fingers snaked down my neck again until he reached the infinity necklace Lucas gave me for Christmas. He tore it off me like it was nothing and tossed it at Reid's feet. "Lucas might want that back. Eternity ends tonight."

"That was mine." I spit in Carver's face, furious.

"I love it when they're feisty, don't you, Reid?" Carver wiped his face with the back of hand before he smacked me again. "I think you'll keep that pretty little mouth shut now, won't you?"

I held back the tears as Carver let go of my hair and balled up the neckline of my shirt in both of his hands. The sound of it ripping in half cut through my ears, and I half-expected Reid to come to my rescue, but he didn't move a muscle. Carver stripping me down wasn't part of the plan, and I didn't know what would come next. The guy was an incubus after all.

"Hey, dude," Reid said from the sidelines. "Do we really have time for *that*, tonight? The demons will be out soon, and we don't want to be caught in here when they do."

Carver didn't answer, and Reid didn't push, letting Carver reposition himself. He separated my knees and pressed his hips in between my legs, grinning as if he was going to get lucky tonight.

Curling an arm around my neck, he gripped onto me and pressed his lips against mine. At the same time, he slipped a hand into my bra.

What the hell, Reid! Do something!

The incubus by the door didn't budge, and I had a hard time believing that he was on my team at the moment. He was letting Carver fondle me!

"Ah," Carver moaned against my mouth, giving one of my breasts a strong squeeze. "Delicious."

"You're disgusting," I spat, at the same time hoping he'd do it again.

Ugh. I hate incubi.

Carver laughed and backed away from me, tossing something to Reid.

Oh, crap. The Liquid Fire.

"What's this?" Reid asked, sweeping his gaze from Carver to me, confused.

"She came armed, old friend. Or did *you* give her that?"

Reid pocketed the vial and shook his head. "I know nothing about it. Come on, let's just kill her and get the hell out of here, man. This place is giving me the creeps."

Either Reid was an amazing actor or the fact that I had the potion hidden on me without his knowledge didn't bother him. I desperately hoped for the latter.

"No need to be in a hurry." The evil glint in Carver's eye made me stiffen and press myself into the back of the chair. Already, I'd been inside this house for too long. "What's the fun in killing her quickly?" Carver lowered himself in front of me again, squeezing my chin between his fingers.

"Look at me!"

I shook my head, shutting my eyes. "Never!" I screamed, fighting the urge to obey him.

"Putting you in a trance defeats my purposes, Carrie. I want you to feel and remember everything. And when Lucas finds your dead body, I want him to know how much pain you suffered before you gave up," he said too sweetly, his hands roaming down my chest again.

I heard the swish of his jeans and the old wood floor groaning as Carver moved back around me. My heart thumped in my ears, and I tried to breathe normally. The others should be outside by now, and whatever they were waiting for needed to happen soon.

I understood they needed to wait. They couldn't barge in and expect Carver to stick around until sundown released the demons into the house. We had a small window of opportunity, and I had to hold on for a few more minutes.

Tied behind the back of the chair, my wrists burned from the rope digging into the flesh. I balled my hands then let them out, hoping to help the circulation flow to my fingers, which were beginning to tingle with numbness.

Maybe that's why I didn't feel Carver grab my index finger until he snapped it. Pain shot through my hand, and my scream ricocheted off the walls. Black fuzz filtered into the corners of my vision. I hung my head, clenching my teeth together. It was crazy given the situation, but I didn't want to cry in front of Carver. More ammunition.

Through the mass of my own hair cascading

around me, I peered over at Reid. Yeah, I realized everyone was waiting for the opportune moment to strike, but by then, I could have all my fingers broken. Reid shifted his weight, his eyes trained out the window behind him.

"Dude," he said. "Sunset is in like five minutes. You don't have time for this shit."

Even though the skies were dark with storm clouds, demons never emerged until the threat of daylight had passed for the night.

"If you want to go, there's the door," Carver instructed, breaking my middle finger like a twig.

I bit down hard on my lip, holding back the wail in my throat. I couldn't take this anymore.

"Reid," I breathed. "Please."

I twisted my head to beg him with my gaze.

Reid's eyes flicked to me. Brows furrowed in a scowl, he crossed the room and stopped in front of me.

"Please," I said again, ready for him unleash his inner demon already and make a move against Carver.

Instead, he grabbed a fistful of my hair, keeping my head still, and slapped me across the face. "Shut up, bitch."

My eyes grew wide at the hatred written all over his face. He actually wanted me dead.

"No, no," I sobbed. Lucas had trusted Reid, and for what? "You're a traitor."

Just as Carver had done before, Reid lowered himself in front of me, smoothing my hair like he cared. Stark. Raving. Mad, he was. "What did you expect, Carrie? I'm a monster, not your friend." He grinned at me, his golden irises beginning to fill in with ink. Still staring at me, his voice lowered as he told Carver, "Break another one."

The sound of Carver's laughter as he cracked my pinky cut me to the core, the agony diving deep into me. Bile rose to my mouth. I swallowed it back, but more took its place. The searing pain spreading through my hand threatened to make me pass out.

Five minutes until the demons would come out and play, devouring the incubi and dragging them to Hell.

There was no way I was going to last that long.

Chapter 25

Pain flowed through me, and black splotches clouded my vision. My legs trembled, rocking my whole body with waves of throbbing. I couldn't think anymore.

Eyes jet black, Reid jerked back on my hair again. "Carver, man, let's break her neck and get out of here."

"No. I want her soul—Lucas's soul."

Reid yanked harder and grinned when I shrieked. "Oh, come on, Carrie. I thought you were tougher than this."

"Yeah, well, I thought you were on our side. I guess we both made mistakes," I rasped out.

Carver snapped another finger at my retort, and I screamed, the pain shooting through me, so raw, so severe that it wouldn't allow me to pass out.

"Let. Her. Go." Lucas's voice rumbled low, stirring a mixture of relief and fear inside me.

No! What's he doing in here?

Through the blur of tears, I made out Lucas's form. He stood behind Reid with a knife at Reid's throat. Horrified, Lucas's gaze rolled over me. I knew what he saw, and I knew why he was furious. My shirt ripped down the middle, face swollen, and four broken fingers.

"You're gonna kill me with that?" Reid challenged. "Won't do any good."

"It'll buy me some time, and it'll hurt. Oh, I'll make sure it hurts." Lucas pushed the blade further into Reid's neck, and a trickle of blood flowed down from the cut.

"Well, well. It's nice to see you again, Lucas." The fake kindness in Carver's voice made me want to barf. "I'm so glad you could join us."

"Get away from her," Lucas growled.

Rushed footsteps on the back porch alerted me to the others' arrival. The door crashed open, and Mike and Jessica ran inside. Stopping as soon as he saw me, Mike wore a similar expression to Lucas's just seconds ago. He narrowed his eyes on Carver, his fists clenched at his sides.

Jessica, however, stared at the knife in Lucas's hand. How could she know that Reid had switched sides ... again?

Cautiously, she stepped toward him. "Lucas," she said, reaching out to him.

Lucas jerked away from her touch. "Reid's a traitor, and he'll die with his maker."

"You have to get out of here—you and Carrie together—" Her gaze roamed over the kitchen until her eyes fell on the stairs leading to the attic. "Oh, no. Too late!"

I didn't know what she saw, but I heard the pounding reverberating on the ceiling.

With the two of us, the power of Incenamus over-powered the containment spell that trapped the demons inside. Now, it was broken.

"Ah! Did Lucas not stick to the plan? He *does* that." From behind me, I could feel Carver rest his hands on the back of the chair. "So, I heard you've been looking for me. I'm here now. What can I do for you?"

"You killed Carrie," Lucas hissed.

"True. But it seems like you fixed that little problem." Carver combed his fingers gingerly through my hair, teasing Lucas. Then he dipped his mouth next to my ear as a hand circled around me and massaged my breast. The other wrapped around my throat. My breath hitched when he squeezed. "As I see it, it's a non-issue now."

Lightning fast, Lucas pushed Reid to Jessica and Mike. My super pissed-off boyfriend stood in front of me, poised to throttle Carver.

"I wouldn't come any closer if I were you," Carver warned, tightening his hold on my neck. I choked on my own saliva as I struggled to breathe. "You wouldn't want to be responsible for her death too, would you?"

Lucas's brows shot up. "Too?"

"Don't listen to him, Lucas. He's crazy," I ground out, half-expecting Carver to hurt me again, but he only laughed that evil laugh of his that struck even more fear into me.

"Reid's been holding back on you, huh? Well, let me enlighten you."

Without warning, Carver swung the chair full-force and shot me skidding across the floor. I cried out as my hands glided over the hardwood. My upper back slammed into the doorframe of the pantry, knocking the wind out of me. With my legs over the threshold, the rest of my body stuck out into the kitchen.

Mike thrust toward me, but Carver growled at him. "Don't. Move."

Desperately, I wiggled my wrists around the rope that tied them together. Pain shot up my arm, but I clamped my lips shut to stifle the wail. The more I struggled, the more the threads dug in, tearing into the skin.

I clenched my teeth and pried my eyes open. Lucas's were locked onto me, and I could see him contemplating how to get me out of this house without jeopardizing the plan.

I'm okay. Really.

He didn't look like he believed me.

"Your sister Rachel wanted me, Luke," Carver said, snapping Lucas's attention away from me.

Standing with Mike and Jessica, I noticed Reid flinch at the mention of Rachel's name.

"Oh, she was delicious," Carver continued, licking his lips seductively at her memory. "No wonder you wanted to shield her, man, but really, you were protecting her from the wrong person. I had no intention of taking her soul that night, just her body—until you showed up." Carver swiveled and nodded at Reid, sneering. "Both of you."

Lucas stepped closer to Carver. "You're pissed off because I saved my sister from you, a demonic asshole? Go to Hell."

Carver snickered and shoved Lucas off him. "If

only it were that easy. You see, you didn't save her, Luke. You doomed her. Right, Reid? I mean, if you'd have let *me* have her, she'd be alive today."

Lying on the floor, I felt Lucas's anger grow in my chest. Heat whirled within me, rising until my face was on fire.

Lucas leered, curling his upper lip, eyes burning with hatred. "You killed my sister?"

Carver held up his hands in surrender. "Oh, no. Not me. Her boyfriend did, though. You know, Reid."

As if in slow motion, Lucas faced the other incubus, brows narrowed in surprise. "You?"

"I guess, he also failed to mention how *you* died?" Carver chuckled, amused by the situation. "Yes? Well, I think it might be time to come clean, Reid."

Lucas's stare turned callous. "Did you—"

Suddenly, Reid sprung forward. Arms outstretched, he locked his hands around Carver's neck. In stunned silence, Carver fell backward, crashing to the floor with Reid on top of him.

As soon as Reid leaped, Mike did too—toward me. He dropped to his knees.

"You okay?" he asked.

I shook my head, fighting the whimper on the tip of my tongue. "My wrists."

"I'm on it."

Mike jumped over me and scooted the chair a few inches forward, releasing some of the pressure on my back. In hurried, gentle motions he began to untie the knots. I bit the inside of my cheek to keep from crying as he tugged on the rope biting into me.

With Mike working behind me, I focused on the fight in the middle of the kitchen floor. Reid's fists pounded into Carver's face once, twice, three times before Carver shook off his shock and responded.

Stronger and more agile than Reid, Carver thrust the base of his palm into Reid's chin, snapping his head back. With Reid dazed, Carver wiped the blood from his nose and sniffed. Then, he pulled his knees up to his torso and plunged his feet into Reid's chest, sending him flying backward.

Jessica dove out of the way, but not before Reid crashed into her and slammed her into the door.

Lucas disappeared and reappeared at Jessica's side. Carver vaulted up off the floor, his maniacal gaze pinned on Reid. Rushing forward, Carver swooped down and picked Reid up from the ground. Holding him by the neck, he plastered him to the wall.

"You're weak, Reid. You'll always be weak."

Reid coughed, blood sputtering from his mouth.

"It's why you couldn't take Rachel's soul when you should have, and why Carrie is still alive. You're nothing, Reid. Nothing." Carver knocked Reid's head against the window. Lines snaked through the glass in a spider web, and like before, Reid fought to remain conscious from Carver's beating. "It's no wonder Rachel wanted me instead," Carver snarled. "She couldn't stand the sight of you."

Reid grit his teeth together and growled, jabbing a knee hard into Carver's crotch. With his other leg, Reid steadied a foot on Carver's hip. Then he stepped up and kicked him on the side of the head.

Carver's hand fell from Reid's throat, and Reid ducked low as Carver's fist wound back and blasted through the window. Shards of glass sprayed out.

Jessica's twelve glimpses of the future rushed back to me. Rain. The kitchen—number one and number two. Number three: People fighting. Four: Glass breaking.

Pulling his hand back through the hole, Carver's skin was littered with small pieces of glass. Blood streamed over his arm, and by the incredulous look on his face, I had a feeling the worst was yet to come.

Mike unwrapped a loop of rope from around my wrists, caught one of my broken fingers, and I screamed, tears spilling over my lashes.

Screaming. Blood. Someone is cut. Five.

Seven more and Carver should be dead.

Come on, guys!

"I'm sorry, Carrie," Mike murmured. "Hang on. I'm almost done."

"Hurry," I moaned, biting back the pain mounting with each of Mike's movements as he unwound the rope.

Jessica lifted her head off the floor. Still dazed, she shook it to clear away the haze. Beside her, Lucas said something, and she nodded. She took his hand, and he helped her to her feet, keeping an arm around her shoulders to steady her. Concentrating on the incubi, her lips separated as she began to chant a spell I couldn't hear.

Now in the middle of the kitchen, Carver and Reid circled each other.

"I will end you," Reid huffed out.

Carver laughed. "You don't get it, do you, Reid? Even if you kill me, I've already taken everything away from you. I. Still. Win."

Reid lunged, his head butting into Carver's stomach. The force pushed Carver against the table on the far side of the room.

"Got it," Mike murmured, setting my wrists free. Carefully, he propped up the chair a little so I could slip my arm out from underneath. I gaped at my four broken fingers and had to look away before I threw up. "Okay, now your ankles. This shouldn't take as long."

Mike jerked on the ropes that secured my legs to the chair. I wondered if, as soon as I was free either Lucas or Mike would rush me out of the house. They needed Mike for the plan to work, but Lucas wasn't even supposed to be inside. Right now, though, Jessica needed Lucas's support.

I swiveled my head to Reid, again unsure of whose side he was on. Hate radiated off him as he dug his fist into Carver's face. My only guess as to why Carver hadn't retaliated was that Jess was speaking some charm to weaken him.

"You're free," Mike said, tossing the ropes into the pantry. He looped an arm around me and helped me up. Once standing, his eyes flew over me in quick inspection, his jaw clenching at what he saw. Tangled hair. A ripped shirt. Blood. Both Carver and Reid's handprints on my face. Not to mention the fingers. "Stay here, okay?"

I nodded. Suddenly, out of nowhere, I watched as Mike picked up the chair I'd been tied to and sprinted across the room, fury raging in his eyes.

"My turn," he said, positioning himself over Carver. Reid stepped aside, and Mike slid in, the chair raised over his head. "You son of a bitch!" Mike smashed the chair into Carver, and it flew apart, wood pieces shattering to the floor.

That's six: broken wooden chair.

Reid picked up one of the broken legs and tossed it to Lucas. "Care to join in?"

Lucas guided Jessica to the stove to lean against. "You good?"

She nodded.

"All right. Time to kill an incubus."

I rushed over, taking Lucas's place next to Jess. "Are you okay?"

"Yeah," she said, pausing long enough to answer me. "You?"

"I've been better. Where's Julianna? It has to be almost sundown, right?"

Jessica checked her watch, frowning. "Two minutes."

"And Megan?"

"Containing the demons. As soon as Lucas bolted in here, the containment spell broke. The last thing we need is demons milling around Villisca too. She's upstairs at the attic entrance."

A loud grunt snapped my attention to the fight. Carver had finally retaliated, and Mike was sliding across the floor on his back. His head hit the hutch, knocking down several picture frames from the top shelves. Some of the drawers popped open with the force of his collision. He wasn't moving.

"Mike!"

Just as I was about to run to him, Reid's body

landed beside him. That left Carver and Lucas.

I stopped and spun around. Really, I shouldn't have been too concerned. Lucas was already dead; Carver couldn't hurt him, right?

"You figured it out by now, haven't you?" Carver taunted him.

"Yeah, I have. And it starts and ends with you," Lucas answered.

"Oh, Lucas … tsk, tsk. That's where you have it all wrong. It started and will end with *you*. You got in my way once, and with your buddy's help, you and your sister paid the price." Without looking, Carver pointed directly at me. "Once I have *your soul* then and only then will it end."

Lucas's voice lowered. "I think you've had enough souls," he said before he disappeared.

Carver crouched, alert, rotating slowly as he peered though the air. "I can still sense you, ghost-boy."

On the floor, Mike and Reid stirred. Mike rubbed his shoulder, groaning. He pulled down the neckline of his shirt to examine the scars left behind from his surgery. That couldn't be good.

A familiar cool breeze circled me, wrapping me in a cocoon of breath.

"Hey, man. You okay?" Reid asked Mike, sitting up.

"Yeah-yeah. I'm good," Mike answered. "You about ready? Julianna should be here any second now."

"Let's bag this bastard."

Reid offered Mike a hand up, and they split up to opposite sides of the room, slipping into the shadows. The play was set.

"Come on, Lucas," Carver shouted. "Let's end this." He reached out to grab a hold of me, but Lucas suddenly materialized in front of him, stabbing the wooden stake through his arm.

"Don't. Touch. Her."

Carver hissed and yanked the stake out. "I'm not a vamp."

"No, but I am." For the first time, Julianna's childish voice created a relieved swell in my chest. If all went according to plan, this should be over soon.

Carver spun around, flipping the piece of wood in his palm. "Nice to see you, Julianna."

"Likewise."

"What brings you to town?"

"I hear you plan to dethrone me. Can't let that happen, now can I?"

Carver chuckled, shaking his head. "Oh, my sweet, I think you've been played."

Her gaze flicked to Carver's weapon, one of the only things that could kill a vampire. "Have I? Seems to me like you've been waiting for me."

"What? This?" Carver held up the stake then threw it across the room. "Not meant for you."

Oh, Carver's a diplomat now?

"Well, that's a shame," Julianna said, a malevolent grin tugging at the corner of her mouth. "I have so been looking forward to this."

With a speed I'd never witnessed before, Julianna sprung at Carver. She landed on the floor in front of him, low to the ground, and swept a leg in a circle at his feet. For a thirteen-year-old, this girl knew how to fight.

Carver came to his senses and jumped right before Julianna knocked him to the floor. He ran to the wooden table, leaping on top of it, flipped backward over Julianna, and landed behind her.

The vampire spun around, and Carver threw the first punch. They were so fast I couldn't make out the movements through the blur.

Beside me, Jessica's breath hitched, her eyes flashing to the stairwell. The heel of a black boot peeked out from the curve of the stairs, before it disappeared again.

"The demons are free," Jessica said. "We must hurry."

She scanned the room until she noticed Reid and Mike, now joined by Lucas, hidden behind opposite walls, ready for their move.

A sound from the stairs alerted me. Megan's boot slipped again, and she stumbled backward, tumbling down the rest of the steps.

"Megan!" I dove forward, straight toward the fighting cambions.

"Carrie!" Jessica screamed behind me. Her hand grabbed the back of my shirt and jutted me backward. I ran into the stove and looked up just as Julianna's fist connected with Jessica's stomach, sending her flying through the air.

Jessica's body landed on the wooden table, breaking it in two pieces down the middle. Her head against the wall and her legs sprawled out in an odd angle, she didn't move.

Seven. A table, split down the middle
Eight. A body—

No. The thought formed in my head, and I tried to push it back. It wasn't supposed to happen like this.

Eight. A body is thrown through the air. The person, they're not moving. I think...I think they're dead.

Jessica's words ripped through me. She'd been wrong about me, maybe she'd been wrong about this too. If she'd witnessed her own death, she would have told me. She would have...

"That witch!" Julianna spat, pausing the fight momentarily to examine her arm. Blood streamed over her skin from the four deep cuts lining her forearm.

The sight took me back to Christmas when Jessica had clawed Stacy the same way.

Nine. Nails scrape over an arm.

Yes, Jessica had sliced into Julianna's arm as she flew into the air.

Pressing myself against the metal, I let my eyes wander to the stairwell. At the bottom, Megan shot her hands forward, a gleaming crystalline barrier erupting from her palms and filling the doorway. Behind it, I could see the dark shadows of the demons tearing at it.

Julianna growled and charged at Carver. Legs kicking and fists punching, they flew around the kitchen. Picture frames fell and holes appeared in the plaster as they ricocheted off the walls. Bodies slammed into cabinets and windows, and the curtains were yanked down. The old wash board in the corner now lay in shambles. Carver kicked Julianna into the side of the hutch, a drawer spilling out and silverware scattered across the floor.

Ten. Silverware falling from a drawer.

Two left and Carver should be dead.

Please...

Both Carver and Julianna sprung off the walls, the stove, even the freaking ceiling, waiting for the other to make a wrong move.

"I can't hold the demons back much longer!" Megan cried out.

At the sound of Megan's plea, Julianna gave the signal—a short whistle in three staccato beats. She swung Carver around and held his attention as Lucas, Mike, and Reid burst from their corners, running head-long toward Carver.

Whose side is Reid really on?

A flashback from the game that ended Mike's football career flashed through my mind, only this time, Mike was playing defense.

From his position, Carver couldn't see them coming.

Lucas and Mike on one side, Reid on the other, the three slammed into him. Lucas and Reid with their supernatural strength causing the most damage.

Julianna gave the final blow to Carver's neck, cutting off his air supply and giving us a few extra seconds to get out of the house before Megan let the demons loose on him.

A stunned glint in his eye, Carver grabbed his throat, wavering on his knees before he collapsed on the floor.

"Get out!" Megan yelled.

Definitely, but I couldn't leave Jessica behind. I

started toward her when Julianna's voice stopped me.

"I don't think so."

I spun around to see her twist Mike up against her body, her legs wrapped around his waist in a half-nelson.

"You weren't part of the agreement, and no one, NO ONE, tells me what to do," she said, her fangs protruding. "Especially not a *Mortal*."

Chapter 26

That bitch needed to let go of him.

Without thinking, I raced toward them with nothing except my bare hands and miniscule human strength. It didn't register that there was no possible way I could take Julianna by myself. But I still ran at her. I circled behind her and grabbed her black ponytail with my good hand, jerking it as hard as I could.

Somehow, it surprised her enough to loosen her hold on Mike, and he ducked out of her deadly embrace. Her legs still around him, though, he rotated until he faced her. Until tonight, I'd never seen Mike punch someone, but with as much as he worked out, I figured he could throw a good one. And he did—right into her windpipe.

I'd learned a lot being around Lucas and Megan. Vampires were soulless creatures, which meant they still had a body…and bodies required air.

I released Julianna's hair and jumped out of the way to avoid the backlash. The vamp's hand flew to her neck, and her legs fell off Mike's waist. She cowered low to the floor, clutching her throat.

"Nice," I said to Mike, shooting him our traditional thumbs-up from football season.

"Yeah, well, don't congratulate me yet."

Julianna bounced back faster than Carver, who still hadn't moved from his lovely spot on the hardwood. She poised herself low to the floor like a cat, eyes drilling into us. "You're both dead," she hissed.

"I don't think so," Lucas said, suddenly appearing behind her with the piece of wood Carver had tossed away when she showed up. "Thanks for your help, Julianna. We appreciate it."

Lucas raised the stake up and slammed it into her back. Stolen blood oozed out of her, soaking her black tank top. She fell forward on her hands, heaving her final breaths, before she plunged face down on the floor.

Worry lines spread over Lucas's forehead as he pulled me into him and kissed my temple. "You okay? Let's get the hell out of here."

"Jessica," I said, pointing to her body sprawled out on top of the crushed table. "We can't leave without her."

"Guys, whatever you're going to do, do it fast," Megan grunted, sweat dripping from her brow. "Really, I can't hold on much longer, and Carver isn't going—"

"Hey, dude," Reid murmured, and Lucas let go of me to follow Reid's gaze. "How long was that stick?"

I spun around to see Julianna's arm twisting around her back. Her fingers clutched onto the wood, and she pulled. Ouch.

Lucas groaned. "Shit. Not long enough."

Reid grinned and waggled his brows. "Let's kill a vampire." His pupils dilated until the whole of his eyes were like black holes ready to swallow anything that came close. Tonight, it seemed, Reid had control over his inner demon.

Lucas nodded, a smile creeping across his face. Then he cocked his head once at Mike. "Mike and Carrie, grab Jessica and get her out of here."

He didn't have to tell me twice.

Julianna's head snapped up, her eyes burning with rage. Yep, time to go.

I ran over to Jessica and knelt beside her. Pressing the pads of two fingers against her neck, I checked for a pulse. When I didn't feel one, I pressed harder.

"Come on," Mike said. "We should get her out of here first."

Mike squatted down beside her. Gently, he slid his arms under my best friend and lifted her up. Completely limp, her head fell back, her hair spilling down.

Around me, I registered the fight ensuing. Bodies crashing against walls and furniture, but I only saw Jessica and how her skin had paled and her lips were no longer pink.

That was probably why I didn't see Julianna standing behind Mike until she grabbed him, and Jessica dropped back down to the floor, landing in a lifeless heap.

"Oh, *hell* no!" Reid growled, running across the kitchen and sliding into her legs like he was sliding into home base.

The force knocked her off her feet, but not before pushing Mike face first into a wall. He slammed against it, blood tricking from his nose. Dazed and on his hands and knees, he shook his head and blinked, trying to focus.

Julianna jumped up and dusted herself off. "I've had enough of this."

No way! She's giving up?

Catlike, she leapt at Reid and sunk her teeth into his neck. He struggled against her, grabbing a hold of whatever part of her he could. Along with his blood, it seemed she drained the energy from him too. Unable to get her off, he dropped to his knees, his eyes reverting back to hazel as the demon inside him retreated.

"You can do better than that, Reid," Lucas mocked, positioning his hands around Juilianna's head. "At least pretend you like it." Then he twisted, her neck snapping, and she let go of the incubus, slumping onto the hardwood beside Mike.

"Um, guys?" Megan groaned.

"Almost done. Hang. On," Reid grunted, slowly making his way to his feet. "I did like it, couldn't you tell, Luke?"

Lucas chuckled as he circled his arms around me. "Carrie, you need to go."

"No," I said. "I have to get Jessica."

Lucas hesitated. "All right. Reid, can you help Mike?"

"Yeah, man."

"Great. Let's get out of here. Carrie, you'd better be right behind me."

Lucas picked Jessica up, nodded at me, and disappeared.

With Jessica gone, I could breathe a little easier. She was safe outside with Lucas. I, on the other hand…

"Reid, we need to—" I said, peering down to where Mike lay, and screamed. Julianna had her fangs delved into Mike's neck. Mike's eyelids dropped, the content grin on his face making him look as if he were enjoying his blood draining from his body.

According to Jessica, three things killed a vampire: the traditional two—wooden stake through the heart and sunlight—and…

Liquid fire…

Of course!

Oh, please let Reid still have it. And truly be on our side.

"Reid, the vial," I said, holding out my hand. "Now."

He dug in his pocket and produced the triangular bottle with bright red liquid. "You know what this is, right?"

"Yeah, give it to me."

Reid placed the vial in my palm. "Hit a vital organ, and you'd better hurry. Carver's stirring."

I glanced over my shoulder and sure enough Carver's shoulders were rolling as if he was loosening them, readying himself for another go.

My hand in shambles, I uncorked the bottle with my teeth. Hopefully, Julianna was too immersed in Mike's blood to notice me.

You've had enough, bitch.

Gingerly, I poured the contents over Julianna's shoulder, hoping it would trickle down to her heart quickly. Thick, redder-than-blood liquid rolled down her arm, seeping over her back and chest. Slowly, it absorbed into her skin and mixed with her victim's blood running through her veins, leaving no trace on the outside.

Suddenly, Julianna's back hunched up, and her mouth slipped off Mike's throat. A drop of Mike's blood dripped out of the corner of her mouth.

Horrified, she stared at me. "What have you done?"

I took my chances and lowered myself beside her. "I guess a *mortal* just killed off a vampire. Pretty sweet, huh?"

From above me, Reid snickered. He set his foot against her chest and shoved her backward, away from Mike. Writhing in pain, Julianna screeched and rolled across the floor, tearing at her clothing.

Then she burst into flames from the inside out. A spark jumped off her and landed on one of the torn-down curtains, setting it ablaze with orange, yellow, and red, reminding me of the fires of Hell I'd witnessed in the attic upstairs last summer. Soon, the whole house would be burning. How fitting.

"Thirty seconds to let go, Megan," Reid said, picking Mike up off the floor. "Carrie, move."

For my sake, and Mandy's, I had to know Mike was safe. No way was this captain going down with his ship.

I shook my head. "No, you first."

"Damn girl, I don't know how Lucas puts up with you sometimes." He shoved past me and ran out the door.

I shot Megan a final nod and followed Reid out.

Scanning the yard on my way out searching for Jess, my eyes fell on Lucas, just off the property line. Vanessa, Megan's witchy mom, stood beside him. I held his gaze for a moment before he rushed toward me.

Already at the end of the wooden ramp off the porch, Reid lowered Mike to the ground and caught Lucas's arm on his way past to me.

"The house is on fire," Reid said as I reached him.

"What?" Lucas's eyes flicked to me.

"I told Megan thirty seconds to release the demons, which was twenty seconds ago, and Carver's stirring."

"I'm on it," Lucas said and disappeared.

Adrenaline surged in my veins as I twisted to run back in the house after him. What if Carver was fully awake now? Worse yet, would Lucas be able to escape after Megan set the demons loose?

Reid chased me and grabbed my wrist halfway to the house. "Don't be stupid, Carrie."

Sure, he'd proven himself to be on our side by what he did in there, but he wasn't going to stop me from rescuing my boyfriend.

"Let go of me, Reid," I said, struggling against his hold.

He shook his head. "There's nothing you can do."

I jerked my arm, making Reid's grip on me tighter. "I said let me go!" I was screaming now, panic rising. Lucas should be out. OUT!

Flames burst from the windows, and Reid tackled me to the ground, covering me with his body. I wrapped my arms over my head, protecting it like I'd been taught in kindergarten.

We were too close to the house. Heat poured over me, burning me. God, was I melting?

"Reid," I heard Lucas say through the thick cloud surrounding us.

Suddenly, I felt lighter as Reid rolled off me, replaced by Lucas's arms cooling my body. The weird sensation of being sucked through a tube encased me, and instantly, I was standing with Lucas on the sidewalk, watching flames pour out of the house.

Sirens wailed in the distance, but they'd be too late. As soon as Lucas teleported her out, Megan combined her power with her mother's. Both she and Vanessa had their arms outstretched, and it was like some force was slowly pulling the flames back inside the kitchen. I doubted they'd have time to fully restore the house magically before the firemen and police arrived, though, especially now that a few neighbors were standing outside their homes watching the house burn.

Good thing weird, creepy stuff happened in this town all the time. Add this to the list.

My back against his stomach, Lucas held me closer, his chin resting on the top of my head. I laced my fingers with his, finally safe.

Over. It was over.

I took a quick inventory of people standing on the sidewalk: Vanessa, Megan, Lucas, Reid, Mike, me. The incubus held Mike up. Still, Mike was alive.

One person was missing, though.

"Lucas, where's Jess?" I asked.

He didn't answer.

I cocked my head up to look at him, but he remained focused on the dying fire.

"Lucas?" I tried again. "Where's Jessica?"

The muscles in his face twitched; he still wouldn't meet my gaze.

Jessica's reminder that we'd be lucky if we all made it out unscathed ate at me.

No, it can't be.

"You're scaring me," I whimpered. Without him saying it, I already knew.

Slowly, those green irises flitted down to me.

"She's at Vanessa's house. Carrie, Jessica didn't make it."

Chapter 27

Fire trucks cried out in the distance, but Vanessa and Megan had already vanquished the flames.

"Lucas, why don't take you everyone to our house to clean up," Vanessa instructed. "We'll be in after we recast the containment spell. Then I can tend to everyone's injuries."

The Miller home was halfway down the block, so we didn't have far to walk. The night had zapped all of Lucas's energy to transport any of us. Reid's strength seemed to be returning little by little, and he insisted on helping Mike so Lucas could walk with me. Now that Carver was gone, maybe Reid could finally be free of him. Lucas and I led the way, my unbroken hand clasped inside Lucas's, the other I held firmly against my stomach, trying not to move it too much.

My head swirled with images of the last...had it really only been an hour since Reid tied me up at the Moore House? Four broken fingers and a whole slew of other crap later, it felt like an eternity.

Images of Julianna hurling Jessica through the

air replayed in my mind. Jess had sacrificed herself to save me from her fate.

The sickening sound of her back crashing into the table rang in my ears. The force of Julianna's punch had to have sent Jessica flying at a hundred miles per hour. Still, even knowing she'd probably died instantly did nothing to comfort me.

In my mind, I traveled further back in time. Back to Christmas when Jessica and Stacy had arrived in Iowa, and Stacy's words filled my memory.

"Jess fell asleep in the car and had a nightmare or something. I had to wake her up; she was screaming."

"Jessica's red claw marks go all the way to my shoulder."

That wasn't all, though. Ever since Jessica had returned, she'd seemed wrapped up in her own world. And at every mention of Julianna, she'd tensed up.

I puffed out a sigh at the realization. Hindsight was always twenty-twenty, as they say.

For months now, Jess had been dreaming of her own death. Seeing herself die over and over again. Knowing—and accepting—that if we followed her visions to kill Carver, it would cost her life.

Without a word regarding my thoughts, Lucas opened the door to the Millers' house and ushered us inside. A freaky sense of déjà vu swept over me. Last summer, after Lucas and I escaped the demons chasing us, Vanessa sent us back here—to her house. She'd even healed my broken bones and lacerations from the car accident.

I scanned over the living room. Exactly the

same.

Ivory furniture spread out at the far end with a glass-surfaced coffee table in the middle. On the opposite wall, a stone fireplace served as the focal point. The same painting of black roses hung above it.

"Let's put Mike on the sofa," Lucas instructed, letting go of my hand and ducking under Mike's free arm.

Together, Lucas and Reid helped Mike across the room. Pale and sickly, Mike collapsed on top of the cushions, his head falling to the side in exhaustion. Four puncture wounds, swollen with dried blood, sunk deep into his neck. I think he may have tried to mutter a thank you, but only a soft grunting sound emerged from his throat.

"Will he be okay?" I asked as Lucas tucked a pillow under his head. "He's not going to become a vampire now, is he?"

"No, he'll be fine. She didn't drain him, and he didn't drink from her. His heart can replace the blood he's lost," Reid explained.

"He'd do well to get some food and water in him before he dozes off, though," Lucas said.

"Yeah, might be a little late for that." I cocked my head toward Mike, soft snores escaping him.

"Hmm. Won't hurt to try, I guess. I'll go raid the refrigerator," Reid said and walked out, leaving Lucas and me.

"Sit." Lucas motioned to one of the chairs. "Let me see your hand."

I'd avoided looking at it. The grotesque angles of my fingers did nasty things to my stomach. Most of the pain had eased into numbness, though—unless I stupidly attempted to move a digit. I bit back a sob as I placed my hand into Lucas's.

"Where's Jessica?" I asked, now that we were all inside and partially settled.

"In the guest bedroom," Lucas answered, examining my fingers as carefully as he could. The coolness of his touch felt good on them.

"I need to see her," I said.

Lucas's eyes flicked to me, his jaw tensing. Gingerly, he brushed the loose locks of hair from my face. "I know. I'll take you up as soon as Vanessa heals this."

"No. I don't want to wait that long." I slid my injured hand out of his, fighting to not wince at the movement. "She was my best friend, Lucas. She died to save me. I want to go to her now."

Lucas rubbed a palm over his mouth. He could deliberate all he wanted; it wouldn't change my mind.

He glanced over his shoulder at Mike. "Okay. Let me make sure Reid can handle Mike by himself."

They'd been best friends in life, and Reid had kept his word tonight. I doubted Lucas trusted him completely, especially without answers about Reid's involvement in Rachel's death, but right now, there were more important things to take care of.

"Yeah, man. Take her." Reid appeared at the door way with a glass of soda, cheese, and crackers.

"You should eat some of that yourself," Lucas said. Already, the puncture wounds in Reid's neck had healed, but he was still pale, and his eyes had sunken slightly inward.

Reid nodded. "I'm going to need another dying soul before the night is over."

"Can you control the monster for a little bit longer?"

"I've been doing good so far. Go."

Satisfied, Lucas helped me to my feet. I wobbled a little, but he steadied me.

"I'm fine," I said, more to myself than for his benefit.

With his support, I ascended the stairs to the guest bedroom. Each step I took brought me closer to Jessica and the reminder that she'd carried the weight of her own death for far too long. Fated or not, Jess's death was utterly unfair.

At the top of the stairs, Lucas reached for the doorknob. "You sure?"

"Yes," I whispered.

He turned the knob and pushed the door open.

"Give me a few minutes alone, please?" I asked.

"Carrie—" His voice rumbled low.

"Please?" I repeated, meeting his gaze. "Go relieve Reid for a while. I'll…" I inhaled and let it out slowly. "I'll be fine."

"If you need me—"

"I know. Thank you."

I didn't watch him walk away. Instead, I took my first step over the threshold, and the end of the bed appeared into view. I moved forward silently, swallowing back the tears.

There she was. My best friend since before I could remember.

Standing beside the bed, I stared at Jessica, reveling in how surreal it was. When I saw her lying there, so still, so colorless, my heart had trouble believing it. The body in front of me looked like Jess's, my childhood sandbox buddy. My confidant. But it wasn't her. The life that made her who she was had evaporated. Before me lay only a body that resembled her.

I threw my hand over my mouth and choked out a sob. Shaking my head, I allowed the tears to overflow. Jessica's life was over. After everything, how the heck did I still have mine?

I moved closer to the bed, the edge of the mattress rubbing against my thighs. Just as Lucas had done to me downstairs, I pushed away the hair from her face so I could see her better. I leaned down and kissed her forehead, my tears dripping onto her skin.

"I'm sorry, Jess. I love you."

Unable to leave her in a strange house alone, I lowered myself on the floor beside her and closed my eyes, crying, until exhaustion gave way to sleep.

***

I awoke to cool fingers brushing over my face. His soft gaze searched mine, and he wiped the dried tears from my cheeks before he kissed me. Lucas understood that he couldn't take away the pain. There was no quick fix to grief. But he did all he could for me—he held me.

After awhile, the door creaked open, and Vanessa poked her head in. "I need to take a look at that hand, Carrie."

I nodded. "Yeah, okay."

With Lucas guiding me, I sat up and leaned against the side of the bed. Vanessa crouched down in front of me.

"I'm sorry about Jessica," she said as I placed my mangled hand in her palm. "What happened is not your fault, I hope you know that. Cambions are tricky creatures, but Jessica did what she did because she wanted to."

"No, Jess didn't want to die," I retorted. "Her stupid visions told her she had to and she listened to them. She walked into it knowing that…" My voice cracked, and I couldn't continue.

"Carrie, just because her death was fated didn't quell her love for people, nor her desire to save them. There is no greater love than to lay down one's life for her friends. Jessica did two great things last night. She saved human lives, and destroyed an evil being. Don't confuse what is meant to be with your own aspiration for doing it. Jess's death was a noble thing."

Vanessa cupped my hand between hers and closed her eyes. She muttered some words in Latin, but I wasn't listening. I was thinking about what she'd said about fate and destiny and our own inclinations to the future. Maybe she was right. Maybe the future hinges on more than a single person's thoughts, ambitions, and deeds.

Maybe that was what Jessica meant when she told me about Mike's involvement—that the future is complicated.

"All done," Vanessa said, releasing my hand.

"You know the drill, it'll be sore for awhile because I'm not a healer. I can only do simple mending, and thankfully it doesn't get much easier than fingers."

"Thanks." I twisted my head up toward Jessica. "What will we do with her? Her family thinks she's in Aspen."

"We're transporting her to Colorado in an hour. Megan and I will be there when the paramedics arrive on the scene, and they'll classify it as a skiing accident, contact her parents, and send her back to Sherman." Vanessa patted my shoulder and stood up. "Lucas, Reid would like to speak with you."

"Sure. I'll be down in a minute."

Lucas pulled me against him as Vanessa left. Tears sprung from my eyes again, and I buried my face into his shoulder.

All lies. Jessica was a hero. She didn't die in some stupid skiing accident on a fake spring break trip. Instead of the honor she deserved, she'd be forgotten as another accidental death.

No one will know how amazing she was.

Lucas's fingers combed through my hair. "Yes, they will, Carrie," he said, reading my thoughts. "Even without her sacrifice, she was amazing, and everyone already knows that. What matters in life isn't how it ended; it's how it was lived."

***

After Vanessa and Megan left with Jessica's body, I shuffled down the stairs. Mike was still passed out on the sofa in the living room, snoring peacefully. Already, color had begun to return to his face.

Voices from the porch drew me to the front door. Outside, the storm had passed and the skies were silent once again. Morning rays poked through the lingering clouds, sending beams of light dispersing over the heavens. Under its vastness, Lucas and Reid sat on the steps, talking.

Somberly, Lucas nodded at the half-cambion. I started to turn around, not wanting to interrupt their discussion, when Lucas twisted and smiled. He cocked his head to the side once, beckoning me to join them.

I stepped outside and sat down beside Lucas.

"Coffee?" he asked, handing me his mug.

"Sure, thanks." I took a sip, the warmth of the liquid seeping through the ceramic and into my palms.

"How's the hand?" Reid asked.

"Good. Vanessa healed it."

"Hey, I'm sorry about what happened with Carver. When I met up with him earlier, I had a hard time convincing him that I was on his side. In the house, I had to keep up the charade or he'd see through it too soon. I didn't mean for you to get hurt."

I stared down at the coffee. "I guess it was a risk we all had to take. Some more than others."

"Yeah," he breathed. Then he dug in his pocket and pulled out my infinity necklace. "You probably want this back."

"Oh, thank you," I said as Reid dropped it in my palm. "I mean, for everything. Not just this." I looped the silver chain around my neck and secured it.

"I'm going to take off, but uh, Lucas, I need to explain what Carver said. He wasn't lying, though, about you and your sister and the role I played."

Lucas raked a hand through his hair, keeping his gaze fixed out into the front yard.

"It was an accident," Reid continued. "I didn't understand what Carver had done to me, and I wasn't being careful. I loved Rachel, man, please know that. I never wanted to hurt her. She and I were in her room when the demon came out, and I had no control over myself. I put her in a trance and took her soul. When I came to, she was on the floor, gasping for air."

Reid paused, the muscles in his jaw pulsing. "I called 911, and they rushed her to the hospital. You met us there, and I told you everything. Every messed-up detail. I don't know if you believed me. Rachel took her last breath before your folks arrived, and you had to get away from me. I followed you, but, uh, you know the rest from there."

Lucas hung his head, squeezing his eyelids closed.

"I'm so sorry, man. Not a day goes by that I don't regret it all."

Reid raised his gaze to me, remorse filtered through his stare, and I felt sorry for him. He'd never be free of his demons. That was probably why he had asked us to kill him when this was over, which none of us would do. And why his human self felt so obligated to warn Lucas about Carver in the first place.

"I'll never be able to make up for what I did," Reid said, his voice low. "I don't know where your soul is, Lucas, but I can give you a place to start. Maybe even fill in some pieces for you."

Still as a statue, Lucas didn't answer.

"Your name is Lucas Reynolds, and you're twenty-one. You attended college at the University of North Carolina at Wilmington studying physics and physical oceanography, focusing on the effects the moon, stars, and earth's rotation have on the ocean. Your sister, Rachel, was eighteen and would have graduated six weeks later if I hadn't killed her. I don't know if your folks are still there—I haven't been back—but they lived in Marion, North Carolina."

Even in the crisp morning breeze, the air felt thick. Reid stood up and dusted off his jeans.

"Good luck, man. Again, I'm sorry."

Lucas didn't lift his head as Reid turned around and walked way.

Chapter 28

When Megan and Vanessa returned, it was midday, and Mike was still asleep on the sofa. Other than the light bruises flushing his skin, he looked good. Well, as good as one could look after a run-in with a vampire.

"Where's Reid?" Megan asked.

I glanced at Lucas, thinking he'd answer her, but he stood up and walked out of the room without a word. In fact, he hadn't said much all morning.

"Reid left," I told her, my gaze on the empty space in the hall where Lucas disappeared.

"Ah." Megan rubbed her palms on her thighs. "Well, I guess now that Carver's gone, Reid can move on. Be free of him."

"I'm not so sure about that," I mumbled, readjusting the too-snug shirt she'd lent me.

"Yeah…"

A few uncomfortable seconds passed before Megan joined me on the floor. "I hate to do this now, but we need to go over your story since you're supposed to be in Colorado with us."

Right. The lie to cover-up the real reason behind Jessica's death.

I hugged my knees to my chest. "Sure. I'll say whatever you want."

"It's for the best, Carrie. Outsiders…well, you know how dangerous our world can be."

I peeked over at Mike. "What about him?"

"Witch protocol says I should wipe his memory, but after all he did for us last night, it's not really fair."

"Ya think?" All of this memory charm crap was getting out of hand.

"He's your friend. What do *you* want me to do?"

I heaved a sigh. "No, don't. Carver and Julianna are both dead, and I don't want to mess with anyone else's head."

Megan nodded. "I respect that."

Then, she went on to tell me the mock details surrounding Jessica's death.

***

Two hours passed and I hadn't seen Lucas. He was, however, inside the Millers' house; I could feel him. Because part of his soul now resided inside my body, our connection had strengthened. Exactly to what degree, though, I had no idea. I still couldn't hear his thoughts.

"Megan, have you seen Lucas?" I asked when she came back to the living room with a glass of water and an apple for me.

"He's in the attic helping Mom with some necro stuff."

"It's been a long time since we've had a necromancer in town," I said, taking a drink.

"Yeah, but there's nothing we can do except wait it out. The chosen one will arrive when they arrive. Until then…" She shrugged.

From the sofa, Mike groaned.

"Finally," Megan breathed, snapping her attention to him. "I'll be right back. I need to get him the potion Mom made to help replenish his blood."

After Megan left, I moved to sit on the coffee table beside him. He shifted, groaning again. One of his eyelids fluttered open, followed by the other. When he saw me, the corner of his mouth curved up.

"Hey you," I said.

"I can't be certain, but I think last night may have been the worst night of my life." The scratchiness in his voice made me giggle.

"How're you feeling?"

"Like I've been bitten by a vampire." His fingers searched and found what remained of the puncture wounds on his neck. "That's quite the hickey."

"Yeah, well, I can honestly say that I don't know what that feels like."

Mike's brows shot up.

"The vampire bite, not the hickey," I clarified, shaking my head. "Well, neither, actually…anyway."

Grimacing, he sat himself up. "That reminds me, Carrie, is Lucas around?"

"He's upstairs with Vanessa," I said, not elaborating, and casting my attention to my lap. I had an idea of what was coming next.

I wasn't wrong.

"I know you explained yesterday about some force binding the two of you, but that doesn't change the fact that he's dead. You understand that, right? He's not supposed to be here."

I flicked my eyes up to him. "And his being dead doesn't change how I feel about him."

Mike stared back, his hazel irises boring into me until I had to look away. Last summer, when I first told him about Lucas, he'd gotten angry and walked out. I think I'd prefer that over this deafening silence between us now. I could almost feel the disappointment radiating off him.

"Good to see you up," Megan said, entering the room holding what looked like a glass of steaming strawberry juice, except even the steam was red. "Here, drink this."

Glad for the interruption, I let Megan take my place, and I went back to one of the armchairs.

Mike took the beverage from her and studied it. "Um, I think I'm gonna pass. I've seen this in a movie before, and I'd like to keep my memories, thanks." He held the glass out to Megan.

She pushed it back to him. "It won't erase your memories. We don't need a potion for that. This is for your blood, so your heart isn't overworked."

"Oh, well, in that case, bottom's up." Mike winked at Megan and knocked the glass back. "Not bad."

"Nice work last night, Captain," Megan said. "We couldn't have done it without you."

"Right. I'm, uh, sorry about Jessica." His gaze

lifted to me for a fraction of a second before landing back on Megan.

I bowed my head, not sure how to feel about the saddened look he shot me.

"We lost a good witch…and a good friend," Megan answered, and I could feel the burn of tears forming in the corners of my eyes.

She was my friend. Mine.

Mike reached out and placed his hand over Megan's, comforting her. *Her!* "Yeah, she was." He offered a slight smile. "So, everything's good now? With Carver, I mean?"

"Yeah, yeah. I watched the demons devour him, he's dead, and thanks to Carrie, Julianna's dead as well. Mom and I recast the containment spell to keep the demons inside the Moore House at dawn— back to normal."

"Carrie killed Julianna?" This time, he didn't peer in my direction even though he said my name.

"I guess Jessica gave her the Liquid Fire potion, and Carrie used it to get Julianna off you. She's a hero too."

"Huh. I didn't know Carrie had it in her."

The sudden indifference in Mike's tone stabbed me, and I needed to get out of here. On my way out, I overheard Mike and Megan laughing like best friends. Like I'd just been replaced.

"Did you feel even a little guilty punching a thirteen year old girl?" Megan snickered.

"Nah. That demonic bitch needed a good ass-whooping." I made my way out the back door and wandered to the garden bench. Bending forward with my elbows on my knees, I buried my face in my hands.

I'm not sure what I'd expected from Mike after all that had happened, but yesterday he said he'd stick by me no matter what. That he was on my side. Now, I didn't know.

First Jessica then Mike.

Am I losing all my friends?

Maybe I was being overly emotional at the moment. Still, the small changes in Mike I'd witnessed inside gnawed at me.

A cool breeze swirled around me, and I felt Lucas's presence in my head, comforting me. I leaned to the side, Lucas's arms welcoming me. He closed me into him, saying nothing. Words were just useless noise to cover-up the pain that we both needed to feel. For Jessica. For Rachel.

For everything.

***

Grandma Renae met me at the door as I walked into the farmhouse later that evening, supposedly back from our skiing trip in Aspen. Her face solemn, she patted my back, leading me inside.

"I wish you would have called us," she said. "Vanessa told us what happened. I'm so sorry, dear."

I nodded, keeping my head down. "I just want to be alone."

"Of course. Do you want me to bring you anything?"

"No thanks."

Upstairs, safe in my room, my gaze met Lucas's.

"Come here," he said, and I flung myself at him, throwing my arms around his waist. By now, my tears had run dry.

He tucked me in bed, and I curled up next to him. The white box my dad had sent me for Christmas poked out of my closet, reminding me that he'd probably be at Jess's funeral at the end of the week. I still had nothing to say to him. Hell, I hadn't even opened the gift yet.

A picture on my nightstand drew my eyes to it. Three goofy faces laughed back at me. Happy. Carefree. Alive. As I drifted to sleep, the memory of Jessica, Stacy, and me in Stacy's swimming pool the day the photo was taken made me smile.

Chapter 29

The drive back to Sherman, Texas was quiet. Mike had wanted to come with us, but Megan told him it would be awkward since he and Jessica only met once—supposedly—over Christmas.

We pulled into Mom's new house at sunset. Even though she'd insisted that all of us stay there, Vanessa and Megan politely declined. They wouldn't be going to the visitation in the morning either. Fewer questions that way.

"Oh, Carrie." Mom rushed out and threw her arms around me. "Baby, I'm so sorry."

All I could do was nod.

After she let go, she turned to Lucas. "And you must be Lucas. It's a pleasure to meet you."

"Thank you, ma'am," he replied. "I appreciate you letting me stay here."

"No trouble at all," she said, waving away his comment.

Lucas introduced Vanessa and Megan so I didn't have to, and the Millers left to check into their hotel, leaving Lucas, Mom, and me to ourselves.

I scanned the outside of the two bedroom house—white with black shutters—Mom purchased after she sold my childhood home. Nothing about this trip felt normal.

The yard was nice and small, and by the presentation of the flowerbeds out front, Mom had been busy with her green thumb that skipped my generation. A porch swing hung on the rafters, complete with a side table. No doubt Mom spent countless hours outdoors as usual.

I took a deep breath and followed her into the house, Lucas right behind me, holding my hand.

"I bought all new furniture for a new life," Mom said when we entered the den.

I swallowed. *New life indeed.*

The room looked nothing like our old one, which had been decorated in neutrals and full of family portraits. Here, Mom had gone all out with color. Lots of color. Tangerine walls brought out the white furniture and trim, and black end tables and shelving served as an accent along with the green throw pillows. One school picture of me from last year rested on the writers' desk. Even though she'd done an amazing job, I couldn't stop the lump forming in my throat. This wasn't my home.

"It's nice," I mumbled.

"I didn't do much to your room. I figured you'd want to decorate yourself." Then she chuckled. "For when you're home from college, of course. Have you decided where you're going?"

We hadn't seen each other in eleven months, and I knew she was happy to see me and wanted to keep my mind off the reason for my early return, but I wasn't in the talking mood.

"Um…no, I haven't."

"There's still time, sweetie. You already received the acceptance letter from the University of Texas, right?"

"Yeah, I think so," I said, trying to remember the logos on the three unopened letters sitting on my dresser.

Lucas and I followed her up the stairs, his presence a constant in my head right now.

"Well, here it is," Mom said, opening the door. "All that's up here is your bedroom, a bathroom, and a small storage room." She pointed down the small hallway. "When school is over and you come home, we'll do some shopping. Whatever you want."

She'd kept the walls white, unlike my old room. Other than that, everything else I recognized. *My* bed and matching dressers. *My* nightstands. *My* stuffed animals. *My* clothes. Even my purple curtains hung over the windows. Still, in this room, nothing felt like it belonged to me.

I ran my fingertips over the footboard of my bed as I walked to the dresser. On top, Mom had propped up framed pictures of Jessica, Stacy, and I at various ages together. Along the edges of the mirror, more photos of the three of us smiled back. I picked up the one from junior year prom, one year ago. Whereas most girls would freak if someone else wore the same dress, we did it on purpose—in three different colors.

"I love that picture." Mom's voice rang out behind me. "They're all good, actually. You three were always inseparable."

Yeah, we used to be.

***

I tossed in bed, unable to sleep. Finally, at two in the morning, I got up and went downstairs. The sofa where Lucas slept appeared empty, but of course it wasn't. As soon as he sensed me, he materialized on top of the cushions.

I stopped in the middle of the room, my jaw trembling. His glowing green irises shone through the darkness, searching mine. And I broke down.

"I don't want to be here," I sobbed. "I can't…"

Lucas disappeared from the coach and reappeared in front of me, and his fingers combed through my hair.

"This house. Everything. I just can't." I shook my head in quick motions. "How can I go tomorrow? See Jess's brother and sister, her parents, Stacy, and affirm this stupid lie?"

He cupped my face, his thumbs wiping away the tears. "And what truth are you going to tell them?"

"I don't know."

Lucas pulled me into him, soothing me. His lips pressed against the top of my head as he squeezed me tighter.

Suddenly, air whipped past me and both of us were on the sofa. Lucas tucked blankets in around me, and I wrapped my arms around his neck, my head against his chest. His fingertips trailed down my back, working in long motions over me. Soothing me. Comforting me until my breathing slowed and my eyelids drooped. As the sun began to rise, I finally drifted off.

***

Lucas and I entered the funeral home for the visitation. Being Jess's BFF, I felt obligated to be there early. That and I hadn't seen Jessica's parents, the Phillips, since before I left for Iowa.

I froze in place when I spotted them up front, standing over Jess's coffin. My heart leapt into my throat, and guilt dropped like lead into my stomach.

With Lucas at my side, my feet moved forward on their own until I reached the end of the aisle. Mrs. Phillips twisted around and saw me. Cheeks red, she closed the distance between us.

"I'm so happy you were there with her, Carrie," she said, hugging me. "That she wasn't alone."

Yeah, I was with her, but not how Mrs. Phillips thought.

"I…" I sniffled. "I'm so sorry. I…"

"It's not your fault, Carrie. They said it was an accident, and there was nothing anyone could have done."

I didn't reply because I knew better.

"She loved you and Stacy so much. The two of you meant the world to her, never forget that, okay?" she said, letting go of me.

I bobbed my head in tiny movements. "'Kay."

"Good. You and Stacy need to stick together now, you hear me? Don't lose each other."

I nodded again. "We won't. I promise."

"Thank you, Carrie, for honoring my little girl."

***

I sat with Lucas in the back row, staring blankly as people streamed in all morning. Students and teachers from Sherman High wandered over to me and offered their condolences. Some asked how things were going in my life, and I said 'fine' because that's what you're supposed to say. I made small talk with them, and when they walked away, I was glad.

But Stacy still hadn't arrived.

Jessica said she'd compelled her to go to Costa Rica with her parents, and I wondered if anyone got a hold of her. They weren't due back to Texas for another two days.

I watched as everyone took their seats before the funeral began. When Mom, Vanessa, and Megan arrived, they joined Lucas and me in the back. Mom's hand wrapped around mine, a handkerchief balled inside her palm.

I stared down at my feet as the prelude played out from the speakers—*Somewhere Over the Rainbow*, sang by Jessica, Stacy, and me. The memory of the night we recorded it flashed through my mind. We were just goofing off, and Mrs. Phillips overheard us and ran to get her camera. With our arms over each others' shoulders, we re-created our masterpiece for her.

A hand rubbed my shoulder from behind, and I twisted in my seat. My dad, Griffin, stood there, a sad glint in his eye.

"I'm sorry about Jessica, Princess," he said.

I hesitated, holding my breath. "Thank you."

It was strange to see him, especially with my mother sitting next to me. Apparently Lucas sensed my apprehension because he squeezed my hand.

"You need to forgive him, Carrie," he whispered so only the two of us could hear.

I doubted that would happen today. Forgiving someone who hurt you that badly took time, but due to the circumstances, I stood up and accepted his embrace.

"You can sit with us if you want," I offered.

"I'd like that." He rounded the row and sat on the other side of Lucas. "You must be Carrie's boyfriend. I'm Griffin, her dad."

"Pleasure to meet you," Lucas said, shaking his hand. "I'm Lucas."

I peered around them just as Stacy walked in. Looking disheveled with her hair not in its usual bustling curls, she pushed her sunglasses on top of her head, and her red eyes met my gaze. I waved at her, hoping she'd join us. Instead, she frowned and shot me a scathing glare as she walked past, sliding into a row on the opposite side of the room.

What is going on?

***

We followed the caravan of cars to the cemetery for the graveside service. When I stepped out, I noticed Stacy standing beside a large tombstone away from everyone else. She cocked her head once to the side, beckoning to me.

"You guys go ahead," I said. "I'll catch up."

Lucas brushed his fingers down my arm. "If you

need me—"

"I'll mentally holler."

He grinned. "That works."

I ambled over to her. The look she gave me earlier still made me queasy. I'd never been on the receiving end of Stacy's bark, but I'd seen it in action before, and boy-oh-boy I did *not* want it to come to that. Not here. Not now. Not ever.

Definitely not after what Mrs. Phillips said about sticking together.

"Hey Stace," I started. "When I didn't see you at—"

"Do you think I'm stupid, Carrie? That I wouldn't figure it out?" she snapped.

Taken aback by her tone, I stuttered, "Um, I—"

"Well, let me enlighten you since your memory seems shaky." Her hands slid to her hips. "I noticed, babe. I noticed every time you and Jessica exchanged your mystery glances and met for your little secret meetings. I told you then I knew you were hiding something, and I warned you. I said I'd find out. I just didn't think it cost one of you liars your life. I'm sorry Jess died, but payback's a bitch, Carrie. So, tell me, how long have the two of you been planning your bestie trip? Since Christmas, or before that? I bet me tagging along to Iowa really ruined your plans."

Oh wow…

"Stacy, you have it all wrong. That's not what happened."

"I've always been the third wheel in this trio. I'm so sorry I didn't live next door to the two of you. I guess I missed out a lot."

She spun on her heel, and I grabbed her arm, stopping her. "Stacy, listen. I'll tell you the truth about everything, please—"

"What? Now you're going to tell me the truth? *Now?* Because the last eighteen years haven't given you enough time to be honest? Yeah, well, I think it's a little late for that. Get your damn hand off me."

"Stacy, no!" I pleaded. "I swear you've got it wrong. We didn't want you to get hurt."

Her blue eyes shot daggers at me. "You didn't want *me* to get hurt? I guess you don't need to worry about that; you didn't hurt me." She took a step closer, her face in mine, her voice low and menacing. "But congratulations, Carrie. You get to live the rest of your pathetic life knowing you killed the only best friend you ever had. Have a nice life."

Stunned to silence, I watched as Stacy walked to her convertible and sped off.

***

The graveside service flew by in a blur. Stacy's words repeated over and over in my mind, and I couldn't help wondering if she had a point. Maybe if we hadn't kept our secrets from her, Jessica might still be alive. The future was strange like that, our lives all woven together, complicating everything. Changing everything.

As everyone departed for their vehicles, I caught a glimpse of red hair poking out from behind the tree that shaded Jessica's freshly dug grave. Reid stepped out and nodded at me. Then he turned and left before Lucas saw him.

Staring at the tree, my brows narrowed as the realization hit. A weeping willow tree.

I recounted the pit stops in Jessica's visions. There'd been twelve, but only ten came to pass before the demons devoured Carver.

Two predictions remained: 314 and a cemetery with a weeping willow tree.

"The visions may not all be connected to the same event."

"Not only did Jessica see her death, she also saw her own funeral," I said. "This is one of her two visions that haven't happened yet."

Lucas cocked his head to the side. "Two? What was the other one?"

"The number 314. I don't know what that means, but the cemetery with the weeping willow is this—right now."

"The numbers may have nothing to do with us, Carrie," Lucas reminded me.

"Maybe…I guess…then why would she have seen it along with all the other events?"

"I don't know," he said, tucking me close to him. "We'll keep an eye out, though, okay?"

"Yeah." I nodded. "Yeah, okay."

After everyone left, I ran a hand over Jessica's shiny, blue casket. I plucked out a yellow rose from the spray of flowers sitting on top. Rolling it under my nose, I breathed it in. The yellow rose represented friendship. I pulled off one petal and pressed it to my lips.

"You're a hero, Jessica, and I'll never forget that."

Then I bent down and tossed the petal into the grave.

Chapter 30

Lucas spooned up behind me. He nestled his face into the back of my neck, breathing in my hair.

We were lying on a blanket in my mom's backyard. Flashbacks of Jessica's funeral earlier that day filled my mind, and I fought to keep them at bay to enjoy the evening. I had a lifetime to think about what happened today, but with part of Lucas's soul living inside me and the other part out there somewhere, I couldn't be sure how much time I had left with him.

Reid had given us a name and a place; our search would begin in North Carolina where Lucas Reynolds died.

He rolled onto his back. "Come here."

I cuddled up next him.

"Look up there," Lucas said, pointing to the sky. "I told you when this was over that I'd show you the constellation of The Sisters of the Seven Stars. It's faint right now, but..." He took my hand and traced the outline. "There's one. Two. Three. Four. Five. Six. And seven—sort of."

"That's the Little Dipper," I corrected, confused. "I actually know that one."

Lucas chuckled. "No, baby, that's over there." He swung his hand in the other direction. "This one is Pleiades, or the Seven Sisters. In Greek mythology, they were the daughters of Atlas, the titan who was cursed to hold the world on his shoulders. Legend has it that the hunter, Orion, pursued the sisters and they cried out to Zeus to help them. So, Zeus transformed them into birds and set them in the heavens."

"I think that's the shortest story you've ever told."

"Haha, funny."

"It's kind of a 'be careful what you wish for' sort of thing, huh?"

Lucas breathed out a sigh. "Yeah, I guess it is."

We lay there, peering up at the sky, our fingers gliding over each other's skin. The tingles his touch sent through me made me shiver, again making me wish my caresses did the same for him.

My eyelids dropped as I concentrated on how Lucas felt next to me—the way his hands enveloped mine; the way his lips pressed against my neck; the feel of his skin as I traced my fingers over the lines of his body; the smell of spring air that wafted around us. My breathing slowed, and I sunk further into his being—into his soul resting inside me. As I did, I felt something slip inside of me, like a veil falling to the ground.

And that's when it happened.

Everything he was thinking, everything he was feeling, flooded me like water bursting through a dam.

He must have felt it too, because suddenly images—*his* memories—flashed through my mind.

I was asleep on Lucas's sofa the night of Mike's football injury. Lucas perched himself on the coffee table and brushed the hair away from my forehead, watching the strands fall from his fingers. All his ghost life he'd been searching for something—his soul, he'd been told—but now he wasn't so sure.

Everything he could ever want or need was within his grasp right before him. His eyes trailed over me. He took in the way my lids fluttered as I slept and how my lips parted slightly when I inhaled. He grazed his fingertips over my jaw and down my neck and shoulder until they reached my hand.

Leaning over me, he lifted it and kissed each fingernail. Like he often did, Lucas fell in love with me all over again. Every detail of me he hungered for; he wanted; he loved. Each part of me was perfect and belonged to him. He closed his eyes, and it was my smile he saw as he pressed his lips against mine.

The scene faded out and another immediately took its place. It was the evening of my eighteenth birthday back in October. He ordered dinner, and we ate by candlelight in his dining room. Through the flames, his gaze flitted over me, and he frowned.

"What is it?" I asked, furrowing my brow.

The thought of the demons chasing us, and how close we'd been to being dragged to Hell surfaced in his mind. As he stared down the demon holding onto him, all he could think about was how he'd failed me. How after they devoured him, they'd come after me anyway. And that killed him more than the idea of becoming demonic himself.

He shook his head, a smile reappearing on his face. "Nothing. Just thinking how much I love you, and how thankful I am to have you."

The emotions he harbored in these memories overpowered me, and I heard myself gasp. I clung to him, pressing my body into his. Sure, he'd told me before that he felt everything inside of himself stronger, deep within his spirit, but until now, I hadn't believed him. Tonight, though, Incenamus was working for me; I could finally see inside his soul—my soul.

Next, he took us back to the cold November night on my grandparents' rooftop. The scene was so vivid and exact that I wondered if he relived this night over and over again in his mind like I did. He imagined the warmth of my body spreading through his fingertips and flowing through him. From within, he could taste my skin and the sweet scent of me—cherry blossom—rolled into the pit of his stomach, making him long for more. Woven throughout his desire, however, I also felt his frustration. Frustration of wanting what he couldn't have. Craving me but never being fulfilled.

From the rooftop, he enveloped me into one of his dreams. Overhead, vines covered in small green leaves hung around us in a curtain. Through them, I could make out the stars glittering in the night sky. I immediately knew where we were: under the weeping willow trees in the middle of the woods where he'd first told me he was dead. In place of our little picnic, though, stood Lucas's bed. On the ground below us, our clothes laid scattered over the grass. Entwined together under the sheets, our bodies moved in perfect harmony with each other. His lips brushed over my face, my neck, my chest as I arched my back into him, losing myself.

As I watched the scene unfold, my heart ached as I felt the regret Lucas harbored swirl into me. This would never happen; it was only a dream.

The last thought he showed me burned me to the core. Two images side by side—our possible futures. On the left, we stood in Lucas's living room. I was older with streaks of gray laced through my brown hair. Lucas hadn't changed, though, except he no longer had the energy to maintain his body. He barely had the wherewithal to even appear to me. Without being reunited with his soul, Lucas was fading away.

On the right, I sat in front of a tombstone alone, the name Lucas Reynolds engraved into the granite. Tears streamed down my cheeks, and I laid a bouquet of wild flowers on top of his grave as I watched him ascend into the heavens.

Before the image completely disappeared, though, I caught a glimpse of another one behind it. By the way it flickered, I assumed Lucas was fighting to hold it back so I couldn't see. There were no thoughts attached, only a picture: me wrapped inside Mike's arms, Mike's lips pressed to the top of my head.

Then it was gone.

My thoughts, feelings, and memories were my own again. I looked up at Lucas and brushed a hand over his face, tracing my fingers over his lips.

"I told you that one day I'd show you what you mean to me," he said.

"I felt everything you felt," I murmured.

Lucas's palm covered my heart. *Because you have my soul now. Always and forever.*

My breath caught, and for a moment I wondered if I'd imagined it.

"Think it again," I whispered.

Always and forever, Carrie. For eternity.

No, I hadn't imagined it. "I heard your thoughts."

The corner of Lucas's lips curved up in a sexy grin. "Now you have all of me."

Did I, though?

The last images Lucas showed me cut through me again. What options did we really have? They both ended the same—us apart. How was that forever?

"Lucas—"

"Carrie, haven't I always said we'd figure this out together? That everything's going to work out in the end?"

I bit my lip, considering his words. "I don't see it. How is that even possible?"

"I wish I had the answers, baby. All I know is that when the time comes, we'll recognize the right choice."

I peered up at the stars again, wondering if Jessica was staring down at me from up there. For months she'd seen herself die, and yet, in that very moment, she still made the choice to put herself between me and Julianna. She could have let me die instead, only she didn't.

The future was complicated, yes, but that was because our decisions were complicated. Our destinies didn't work themselves out alone as if we had no hand in how it played out. Jess knew what she was doing.

And no matter where the future took Lucas and me, regardless of the outcome, I finally knew what I wanted.

Lucas's soul was out there, waiting for us to find it, and I'd stick by him every step of the way until we found it. His death may have merged our fates, and Incenamus may have anchored them, but our love would forever seal them. No matter what tomorrow would bring, nothing would ever change that. We were meant to be.

Sharing the same soul, we were one.

"Together?" I asked.

Lucas shifted to face me, two fingers gliding down my cheek. *Always.*

THE END

Acknowledgements

As I look back and reflect over my writing journey thus far, I am amazed. Amazed at myself for the growth I've seen not only in my writing, but in myself. Amazed with the amount of support I've received from author friends, bloggers, reviewers, and my publisher. And amazed with the love and comments from readers. Seriously, I'm just blown away.

So, this is my chance to say "THANK YOU" to everyone, and I sincerely hope I don't leave anyone out.

First and foremost, I thank God, for without Him, none of this would be possible.

Secondly, my husband. I will forever be grateful for your encouragement, especially when I'm feeling frumpy about my books and my writing. Your support of me in all areas of my life is astounding, and I'm so honored to be able to spend the rest of my life with you.

To my children, all four of you. You guys are crazy! And I love each of you very, very much. Your vastly different personalities and all the cute things you say are inspiring. Thank you for bearing with me as I worked hard to finish this book. The four of you are the best!

Next, to my parents, siblings, and in-laws for being there for me throughout my life. For all the good and bad memories. Each one has helped shape me into the person I am today.

Thank you to my friends and beta readers who read through this book with a keen eye. I'm glad I can count on you for your honest feedback. Tonille Burrows, Kim Jackson, Logan Keys, Amy Bartelloni, Laura Thalassa, Heather Jelsma, Sunniva Dee, Temperance Elizabeth, and David Negley.

A special thank you to Heather Jelsma and Angela Rothfus for your help and insight with my website. I wouldn't have one if it weren't for the two of you.

I've been blessed with amazing CP's, and I'll never be able to thank them enough. Did I mention that they're amazing?

Sunniva Dee: At the time this is published, we've been through three novels together. THREE!! Can you believe it? From the first time we "met", we clicked. We've been through the ups and downs of publishing together. We've laughed together; we've cried together; we've been frustrated together. And then we've laughed together some more. Over writing and life. I love how we encourage each other, and I can always count on you to give me your very honest opinions. I totally love you for that. Thank you, seriously, for everything.

Temperance Elizabeth: I know the timing for this book wasn't the greatest for you, but you still took the time to go through it and give me your awesome feedback. With all my heart, thank you. And you realize you're next right? I can't wait to see *The Thirteenth Oak* in print, because it so deserves it!

Laura Thalassa: I've probably never told you this, but I remember the very first we "conversed" when you commented on my query letter for *The Spirit*. You complimented the crap out of it, and I read your comments a thousand times, shouted to Sunniva and my husband about them, and didn't sleep for two days because I was so ecstatic. A real life editor loved my query!! Talk about huge boost of encouragement. Yeah, I'm lame, and I'm cool with that. You rock, you're awesome, and I'm so thankful for you!

To my street team for pimping me like, well…uh, anyway. You know what I mean. Thanks for being there for me. Thanks for loving my books. Thanks for promoting my books. Thanks for the fantastic teasers. Thanks for a whole list of stuff that is too long to mention here. I appreciate you more than you know.

To the bloggers and reviewers who have supported me and this series. I'm too scared to list you all because I'll probably leave someone out, but you know who you are. Bloggers are the bread and butter for authors, and I want to thank you for welcoming me with open arms. Keep up the great work!

Okay, I'm almost done, I swear!

To my editor, Toni Rakeshaw. You have been a joy to work with. Thanks for picking apart this book and giving me all your fantastic comments. There were a couple things in there that I'd have been seriously embarrassed to have had published if you hadn't have caught them. ☺ Thank you, thank you, thank you.

A huge thanks to Redbird Designs for the freaking sweet cover. It is beyond perfect.

Thank you to Limitless Publishing! Jennifer O'Neill, Jessica Gunhammer, Dixie Matthews, I appreciate all of you. Thank you so much for taking a chance on me.

And last but certainly not least, to the readers. Without you, there'd be no books! So, as long as you keep reading, I will keep writing. A huge, sincere round of applause to each and everyone one of you. You're the best!

Sweet Dreams,
d.

About the Author

Born and raised in Iowa, d. Nichole King writes her stories close to home. There's nothing like small-town Midwest scenery to create the perfect backdrop for an amazing tale.

She wrote her first book in junior high and loved every second of it. However, she couldn't bring herself to share her passion with anyone. She packed it away until one day, with the encouragement of her husband, she sat down at the computer and began to type. Now, she can't stop.

When not writing, d. is usually curled up with a book, scrapbooking, or doing yet another load of laundry.

Along with her incredible husband, she lives in small-town Iowa with her four adorable children and their dog, Peaches.

Facebook:
https://www.facebook.com/authordnicholeking

Twitter:
https://twitter.com/dNicholeKing

Goodreads:
www.goodreads.com/author/show/7762889.D_Nich ole_King

Website:
www.dnicholeking.com